BREAKING SASS

DIRE WOLF MATES
BOOK TWO

C.D. GORRI

COPYRIGHT

Breaking Sass:
Dire Wolf Mates 2
by C.D. Gorri
Edited by BookNookNuts

Copyright 2022 C.D. Gorri

For my ARC team and all the rest of you bad asses out there,
never change!
Xoxo, C.D.

Before you begin sign up for my newsletter here:
https://www.cdgorri.com/newsletter

BLURB

What happens when a sassy Dire Wolf, with a penchant for breaking rules, and a Lion, who's in love with the law, clash?

She's a sassy Dire Wolf with a fondness for speed, and he's a lethally sexy Lion who knows how to lay down the law. Get ready for fireworks when these two dominant personalities clash!

Sheila Rand is the only female member of the Dire Wolf Motorcycle Club. Rare and powerful Shifters, the Dire Wolf MC has decided to make Blue Valley their permanent home. As the Alpha's cousin, Sheila's outspoken nature, and habitual defiance are overlooked by her Packmates, but not by *him*.

Mr. Law and Order thinks he can break her, but he doesn't know who he's dealing with. This she-Wolf does not want a mate. Especially not a puffed up pussycat!

Leonard Crowley is one of Blue Valley Police Department's only Shifter Detectives. He's worked hard to keep the Shifter secret, doing his utmost to blend in with mainstream life. With his father ailing, Leo is called home to confront certain issues that have popped up in the Blue Valley Pride. The elders insist he name one of their females as mate to assume his rightful position as King of the Pride, but Leo has a surprise for them.

Leo has already met his mate. He just has to claim her.

Will the feisty couple discover breaking sass is much more fun together?

PROLOGUE

Damn. Damn. *DAMN.*

Sheila Rand pulled her Harley Softail Convertible over, coasting to a slow roll and eventual stop on the shoulder of the four-lane New Jersey highway. She'd been out for a spin on her bike alone after closing the bar tonight. It was nothing she hadn't done a dozen times or more since they'd opened Serious Moonlight in the South Jersey town of Blue Valley.

She tore off her helmet and tossed her mane of fiery red over her shoulder, huffing out an angry sigh. All she'd wanted was some time alone. A few minutes with the wind rushing all around her so she might try to weed out the negative thoughts and worries that had plagued her throughout the long and surprisingly busy day.

Business was good. Her Alpha was happily mated. The female he'd chosen was a real spitfire, and Sheila thoroughly approved of her. Lucy Corwyn was the name of the now pregnant feline Shifter Derrick was completely smitten with. They were downright cozy and wasn't that annoying in an adorable sort of way?

Grrr.

Easy, girl.

Sheila's inner beast prowled inside the metaphysical plane where she rested till called. Her evening rides usually helped settle her animal, but of course, tonight was all wonky. Her favorite thing about Blue Valley, the new place of residence for the Dire Wolf Motorcycle Club, was its easy access to the highway. Sheila could really cut loose on the miles of smooth, sleek asphalt in the wee hours of the morning.

Her Pack was off doing whatever they did when they weren't working or riding. She'd chosen to run with Derrick and his boys when she'd still been young enough to appreciate their wild ways. Oh yeah, their branch of the DWMC had started as a real ragtag group of renegades and nomads. Like all Dire Wolf Shifters, she supposed.

Only they were different. Very recently, Derrick, the boys, and Sheila had all decided to end their time on the road. Dangerous for their kind, but necessary if they wanted to lay down roots, build homes, have families. Her stomach clenched with butterflies, thinking about Derrick and Lucy's cub.

Lucky, lucky couple.

Sheila didn't know if it would work in the beginning, them staying in one place. But now that Lucy was growing her cousin's baby inside her belly, well, it gave all of them a reason to settle. A reason to protect their land and their business. That cub was the future heir to the throne, and the entire Pack couldn't wait to meet the little blessing.

The fact their kind usually attracted unwanted attention in the form of challenges and brawls with other Shifters didn't worry Sheila. Because of their size and strength, Dire Wolves often kept their Packs small, but that did not make them any less tough. The elusive Shifters usually stayed on the road to avoid altercations, but they'd staked their claim and they would defend it with their lives.

She liked Blue Valley, contrary to popular belief. Sheila wasn't trying to leave or missing her old life when she went on these runs. It was just, *well,* riding a motorcycle was a lot of fucking fun, and she was fond of fun.

Hell to the yeah.

She trusted Derrick, and not just because he was her cousin and Alpha, but because the man had a nose for things. When he'd announced his plans to settle, the whole lot of them had agreed to join him. Tired of life on the road, they all agreed to make a claim on some land and build a home, a Pack house, together.

So, here they were. And here she was. But there was something else in the air Sheila hadn't counted on when they'd landed here, and that was a restlessness she didn't want to name.

Shit.

She was no coward, and it was time to face facts. With their Alpha just mated, hope had sprung eternal. The rest of the Pack had started mooning around and looking outside, all of those big, dumb boys wondering if they too would find their fated mates in the small town.

All except for Sheila.

This spunky little she-Wolf was perfectly fine on her own. She didn't need a man to complete her, or whatever horseshit the graybeards from her old Pack had tried to convince her of when she'd been just a cub. What could a man do for her that Sheila couldn't do for herself?

Puhleeze.

She was stronger, smarter, faster, and worked harder than most of the guys she knew. Sheila could out cuss, out ride, and shoot more whiskey than half the Shifters she knew, and that was saying something.

Plus, she already knew where her g-spot was. The last guy she dated couldn't find it with a hand-drawn map or satellite guided assistance, for fuck's sake.

Pack house was getting stuffy with all the sighs and whines of the lovesick men she'd pledged to ride, *and land,* with. Overgrown cubs, the whole bunch of them, crying in their beers about needing a mate. Still, Sheila could deal with them. With her Pack.

They'd picked Blue Valley and that meant she did, too. But she'd never ever, *never ever* signed on to deal with *him*—that butt-sniffing, post-scratching, lazy feline pain in her ass.

Nuh uh. Not her. No way.

She looked in her rearview mirror at the sedan that had pulled over onto the shoulder behind her with one end sticking slightly into the traffic lane, to protect the person being hassled, of course. The customary siren was perched on the roof, lights flashing. At least the bastard hadn't turned on the sound.

Silver lining.

Oh, whatever.

He'd been waiting for her to ride by, of course. Crafty fucker. Darn speed traps should be illegal, in her humble opinion. What harm was she doing, taking her frustrations out on the road when no one else in their right mind was out and about at this time? It was the witching hour, after all, and Sheila was feeling mighty crafty.

Should make a big, fat voodoo cat and stick pins right in his you-know-what, she thought with an annoyed snarl. Would be a shame, though. Truth be told, the boy was quite good looking. Nice, big, hard body, and from the semi bulge in his pants, Sheila would bet the Lion was packing something mighty girthy behind his zipper.

Grrrr.

Hush up, she told her horny she-Wolf.

The man certainly was taking his time, but finally, after a few minutes, Sheila's supposed *fated mate* stepped out of his vehicle. She watched as he straightened up, and up, and up—he sure was big.

His gold eyes flashed in the darkness, and was that a purr coming from his chest as he raked over her body with that possessive gaze of his?

Sheila frowned. She was not an object. He did not own her. And furthermore, she refused to let her inner beast dictate her reactions to this, this—*really hot fucking guy*. Her she-Wolf could be somewhat pushy at times with her invasive thoughts.

Ugh.

"Put your helmet on the ground, please, and show me your license and registration," Leo Crowley said in his usual gruff voice.

Gives me goosebumps every single time. Bastard.

"Make me," she countered.

"Sheila." His tone held a warning note, but she didn't give a fuck.

"Detective," she replied, tossing her hair arrogantly.

"You know, you were doing ninety-five. It's dangerous on the road at night," he started.

"For you, maybe. But I was born on the road, detective. Just one more difference between you and me. Now, are you giving me a ticket?"

"Not tonight," he said, hands on his narrow, rodeo cowboy hips.

"Then can I go?"

Leo growled deep in his chest before nodding sharply, staring at her with those big, golden eyes of his.

"Get home safe, Sheila."

She ignored his parting words, revved her engine, and shot off like a bat out of hell. Inside her, a storm was brewing, and the reason was that man. Why couldn't he just walk away? She'd told him now a hundred times.

So, what if her she-Wolf was up in arms over the man? Sheila the human was decidedly not. He was all wrong for her. A cop, for fuck's sake, when she'd been raised to flout the law.

No, no, no. Leo Crowley was not for her.

Mine.

No.

Grrr.

Quit it.

Fate might have decided Detective Leo Crowley was her mate, but Sheila wasn't about to go down without a fight. She was going to break that crush right out of that man, one sassy comment at a time. Then Sheila would have what she'd always wanted above all else.

Her freedom.

CHAPTER 1

"Leo, come home," George whined over the phone.

The grating sound his younger cousin had perfected at seven years old still made Leo's Lion hiss in annoyance. His inner animal seriously did not care for George's manners or attitude.

It's not that he was blatantly disrespectful, but George was a bothersome prat. A pest. An annoyance. An irritation. But he was still his cousin—something Leo would very much like to forget.

His beast chuffed in response to the whining imbecile on the other end of his smart phone. If he were here, Leo would have already shifted and played a little game of cat and mouse with the much smaller male.

Grrr.

As it was, he had to count to three before replying. A little technique he'd learned in kindergarten to help him reassert his self-control. After all, it was unseemly for the future King of the Blue Valley Pride to lose his shit at a subordinate. Especially over the phone.

"I have a job, George. I cannot just come home when summoned. If you have an issue, tell the King."

"That's just it, Leo. The King is not seeing anyone these days," George whined.

"What? Come on, that can't be true. Dad is always available to the Pride. Besides, I'm on a case investigating an attack that could lead to a possible leak in our *organization*," he said, alerting his cousin to the fact some humans had gotten wise to the Shifter secret.

If word spread about the existence of the supernatural world, it would be pure chaos. Every Shifter, Vampire, Witch, and whatever would be under fire. There was a reason they kept hidden. Humans did not respond well to the unknown, and paranormal creatures would suffer grave consequences if discovered.

"Officially, I am investigating the bombing at *Serious Moonlight* that occurred last month. Unofficially, the Council has me poking around to try to find the mole. They want me to shut this shit down, George. It's important," Leo said, working hard not to let his Cat override his sense of serenity.

"So is the Pride."

"The Pride can wait," he snapped at the younger man, his beast's growling growing louder by the second.

Shit.

There were too many humans milling about. Leo closed his eyes and rolled his shoulders. He gazed out over the horizon outside of his small kitchen. He'd chosen this house for one reason only, and that was the view.

Magfuckingnificent.

The structure was small and cramped, but its location was sound. On the edge of town, his home was far away from the hustle and bustle of the otherwise idyllic community of Blue Valley. Sure, he missed the Pride sometimes. Conversations with his father, and the small patch of woods where he used to roam as a cub, but Leo had a different life now—a new purpose.

"Leo, please," George whined again.

"Rroarr!"

"Eeek!"

Leo roared into the phone, unable to hold on to his patience any longer. Thank fuck he was home. His idiot cousin actually squeaked in reply, and the sound made his animal want to hunt.

No. No. NO.

"Christ, George, enough," Leo grumbled and rubbed his hand over his face.

His Lion was a damn nuisance. Being born dominant meant always battling the beast within. His Lion was violent, bloodthirsty, volatile. He liked to growl, hiss, bite, and claw—tear into anyone who even thought to challenge him.

His list of enemies now, unfortunately, included George, his idiot cousin. The fool obviously thought it was a good idea to try to order him around. But Leo's dominance was a real thing, even over the phone. He looked around quickly, making sure no one had heard his little slip.

Fucking hell. 1, 2, 3...

"Sorry, Leo," George mumbled. "I mean you no disrespect, your majesty. But your father, *the King,* is not doing well. His illness is progressing, and the elders have called a circle—tonight, Leo."

"Tonight?"

"Yeah. It's serious. You really need to be here for this."

This time, George's whine was coming from his animal. The difference sounded distinct over the phone, and Leo knew he was agitated. His Lion growled softly. The beast was a natural born leader. He wanted to soothe the younger male, while maintaining his position as the stronger, more dominant Lion. It was all part and parcel of being born the next true King of the Blue Valley Pride.

Other Shifter groups had *Alphas*, *Netas*, and *what-have-yous* to guide them, but Lion Shifters were led by either a King or Primus, depending on their Pride. The Blur Valley Pride had Kings and Queens to rule them.

Leo Crowley had flouted tradition by leaving to become a cop, but it did not matter. His future had been set in stone the day he was conceived. It was easy to forget since he'd moved away from the Pride. But George was right. Leo had a duty, a responsibility to his father, and the Pride.

No, he was not particularly fond of politics. The slimy, greasy, double talk of the Pride's circle had never sat well with him. Hence the reason he chose a profession where he kept law and order, not talked about it.

There was another reason he wasn't feeling particularly gracious at the moment. Everyone knew the best Kings had Queens by their sides. Fate often played a hand at bringing Shifters together, but Leo's own potential mate had found some pretty unique and off-putting ways to turn him down.

Telling him *no* was a favorite pastime of Sheila Rand's. One of her favorite methods was, of course, the one-fingered salute she waved whenever he even walked into the bar her Pack owned and operated, which was daily, since—*stupid fuck that he was*—Leo couldn't seem to stay the hell away from the ornery female.

Sassy, sexy, fiery-tempered woman.

Leo's beast chuffed whenever he pictured the voluptuous Miss Rand. The Lion grunted, baring his teeth where he rested inside the metaphysical plane where all Shifter beasts existed till called. Leo had a special connection with his Lion, and he could see and hear him quite clearly inside his mind's eye. The Lion was annoyed at his human side's fretting, but whatever. Leo had plenty of things weighing on his great leonine mind.

Curvy, redheaded, sweet-smelling things.

"Well? Leo, will you come?" George interrupted.

He'd forgotten he was still on the phone with the annoying male. Leo sighed heavily. The younger Lion had a point about the elders calling for a circle on such short notice. It was unusual and suspect. But he had no desire to be sucked into Pride politics. Not at the moment.

His Lion wavered. The primal need to take care of those weaker than him was strong. Right up there with his need to crush anyone who dared challenge him. Instinct won out. His Lion was riding him hard, urging his human side to offer comfort to his Pride and kin.

Years of practice pushing his dominance aside in order to get things done, Leo tapped the countertop and exhaled slowly. Working with one foot in the human world and one in the supernatural world required balance. But if he was any sort of son to his father, *the King*, keeping tabs on the Pride was a matter of familial obligation and duty. What other options did he have?

"A circle, you said. And it is taking place on Pride territory tonight?"

"Yes. It's not good, there's been talk of a coup," George replied quickly.

"A coup?" growled Leo.

Bad enough they were calling a circle, but if this was a plot to overthrow the King without a direct challenge, heads were going to roll. A circle usually just meant the elders were getting ready to announce something. His guess was it was something big, and possibly annoying.

These things did not occur for no reason. Leo's experiences on the force and his heightened supernatural senses made him superb at finding out people's motivations. Leo was his father's heir. Whether or not he wanted to rule, Leo would have to accept formal challenges for the title once he ascended the throne.

Anyone trying to flout that law would be dealt with. Lion laws were complex and intricate, dating back to ancient times. The elders knew this. If they were plotting a coup, what did they have to gain by trying to circumvent their own traditions? That was the real question.

"I'll find someone at work to cover for me."

"You mean, you'll come?"

The younger man's excitement made Leo wince, and he growled into the phone loudly before he stifled the sound.

"Yes. I will be there, George," he returned.

Feelings of duty, honor, and loyalty welled up inside Leo as he tapped the end call button on the small screen. They were strong character traits of any Lion of worth, in his opinion—any person, really. He had a strict view of his responsibilities, and the Pride was both duty and obligation at the very least.

With over sixty adult members, the Blue Valley Pride was one of the largest Big Cat groups in the northeast. And that was not luck. No way. Leo's father, the current King, was a total badass with a reputation for being strong and decisive, while maintaining a gentle paw on the pulse of his Pride mates. Happy Lions meant a happy Pride, and a happy Pride was a fruitful one. The Blue Valley Pride was extremely productive in that respect.

Eat Well Live Proud, their import and export business, worked with the finest organic meat products in the world. The business was profitable and kept the Pride's coffers healthy. They had business dealings with top sheep, goat, bison, and of course, cattle ranches around the world, including but not limited to Colorado, Texas, New Mexico, Brazil, China, Australia, and of course, Argentina. Not to mention their fish and poultry connections.

EWLP products were shipped to all the top supermarkets, specialty stores, hotel chains, and restaurants. They even had a *ranch to table* delivery service where families could order top quality meat in bulk. He knew the importance of this business and its connection to the Pride, and Leo was proud of his father's success in making it all happen.

The US Department of Agriculture's Animal and Plant Health Inspection Service had been a constant figure in young Leo's life. He still kept tabs on new regulations and requirements and made sure his father and his advisors were aware of any new laws and rules that crept up on them.

Eat Well Live Proud kept the Pride in the black. Every one of his Lions shared in the profits of the company with quarterly dividends. Most of the adults in the Pride worked for the company, and those who retired did so with excellent packages and still kept a portion of the proceeds.

Donovan Crowley was no fool. His father had always been crystal clear during his reign that greed had no place within the Pride. He was a philanthropist, using most of his own wealth and his share of the proceeds to see to his community's needs.

King D had built an entire community of houses for his people. A gated community where he managed to separate his Lions from the normals who would likely shit themselves if confronted with a couple of changed adults from the Pride.

Smart. Very smart.

It was the duty of every Shifter to keep their

secret. Leaders had to be strong, decisive, and capable of keeping the peace. King D was all that and more. The Blue Valley Pride's gated community, called *Blue Valley Homes*, had three recreational parks for their cubs, several grassy knolls, and over fifteen acres of surrounding forests to roam.

There was plenty of room for Pride members to move about. He also reinforced their sense of fellowship with scheduled runs and Pride meetings. Yes, Leo's father was a good King. And yet, the elders were calling a circle.

Grrrrr.

Of course, Leo had been absent lately. He didn't have much hands-on experience with his father or the Pride since he'd been elbows deep in doing his job—not to mention *other* distractions.

Redheaded, big-bosomed, sassy, sexy as fuck distractions... Prrrrrr.

The truth was simple, if a little embarrassing to admit aloud now that he was an adult—but here it was. Donovan Crowley was Leo's personal fucking idol. The King had always been larger than life to his son. A true example of the best of what their species had to offer. Powerful, just, fair, and stronger than any other Lion Leo had ever seen.

True, he'd been distant. But he was a caring

father. He just always put duty first—something his son had learned to emulate. One thing was certain, the Pride sure loved Donovan Crowley, and his people were loyal.

There just hadn't been much room for Leo in his busy life. But that was okay. Leo understood all about duty, and he wasn't whining about it. He was never mistreated. Nothing could be farther from the truth.

If anything, Leo was a little spoiled. Growing up Lion royalty had given him the best. He had an excellent education—best that money could buy. As for the whole Dad being too busy to toss around the old pigskin, well, Leo had plenty of friends and buckets of affection from his dearly departed mother, and the other Lionesses in his family.

He literally had dozens of female relatives, all doting on him throughout his child and young adulthood. He had been afforded all the benefits a man of his position was entitled to. And when he was old enough, he'd left home for college. That had been a very turbulent time in Leo's life.

At the end of his first semester, he'd returned on a weekend visit to find his human mother ill, and his father tending her bedside alone. He'd been stopped at the door, told by his father's loyal valet—a man who was a pillar of the palace—that his father thought it best if Leo did not visit during that time. The King needed his Lion settled before he could handle the dominant male his son had become.

Of course, seeing his mate decline in health had upset his Lion, and Leo mourned the loss of both mother and father during that time. He hated not seeing his mother, but he managed a handful of visits when his father was away from the palace, during her illness, before she'd finally succumbed to it.

Yes, he resented his father for keeping him away from his mother for all those years. Partly why he'd become so distant. Donovan Crowley had ordered his son away from the palace and kept his mate to himself, denying Leo access to his mother, and that broke something between them. It damaged the bond Leo should feel to his King and father. He knew it. The King knew it. But both ignored it, pretending everything was okay over brief emails and even briefer phone calls.

He did not want to deal with all this Pride business right now. Fucking George. Why couldn't he just leave Leo alone? Being heir to the crown was simply a fact he did not have time for. But Leo knew his duty. Even if he'd conveniently forgotten it as he'd set about making a life for himself outside the Pride.

He'd always known he would have to return one day. Leo just wasn't prepared for it to happen this soon. He stood looking at nothing and thought long and hard about his position.

A Crowley had reigned over the Blue Valley Pride since the late 1790s. His father was a firm believer in the old ways. Donovan Crowley followed those old beliefs to the *t*, including alienating his only son.

He'd even kept a *circle of elders*, a sort of council of advisors to help keep the Pride on a healthy track. Their job was not to dictate, but to ask questions and to make suggestions. Should a King not be able to perform his duty, they had the power to call for a challenge for new leadership.

That meant they would have to pick a challenger who would then fight the King in a battle to the death either on two feet or four. Those were the only rules. And it had never happened. Not in the history of the Blue Valley Pride. At least, not as far as Leo knew.

Born with the Crowley lineage's powerful streak of dominance, Leo's Lion was strong, a true Alpha male. It was logical for Leo to leave the Pride until the time came for him to lead it. No one wanted a challenge between father and son. Heartbreaking though it was to be parted from his mother, Leo understood his father's reasons for keeping him at bay. Sometimes a King had to make difficult decisions.

"Son, I have no wish to harm you, but the elders say it is inevitable. When two dominant males, each with the predisposition to be King, are locked inside of the same Pride, one usually winds up dead. I will not have any harm come to you. I owe your mother that."

His father's voice echoed in his ear on the day of his mother's funeral, and he realized it had been one of the last times he'd actually talked to the man face to face. Leo knew stories of Lions killing each other, of sons and fathers at each other's throats to claim the throne. According to his father and the elders, this happened when dominant males could not control their natural urge to rule.

His grandfather had been killed in an accident before his father had cause to test this theory himself. Leo understood he did it out of love for his son. But understanding and accepting it were two different things. Would he change the past if he could? Maybe. But that was not within his power.

Pride life was bloody and complicated. Keeping

the Shifter secret by working alongside human law enforcement and covering up those incidents that would have leaked the truth had become his duty and obligation in place of the Pride. It had been hard, very hard, to stay away when his mother had become ill. But he did. For peace.

He'd tried to forgive his father. Tried to patch the bridge. Even made the best of it when he'd been told to leave and not return in that hated letter Montgomery, his father's valet, had given him. But Leo was loyal and good at following orders. He did as he was commanded by his King and father. He moved on, only visiting a few times over the years. Of course, ever since his mother had passed away, the visits had lessened.

According to George, he had to return. His father's health was declining, the Pride at risk. Shame filled him as he thought of all the time he'd allowed to pass. The gap between him and his father growing wider all the while. Leo walked outside of his house, into the warm night breeze that greeted him like a blanket against his skin. It was not balmy, just mild. Agreeable for the season.

Kind of like the warm air that blew from the expensive dryer he'd ordered through his barbershop. Like most Lion Shifters, Leo was big on maintaining his mane. He wore it a little shorter than most males in his Pride, but it was thick, glossy, and golden and he treated it well with conditioners and organic, sulfate free shampoos. Good hair care was a Lion thing.

He shook his head at the errant thought. He'd need his wits about him if he were to enter the *elder's circle*. Those felines were cunning and slick as most hunters were, and everyone knew Lionesses ruled the hunt in any Pride. Four women from the oldest, most loyal families made up the circle. He'd been away long enough to lose sight of their agenda, but not of the fact that they were dangerous.

Distance can be good, his Lion grunted, *they will have forgotten who we are.*

"Well then," he said aloud.

"Let's remind them."

L ater that night...

T he sky seemed lit with thousands of stars, and he took a moment to look at them before he sat down in his custom 1965 Corvette Stingray.

The red convertible was pure cherry, in his not so humble opinion.

It took him a few years to track down that particular model of his favorite sports car, but it had been worth it. He'd spent weeks rebuilding the engine, adding perks, and modifying the interior to fit his larger than normal frame. Leo was a big fucking Lion, and he needed the extra room.

He'd tried to maintain the original body, right down to the accents. The color was not just simple red. It was the original *Rally Red* made by GM with the same luster and deep shine the car would have come with brand new from the factory.

It was the best of both worlds. Classic car, modern comfort, and fuck, he loved the damn thing. Especially the way the powerful engine felt beneath his hands and feet. The sleek automobile had taken a long, long while to hunt down. But Leo was a patient Lion when it came to things he wanted.

The image of a certain seductive she-Wolf flitted through his head, and his Lion growled, rising within him to contemplate the object of his current hunt.

Sheila Rand. Beautiful, dominant, sexy as fuck Dire Wolf.

Mate. Mate. MATE.

Leo's growl rose and rattled the interior of his ride. He closed his eyes and counted, trying to rein in his inner beast. Fate sometimes played a hand in bringing Shifters together. Leo had never really thought about it. At least, not until the day he'd met his in a curvy little package who wanted nothing to do with him.

Fuck. Fuck. FUCK.

The confounded woman knew they were mates. At least, he was 99% sure she did. For whatever reason, she was completely unwilling to talk about it. So, he did what any self-respecting Lion would do. Leo visited her at her job. Waited for her when she left for her nightly rides. Watched. Protected. Lusted from afar.

Fine. He was stalking her. What the fuck choice did he have? The animal would not let him leave her alone. He tried for patience. Wanted to take his time, to woo her with his charm, wit, and looks, which were not half bad—if he did say so himself.

Sheila Rand was worth it. And Leo would not, could not, rest until she was by his side.

Grrrr.

But first, he needed to focus on what lay in wait for him at the Pride house. Afterwards, he'd worry about the sassy woman who'd already laid claim to his fierce predator's heart.

Mine.

"Yes," he agreed with his beast.

"Mine."

CHAPTER 2

Sheila heaved out a sigh and wiped up yet another spill on the otherwise gleaming bar top with a clean rag. Normally, she liked her job, but tonight she was a bit preoccupied.

He walked in a half hour ago. Stupid Lion, with his stupid, thick, glossy hair, tempting her to walk over, straddle his lap and run her fingers all through the perfectly tousled golden locks. It was ridiculous for a man to have such good hair! He looked like he hardly did a thing to it, but it was way too perfect for no effort. She'd bet half her tips he spent an hour on that head every damn morning.

Fucker.

Cute fucker.

Whatever.

It was all Sheila could do to keep her animal away from the dumb pussycat—tempting, dominant beast of a male. He'd been showing up daily for weeks now. Just pranced on inside her bar every damn day, like he owned the place.

Irritating, heavy handed, sexy, muscular, gorgeous— wait, what?

When did she start complimenting the big pussy? Nuh uh. Sheila wanted nothing to do with that badge-wearing overgrown house cat!

Leo Crowley was law and order, and Sheila Rand was anything but. She was a ripped jean wearing, motorcycle riding, fierce as fuck Dire Wolf Shifter. She did not need some Alpha male Lion in her life. Hell, she knew all about those ridiculous males, needing females to do all the work, wanting her to pander to his every wish and need.

Hard pass. Seriously.

Sheila leaned down to pick up a speck of invisible dust, needing the break from the rather intoxicating view of his golden-eyed stare—yes, he watched her. She felt those eyes on her like hands. Secretly, it thrilled her. She wondered what it would be like to give in to the undeniable attraction she felt for him, but no! She was so not falling down that rabbit hole.

Her inner Wolf whined, the beast barking a sharp, sad sound that echoed in her mind's eye. The animal wanted Sheila to greet her mate. To rub her fur on him. Mark him with her scent.

He is not my mate.

Yesssss. Mine. Mate.

Shut it, she growled at the beast.

This was ridiculous. She was not one big, throbbing hormone, for fuck's sake. She had to concentrate. Sheila tilted her head to better hear the conversation taking place on the other side of the front bar at *Serious Moonlight.*

A lifelong David Bowie fan, Sheila had enthusiastically approved of the name immediately when Derrick, her cousin and Alpha, had come up with it. After some debate with the ornery fucker, she'd been granted permission to come up with the logo.

Sheila had taken great pleasure in designing the logo and overall theme for *Serious Moonlight.* After all, this was the first official home of the Dire Wolf Motorcycle Club. Blue Valley had welcomed them with a healthy flow of patrons courtesy of Rafe Maccon. That powerful Alpha of the Macconwood Pack had come in with his mate and infamous Wolf Guard during their first week in business. After that, he'd sent plenty more customers over to them.

She'd been nervous at first. Had heard the rumors of the powerful male and knowing how other Wolves often reacted to their small, but potent Pack, she'd worried about her cousin. Challenges would, of course, be directed at him as Alpha. But Rafe, and his mate Charley, had surprised Sheila. They were not interested in fighting. Charley, a human, had been more intent on discussing the logo Sheila had designed, to her great pleasure.

The curvy little Alpha fem had loved the brash, hot pink scrawl Sheila chose to go on top of the glowing image of a large, white, full moon. It was both eye-catching and memorable. Sheila had liked the neon incarnation of the design so much, she'd ordered a mini sign for behind the front bar. She'd also slapped the logo on custom ordered black t-shirts, tank tops, and aprons for the staff.

Only recently, their order of printed napkins and place mats had come in. Sheila could not wait to use them. It was a branding thing. Guaranteed to make their customers remember their time at *Serious Moonlight Roadhouse & Bar*.

The Pack had plenty of start-up money, and though they each had their own bank accounts, there was one central business account that detailed their gross earnings before they got their shares.

Some of the Pack had bitched about the pink neon, but after a few months of raking in the crowds, they'd shut up.

Jerks.

She snorted at the thought. They might be jerks sometimes, but they were her Pack, and she loved them. Not like *loved* them loved them, but they were all family. Derrick was a good leader, and she supported his decision to settle down. It was not easy for their kind to do—nomads, the lot of them. But they managed.

Derrick was smart for a boy. He doled out jobs and responsibilities as evenly as he handed out shares of the proceeds, keeping their minds focused and their Wolves too busy to notice their surroundings. Money was good, but it was not everything. They had a few regular bills, but other than that, little use for money. Most of their cash went to motorcycle maintenance, and the rebuilding of whatever old school bikes they found, of course.

None of them had any particular love for material things. Too much time on the road was good for that, at least. Stuff was stuff. The important things in life were free. Sheila knew that deep inside her heart and soul.

Not that she wasn't loving the little conveniences

living in Blue Valley offered. Having a house with running cold and hot water beat sleeping in the dirt and washing in a cold stream any day of the year.

Hell yeah.

She was more than glad they'd found a place to settle, but just lately she'd felt a little anxious. Of course, it wasn't Blue Valley or her Pack that was making her restless. It was more likely the six-foot something hunk of man, staring at her from the other side of the bar, driving her bananas.

"Can I get another beer, baby?"

Sheila's attention snapped to the older customer, who'd interrupted her train of thought. Blue eyes flashing their annoyance, she frowned at the too familiar male, disapproving his use of a term of endearment with her. Sheila growled a little, grabbing a bottle of his preferred brand from the cooler, opened it, and placed the bottle on the bar top in front of him.

"The name's Sheila, Irv. Not baby. Not honey. And not sugar tits. I told you that already," she said curtly and made change for the twenty he'd put on the bar.

"My bad, Miss Sheila. But you sure should be somebody's baby," he grinned widely, showing off the big gaping hole where a tooth should have been.

"You flirtin' with me, Irv?"

Sheila smirked, shaking her hair back off her shoulders. It was hot inside the bar, and she'd have to adjust the thermostat, so she didn't start sweating.

"Heck yeas, I am. I'm old, not dead," the man replied readily.

Irv's eyes gaped, his head dropping as he stared at the way her tight tank top outlined her curves. Sheila rolled her eyes. Men were so damn predictable. Her tank top was useful for tips, but the truth was, she had zero hangups about her body. Yes, the uniform was tight, but the material was soft and stretchy, and she enjoyed wearing it. Fuck what anyone said about her.

Yes, she had curves. She also had muscle. Tattoos. And five piercings in her left ear. Sheila was a motherfucking Dire Wolf Shifter. Her body was hers and she wore whatever the hell she wanted when she wanted.

Period.

Were it not for the fact he was seventy years old, if he was a day—Sheila might have popped old Irv right in the jaw for smacking his lips together like she was a slice of pizza. Extra cheese. Lucky for him, she was feeling gracious.

"Irv, you leave that young thing alone," one of his companions butted in.

"Oh hell, now don't you go embarrassin' me in front of my boys, Miss Sheila. Tell him we're just talkin' here," Irv said, taking a pull from his beer and blushing all the while.

He met her eyes for a second, averting his gaze almost immediately, which was just as well. Her Wolf was riled. Of course she was. Leo's eyes were trained on her and Irv.

Nosy pussy.

"I would never think of embarrassing you, Irv. Next one's on me, okay?"

She winked at the older man, whose blush turned even redder. Sheila laughed and Irv waved before taking his beer and turning to chat with his buddies. She dropped the change he'd given her in the tip jar and went back to wiping the counter and eavesdropping on an unhappy couple in the corner.

Always be nice to the customers.

It was an unwritten rule all entrepreneurs adhered to. Sheila more than most. She was tough, levelheaded, and business oriented in ways that even managed to surprise her. But there was something going on in the corner she didn't quite like.

Sheila was manning her station solo tonight. Her

usual co-bartender, Weylin, was busy covering the back bar for Lucy, who was taking time off for the next couple of days because of her ever-growing abdomen. The she-Cat was pregnant with Derrick's young, and Sheila could not be happier for them.

Cubs, her inner Wolf whined.

Just thinking of them terrified Sheila. They were so tiny, so delicate, and fragile. How could anyone take care of something so small? It gave her the willies just thinking about impending motherhood. And if that was not frightening enough, how about dealing with some overbearing Alpha breathing down her neck?

Ugh. Poor Lucy—though, truth be told, she did not look like she minded. Thank fuck for the new soundproofing insulation the boys had installed in every room. Last thing she needed to hear was her cousin and his mate getting it on night after night.

Sour grapes much?

Fuck off, Wolf.

Anyway, Sheila was working her station alone, and typically, that would be fine. Sheila was no slouch. Besides, if Derrick had his way, the Alpha fem would be off every night, but Lucy was a stubborn kitty. Sheila's new cousin-in-law, a Bobcat Shifter, was fiercely independent. It drove Derrick nuts, which, of course, amused the rest of the Pack to no end.

Sheila liked Lucy very much. She respected the woman's natural grit and her determination to work by her mate's side. Tonight was a special occasion—Sheila had it direct from the source. Derrick was finally going to pop the big question over dessert. He'd chosen to take Lucy on a picnic, complete with a fancy supper prepared for them by Brock, their Pack Beta, and head chef at the roadhouse.

It sounded romantic and sentimental—just perfect for the couple, as far as Sheila was concerned. Not that she went in for mushy shit most of the time. Sheila was more a get it on and get out the door kinda gal. Even if it had been a hot minute since the last time she'd felt the need to get sweaty with a member of the opposite sex.

Sheila was not the *settle down with a mate* type, and it surprised her to find her cousin was. Good for him, though. She supposed it helped that Lucy and Derrick were so much alike. The little hybrid Cat Shifter loved the outdoors as much as the giant Dire Wolf did.

Yes, this was good news. Important too, for the whole of them as a Pack. It was about time Derrick claimed the female in a traditional if old-fashioned way. Lucy had already started showing, and Sheila was definitely in favor of their cubs bearing the Rand name.

Of course, Lucy was going to give him hell. Sheila grinned, thinking about it. Ha! Poor big cousin. But she knew the little she-Cat loved Derrick like crazy. Besides, they were already mated. Marriage was just a nice way to tidy it all up. Not that Sheila wanted to get married. Like ever.

Never ever. Not me. No way.

Even if a certain pussy kept prowling around the bar, trying to get her attention. She was having none of what that tomcat had to offer. IN fact, Sheila pointedly ignored Mr. Law and Order every single night. She would've thought he'd have gotten the hint already. But no. He still came strutting through those doors like clockwork.

The damn man had even stopped in front of her tonight, giving her one long, thorough look before heading over to where Weylin was working the back bar to grab his usual IPA. He was wearing fitted slacks and a neat, button down that made her want to run her hands all over it, wrinkle him up good.

There was just something about his good boy clothes and bad boy hair that was so damn appealing to Sheila. He was a series of contradictions—tiny little mysterious quirks she wanted to work out and discover for herself.

Grrrr.

Watching him walk away, fine ass outlined in his tight pants had set her Dire Wolf into immediate annoyed mode. Her beastie was pissed he'd gotten his beer from Weylin—but she was not mad at him. Oh no. Never that. Snarky, territorial female that she was, her she-Wolf was pissed off at her human side, at Sheila, for driving their mate away with her off-putting manners and sassy nature.

Oh well. This is what I wanted, anyway. About time that overgrown throw rug left me alone.

Mine.

Shut it.

Sheila heaved a sigh, frustrated with her inner arguments. She told herself over and over again that pussycat was not hers. And yet, every time she caught sight of his golden hair gleaming or heard his raucous laughter boom out from the other side of the room, her Wolf snapped to attention.

Her Pack mates were fond of him. They enjoyed his stories about working as a detective and often had a joke or two for the Lion when he came in. Ever since he'd helped out with the little bombing incident, he'd earned the respect of the DWMC, and maybe a little loyalty, too.

Fine. He was alright, she supposed. Leo had helped them identify the culprit behind that attack, and he saw to it Derrick was not charged. Afterwards, her cousin had announced that Leo Crowley's money was no good at *Serious Moonlight*.

In other words, the big ol' pussycat was not to pay for a single beer as long as he lived. Of course, that didn't stop the *by the book* Lion Shifter from leaving a couple of bills on the counter every night.

What a hard ass!

He couldn't even accept a beer without getting his tail in a bunch. Sheila's stomach clenched. Her pulse raced, and she found it hard to focus on her current task, which involved tossing a few empties into the recycling bin. He was just so, so—*what was the word she was looking for?*

Gorgeous? Sexy? Ours?

No. No. NO.

How about infuriating, annoying, and ridiculous?

Bingo. Those would work. The man was all those things, mostly though, he was distracting. Leo the Lion and all his steady persistence were proving to be something more than just a nuisance. Everywhere she looked, he was there. Stopping her when she was speeding. Showing up at the bar at all hours. Insisting they were mates.

Grrrr.

She ignored her Wolf's unhappy growl. Whatever the Fates had decided, Sheila was convinced they'd made a mistake. She was not the one for that uptight pussycat. Pushing the man out of her mind, she inched closer to the couple sitting at the end of the bar.

They'd had her attention from the moment the pretty, young woman came in about twenty minutes to join the man, who had been drinking beer on tap steadily for over an hour. She'd been happy, smiling, confident, until the moment she sat next to him.

Sheila had walked over to take her order, but the man waved her away. She left to take care of someone else. After all, it was none of her business. But Sheila kept one ear on their conversation—not picking up any words, just the overall tone. The woman was silent, but the man, whose face was longer than average with thick gray sideburns and matching salt and pepper streaked hair, was speaking in furious undertones to the no longer smiling female. She looked near to tears now. Her face was flushed with embarrassment, and that was not at all cool with Sheila.

"Fucking good for nothing, leech," the man sneered at the woman. "You didn't pick up my stuff, even after I told you I needed it."

"But you know I don't get paid till Friday. Besides, I don't like that man, he scares me—"

The woman tried explaining, her soft voice catching at the end. But the man cut her off, slamming his empty glass down on the bar angrily. Sheila frowned hard as she eavesdropped.

"You're just a selfish, lazy bitch," he snarled.

"Al, you don't m-mean th-that," the woman stuttered.

"You don't do a damn thing 'cept sit on your fat ass while I work hard every day. Shit, at least you used to look good. Now look at you. Saggy tits, fat stomach, stretch marks all over you, fuck. I could do so much better than you," he said, not even bothering to turn his head while he belched in her face.

"Al, please, people can hear you—" the woman begged.

Sheila growled low and deep. Her Wolf was getting mighty pissed off at Al. She handed another customer his change, listening, waiting, and wondering where the fuck Thor was. Usually, she could signal her Pack mate and bouncer when something was going to go down, that way they could nip it in the bud before it grew out of control.

"Shit, woman," Al, the charmer, continued, and Sheila was really getting angry, now. "You're lucky I invite you here at all. You don't bring my shit. You look like a fat mess. And then, you come up in here, start acting like I'm supposed to buy you a drink and shit. Hell, no! You don't earn shit. You don't get shit! Fuckin' waste of space."

Mr. Boyfriend of the Year slapped his hand on the table and signaled Sheila. Oh, this motherfucker wanted another round, did he? She narrowed her eyes. The cheap fucker had ordered plenty of beers for himself ever since he'd first sat down. He'd paid, too, so she knew he had money.

Whatever it was he wanted her to get for him, Sheila had a feeling it was not savory. The woman looked down, unable to hide the tremor that ran through her at the man's harsh words. Sheila hated bullies. She walked over with a glass of water for the lady.

"Hey, I need another," he said, but Sheila ignored him, speaking to the woman only.

"Can I get you something, honey?" she asked gently.

The female looked up, shocked. She bit her lower

lip, looking like she wanted to cry, and it was all Sheila could do to not let that jerk have it with both fists. She was too far away, and there were too many scents for her to make out if they were human or supes. Not that it mattered. Mistreating your significant other was a shitty thing to do whatever your species.

Al the asshole glared. He was clearly pissed Sheila was not serving him, but *whatfuckingever*. Dumbass should be grateful her attention was focused elsewhere.

"Oh, um, th-thank you," the woman replied, and Sheila nodded her understanding.

Sometimes, kindness was a foreign language to people who'd been denied it too long. Sheila understood. She offered the stranger another smile before walking away, adding something before she turned to help other customers.

"If you need anything at all, just let me know. I'm Sheila."

"Hell, Sheila, I need something. I need a fucking beer," Al said, trying to get her attention, but Sheila ignored him.

"Rudeness will get you nowhere here, mister," she said, and walked away, giving him a hard look that had Al squirming in his seat.

The man was a dickhead and a bully. His eyes glowed a little, so yes to being something other than human. He really ought to know better. Sheila let off a low growl, and Al the asshole gulped.

Poor woman. Stuck with a mean man. Sheila was not judging her. She was sure she had her reasons, but if she needed help inside this bar, Sheila's Dire Wolf was there for her. She'd grown up with strong female role models. Her mother, her aunt, and the other women of her Pack who'd broken off, forming their own MC had taught her many things. Mostly, to have other women's backs.

She was proud of those she-Wolves, even if her place was not among them. And Sheila took their lessons with her wherever she went. Female solidarity was alive and well in the Shifter world. Male dominance could go fuck itself. Sheila was a mother-fuckin' badass. Anyone in her bar was hers to protect.

It was the Wolf in her that demanded. Her beast was a protector. Derrick knew it and loved that about her. It was why out of all the other Wolves, whether bigger or stronger, he had selected her as his mate's Guard. Sure, they were not as formal as other Packs, but Sheila understood her role.

If and when shit went down—and it always did—

her job was to get Lucy to safety. She could do that. To protect her own, no ask was too big or small. And right now, as she sat at the bar Sheila was tending, that woman was hers. Even if only temporarily.

If the lady had said yes to a drink, she would have bought her a damn beer herself. Maybe she still would. Sheila finished with her present customer and turned to head back in the bizarre couple's direction, but someone beat her to the punch.

There he was. Mr. Law and Order to save the day. Damn interfering pussycat. She grumbled but could not stop her feet from heading over there. She was curious at how the straight as an arrow detective would handle Al, the dickless wonder.

Sheila continued to edge closer to the trio. Okay, maybe she was curious as to how the lawful Lion would handle the situation. True, the Pack might like the detective, but something told her they would be right pissed if Leo went around arresting their customers.

Shit.

She had better stick close to him then. Just in case she needed to intervene. No other reason.

Yeah. Right.

Her enormous, red-furred Dire Wolf snorted from inside her mind's eye, and Sheila shook her head to clear the sound from her brain. She was getting a little tired of her irritating animal's snide remarks.

Pfbbbbbtt.

Crap. Did Dire Wolves even know how to blow raspberries?

Apparently, was her only response.

FML.

Sheila growled and wiped the bar once again. It was an endless exercise, but a necessary evil. She refilled shot glasses, served a couple of cold long-necks to the good patrons of her Pack's establishment. All the while, she kept tabs on what was happening between the three people at the end of the bar.

Leo, the pain in her ass Lion himself, was one persistent pussy. Al was showing signs of completely losing his shit, and his female companion was biting her lip, eyes huge as Leo struck up a conversation with her. The man just couldn't take a hint, from her or anyone else, it would seem, but if she were being honest, Sheila would admit the big, furry butt face was growing on her.

Kind of. Like a fungus. Ha ha!

CHAPTER 3

The band was playing a rock ballad, and the flow of customers was steady for a week-night. Food was coming from the kitchen in spades. Their new hires were hustling from table to table, making sure everyone was happy.

All in all, Sheila could not complain. It would have been just like any other night if only the volatile moron at the end of the bar had used his brain and walked away. Leo was perhaps the most gallant and chivalrous male she knew. There was no way he would walk away from Al the asshat, leaving that female alone with the man who'd been ripping her a new butthole in front of everyone.

Sheila inched closer to the trio and listened intently as Leo flashed one of his patented, panty-melting smiles of his. Al was shaking, frowning hard at Leo's invasion, but the woman, his girlfriend or whatever, seemed happy at the intrusion. Who wouldn't be? She was blushing a bright, pretty pink under Leo's attention—*as any red-blooded female would.*

Sexy, hot, golden boy. Kissable lips, hard body, and that delicious spicy musk wafting off him in waves. Yummy. Sooooo yummy.

Grrrrr.

Sheila stopped short, almost dropping the bottle of vodka in her hand. Leo's gaze flashed over at her, one brow raised in question, but she ignored him. Replacing the bottle on the shelf with the others, Sheila pretending to concentrate on wiping the bottles and making sure the labels faced front.

What the heck was she doing? Getting jealous of the attention he paid that poor mistreated woman?

He was just being kind. Probably heard the hell the man was giving her and wanted to make sure she was safe. But did he have to be so good-looking while he maintained order?

Down, girl.

Sheila never said she didn't find him attractive. Leo Crowley was a Shifter. That alone ensured he was physically fit and attractive. Exceedingly hot. Hell—she'd have to be dead to think otherwise.

He was a straight up eleven on a scale of one to ten. The detective's pearly whites sparkled in the dimly lit bar, his platinum-streaked blond hair was pushed back off his forehead, making him appear approachable and friendly even. He had tanned, flawless skin beneath the scruff of facial hair that was already showing, despite his having shaved that morning. Yes, she knew of his impeccable grooming habits.

Truth was, she knew more about Leo the Lion than she cared to admit. He was model hot. And, sad as it was for her to admit, this was the first time he'd even looked at another woman, and she was jealous. Embarrassingly so.

Jealousy simmered beneath the surface, but she knew better than that. A woman was being mistreated by her male friend, and the good detective was doing something about it. Smile trained on the little lady, he opened his mouth and spoke.

"So, Marilyn, now that we have been introduced, what will you have?" Leo said, picking up on where he'd left off.

He was speaking loud enough for Sheila's Shifter

hearing to pick up on the conversation, and she bit back her smile.

Cheeky fucker.

OMG. Did he know she'd gotten slightly miffed?

Sheila cleared her throat, trying not to grin while Leo completely ignored the blustering male beside the now openmouthed woman. Al the dickhead was turning beet red, but Leo did not seem concerned in the slightest.

"Oh, um," the woman, Marilyn, replied.

Her big eyes went round in surprise, and she blushed prettily. Sheila spared a glance at Leo, but his gaze was on the shorter woman, even if his attention was on the man beside her.

"Hey, she's spoken for," growled Al, the ass, who, as it turned out, was an actual Ass.

Sniff.

Huh. Why hadn't she noticed that before? Sheila's nostrils flared as the Donkey Shifter brayed at Leo. The hair on the back of her neck spiked, and her inner Dire Wolf pressed at her skin. Her inner Wolf didn't particularly like the way Al was speaking to her mate.

Shit.

There was that word again.

Mate.

That itty bitty little word was something she'd been denying herself for weeks now. Fate had a plan, but Sheila was fighting it tooth, claw, and nail.

Mate? Nope. No fucking way.

Yes way. A whole lot of fucking way.

Her inner bitch had a way of really getting on her nerves. But now that she'd admitted the word to herself, it was all she could think about.

Mate. Mate. Mate.

There it was, flashing in her brain like the pink neon sign she'd craftily concocted.

MATE.

Ever since she'd scented his rain-washed scent, her Dire Wolf had known what he was to her. Sheila's denial was about to end.

Well, fuck me, she thought.

Yes, please, inserted her Wolf.

Exhaling slowly, she prepared herself for the moment his scent invaded her nostrils. It was pure Shifter biology. Easily explained, but every time she caught a whiff, her hormones threatened to go completely crazy. Her ovaries were working triple time, going off like roman candles around the man. She could feel her heat simmering below the surface, that primal biological instinct that ensured the propagation of the species when one fated mate ran into another.

Not now. Think about something else, Sheila.

Immediately, her brain flashed back to the first time she'd caught sight of him. It was the night those humans had tried to set off a bomb in *Serious Moonlight*. Detective Crowley had been the lead investigator on the scene. One sniff of the Lion Shifter's fresh scent, and Sheila's Dire Wolf had gone gaga for the big pussy.

He smelled the way a grass field did after a good, cold, crisp rain. Clean and untainted, tinged with ozone and budding with life. It was her absolute favorite fragrance. One she wanted to roll around in and coat herself with. *Damn biology,* she grunted and ignored the flash of gold from his eyes as they landed on her for a second before returning to the other female.

Grrr.

Awareness raced through her veins. A wave of his scent hit her again, stronger this time. She closed her eyes, willing herself to calm down. But how could she when he was so close and smelled so damn tempting? It was all she could do not to throw herself over the counter and attack him like the animal she was.

Sheila had a little bitty reputation for being reckless. Derrick had given her hell for that for as long as she could remember. Especially for her habit of riding her Harley during the fiercest rainstorms.

When she could, she'd take off in her fur, but that hadn't been too often when they'd lived on the road. Blue Valley was their last chance to find a permanent place in the world, and so far, so good. She couldn't wait for the next storm. She'd get to run through it in the safety of the woods they'd claimed behind the Pack house. It was nice to think she could do that anytime she wanted.

Strange. Different. Good.

The house was big, yet a little crowded for a Pack of adult Dire Wolves, in her not so humble opinion. Still, it was theirs and she had space that was just her own. Finally—and wasn't that awesome? She wasn't ready to give it up. Did not want to lose herself to anyone, mate or not. And no, not even to the yummy smelling pussycat.

"I said she's spoken for," the Ass said again.

Sheila watched Leo's golden gaze find the imbecile. She waited a beat, ready to smack the Donkey down if he got out of hand. Protectiveness welled inside her. She'd deny it in the light of day, of course. But just then, every fiber of her being was attuned to the heated situation developing. She'd started wanting to protect the woman, but she had a bigger mission now.

Protect her pussy—and not the one between her legs. She meant the six and a half foot tall Lion Shifter whose golden gaze haunted her dreams. The Donkey narrowed his eyes, blunt teeth bared, as he tried unsuccessfully to hold Leo's predatorial stare.

Good boy.

Leo growled low and deep, but his body was too relaxed. He could get hurt if he was not battle ready. Now, he might have to follow the law as a cop, but she didn't. Sheila Rand was a law unto herself. A fierce Dire Wolf, Sheila could more than handle the situation. She waited and watched, surprised when straightlaced Leo moved so quickly, she barely caught it. He had Al's hand under his, pinned to the bar top, and that was when she saw the switchblade.

"You brought a knife to my bar? Oh Al, you imbecile," Sheila muttered, taking the thing from his hand, and tossing it in the trash.

Leo nodded at her, gold eyes flashing briefly, then he curled his lip in disgust at the man. Sheila's inner Wolf was practically tripping over herself to get closer to him.

Sexy, powerful, dominant.

Fine. So he could take care of himself, she admitted reluctantly. Leo wasn't done either. He revealed his long, wickedly sharp canines in a not-so-friendly reminder of what he was. A predator. A Lion. King of the beasts.

Normally, she would snort at the thought. But not now. Not when he was flexing his badassery to protect a strange female while keeping it secret from the humans in the bar. The Leo she knew was a cut and dry kind of man. But not this side of him. He practically oozed dominance, and she had to admit it was sexy as hell.

Gulp.

Sheila was getting a little hot around the collar at this hint of Leo's baser, ferocious nature. Okay, so she had a thing for dominant males. She had always known she could not settle for a submissive. Sheila was too damn sassy for that. She would kill any lesser man's spirit with her snark, not to mention her thighs. Her strength had been a slight problem once or twice with past lovers, and she really fucking hated holding back.

Not Leo. He can handle us.

Her Wolf was very dominant, and the beast inside her enjoyed the byplay between her would be mate and the lesser male. Especially when the Ass actually started shaking in his seat. Sheila couldn't help it when her belly tightened, and her skin grew heated. Leo was hot as fuck when he was being all growly.

"Marilyn, are you spoken for?" Leo asked the woman, eyes trained on Al.

"Oh, well, I um—"

"Dammit Marilyn, I'm your husband!" Al shouted, wincing when Leo appeared in a blur on his other side.

He had Al's collar in his fist and was snarling deep in his throat as he pulled the fucker off the stool to stand in front of him.

"Do. Not. Speak. Unless I talk to you first, understood?"

"Yes?" Al whispered.

The word came out more like a question. He whimpered and Sheila's nostrils flared. The Ass might have just peed a little. Oh, fuck no. She was not cleaning that if he made a puddle. Eyes narrowed, she leaned over the bar to check, but thank goodness, the floor was clear. His piddle was still in his pants.

Gross. So gross.

"I think you've worn out your welcome, Al. Why don't you get on out of here?"

"No, uh, well, I can't. She's my ride?" Al squeaked.

"Your ride?"

"Well, yeah. Marilyn is my wife. We, um, live together?"

"This lovely little woman is your wife? A slovenly, foulmouthed, foul smelling Ass like you? Marilyn, is he lying to me?"

"Um, sadly, no, he's not," the female whispered her reply.

"Do you always mistreat your wife in public?"

"Sometimes. Mostly he just does it in private," she told him, her eyes gaining some of that confidence Sheila had spied when Marilyn had first come inside the bar.

"I-I'm sorry, Marilyn. It's just, well, you know how I get when I don't have my, *uh*, medicine," the Donkey whispered, eyes wide, pleading with his wife to understand. He still couldn't quite meet Leo's predatory gaze.

"What medicine?" Leo asked.

"Oh, he means drugs. He's a Duster," Marilyn said with distaste, referring to a type of bespelled drug that could give supernaturals an unnatural high—Shifters included.

Sheila frowned hard. She didn't want any Dusters in *Serious Moonlight*. Making a mental note to tell Derrick and the boys to look out for dealers, she clenched her jaw angrily. There was just no excuse for Al's behavior. He could blame it on magical drugs, but ultimately the fault was his own. He needed help, but before she could speak up, the Ass was sticking his foot in his mouth.

Again.

"Wait! Don't tell him that, he's a cop! She can't say nothing about me. She's my wi-wife," Al stuttered and swallowed as well as he could with Leo's hand wrapped around his throat.

"A Duster, huh? What was it you called your *wife* a moment ago? A leech?"

"I, well, uh, that is—"

"Do you know what a leech is? It's a parasite. An amorphous bloodsucker who lives off others. Does she look like a leech to you? Using Witch Dust is a disgusting habit, very dangerous too, Al. I'll need to call to the Council," Leo muttered.

"Oh, you don't have to do that," Marilyn began. "He's really not worth it."

Sheila was standing right in front of them now. Her eyes and ears were attuned to the surrounding crowd. There were mostly Shifters, but some humans in the mix. Best to keep things friendly. She ran her hand over Leo's arm, and he dropped his hold on Al, gold gaze flashing to hers.

"Shut up, Marilyn," hissed Al, turning to stare at Leo with wide eyes. "Sorry, uh, sir. Look, we will just be going. This isn't your business, anyway."

"Al, because you know I am a cop, I do not have to tell you this is very much my business. Domestic abuse is a punishable offense," Leo growled. "Give me your phone. I'm installing a tracking app, try to remove it and you will have a dozen of the Council's Enforcers on your ass faster than you can say the word help. Now, until someone from their office contacts you, I suggest you go home and wait—"

"Okay, fine. Thank you," Al mumbled, standing to go, eyes flashing at Marilyn.

"Before you run away, Al, listen carefully. I need you to understand this female of yours is a treasure. She deserves a worthy mate who makes her feel special, protected, loved, and cherished. All females do. This second number I am putting into your phone is for a counselor, someone like us who can help you with your addiction problems. Now, I am also putting my number in Marilyn's phone. I will check in with her about your progress and coopera-tion with the Council."

"What? You're gonna spy on me?"

"You're damn straight, I am, Al. This is my town. You do anything wrong, and I will find out. Now, tell me, Marilyn, do you have children with this person?" Leo ignored the man and spoke to his mate once again.

"Yes, we have t-two. A boy and a girl," she said shyly.

"I see, and you take care of them?" he asked.

"She's supposed to!" yelled the harried looking Donkey Shifter.

"Interrupt me again, and I will remove your ability to have any more children, understood?" Leo's quiet threat had more effect on the man than if he had yelled.

Sniff.

Sheila almost gagged as the scent of urine grew thicker. She looked once more at the floor, but it seemed Al's jeans were soaking it all in. It was the only thing saving him at this point. Leo looked down, disgust etched on his handsome features as he snarled at Al.

"Will you man the fuck up, please?"

Sheila was impressed. She'd expected the Lion to strut and roar, to announce his dominance and flash his badge with all the suavity of a fucking parade, but he didn't. Surprising both her and her she-Wolf, who watched the byplay with keen interest. The man nodded. His long face went ashen, and Sheila approved.

Asshole.

"Sorry about the interruption. Now, do you cook? Clean? Care for your children and your mate?" he'd turned his attention back to the female.

"Yes, but I don't have a job, so it's fair," Marilyn said.

"No, you don't have *a* job," Leo said.

Sheila narrowed her eyes at him. What the hell did he say? Was this it then? The moment he revealed his true leonine assholery? Leo Crowley was a secret chauvinist—something did not feel right, but she did not have to wait long to see where he was going with this. With Leo's next sentence, he redeemed himself and Sheila released the breath she did not know she was holding.

"Sounds to me like you have three jobs, Marilyn. Probably more if you count chauffeuring the children to school and extracurricular activities. Not to mention the shopping and million other chores that crop up every day, am I right?"

"You're not wrong," the woman replied, and yes, she was blossoming under Leo's praise and acknowledgement.

Sometimes that was all it took. A little recognition, a modicum of respect, and some affection. Those three things could save any failing relationship be it romantic, business or whatever. Everyone liked to feel needed, valued, and appreciated. It was human—*and not so human*—nature.

"You do it all, don't you, Marilyn? Unappreciated, unrecognized. And you," Leo's quietly intimidating voice was aimed once more at the Donkey Shifter, whose expression had gone from angry red and confrontational to *shitting his pants* green.

Oh, he better fucking not, her Wolf chimed in, and Sheila snorted. Leo's head tilted, so he heard her, but he did not miss a beat.

"You have one silly little job compared to all she does, and still, you think you're more important. You really think you are the irreplaceable one. How delusional are you, Al?"

"Well, I, I mean, I bring home the money."

"So. Fucking. What? Do you even know how to care for your children? Do you cook, clean, wash the clothes? Would you know what food they prefer if you even bothered to do the shopping? Hell, do you even know what day the trash gets taken out or when to change the lightbulbs or the smoke detector batteries?"

"I do, well, *er,* no, but still I have a job," Al said, but he didn't sound so sure anymore.

"One job. You *pathetic waste of space*—sound familiar? I heard what you said to her. All of us did," Leo growled, and when he jerked his head, Al looked around, Sheila too, and saw every male Shifter glance their way, their golden eyes flashing anger at Al.

Leo had rallied every male in the bar without raising his voice even once. And all to protect a stranger.

Fuck. That is so hot.

"For your one job, Marilyn accomplishes dozens, and she gets them done without a hand from you. You called her the leech, you sorry excuse for a male. She is way too fucking good for the likes of you, *Duster.* Now, apologize to her, or so help me, I will drag you outside, and show you three good reasons why you should."

The Donkey Shifter swallowed loudly. He looked from Leo to his wife and then back again. Sheila waited. Would the man prove smarter than he looked? Or would she get to find out what those three good reasons were?

"You really don't want to argue with me, son,"

Leo growled. "Apologize. Now. Or I will forget my job is to uphold the law, not break it."

"Okay, okay! Look, uh, I'm sorry. I won't do that Dust no more. I swear. I will call that counselor. Marilyn? Baby? I didn't mean nothing by it. I'll get help. Um, here, let me get you a glass of wine, and some buffalo wings too," he said, scratching his head and raising a hand towards Sheila.

"Thank you, Al. That would be nice after the day I've had," the smallish female said.

Marilyn straightened her shoulders and nodded at her husband. Her whole outward appearance seemed to have risen along with her self-esteem in the last few minutes. She turned back and looked at Leo, smiling at the big ol' pussycat like the sun rose and set on the man. Sheila might have found it a tad annoying, but she could not blame her.

Pretty damn impressive, pussycat.

"Just remember, you deserve respect. You don't have to take attitude from anyone. Society might not place high value on the roles of females who stay home to raise their families, but Shifters should know better. Don't hesitate to call. Especially if he doesn't straighten up his act."

"Alright. Thank you so much, officer," she said.

"It's detective, actually," Leo replied, and the woman smiled even wider.

Sheila slapped her rag on the bar in front of the cozy pair and placed the empty glasses in the sink.

"Can I get anyone anything?"

Golden eyes flashed at hers, causing an unwanted reaction deep within her core. Fucking Shifter biology. She tried not to notice the smirk on the corner of Leo's handsome face and focused her eyes on the smallish female. Far as Sheila could tell, the woman might be a Squirrel or Chipmunk Shifter. That would account for her large, round eyes, and that cutesy, vulnerable little overbite.

Grrr.

What was it about men who just loved a damsel in distress? Sheila wasn't a damsel, never had been and never would be. She could handle herself. The way *Ms. Chipmunk* here was batting her eyes at Leo wasn't something she could ever mimic. And if that's what he wanted in a mate, well, he wouldn't find it here. Wasn't that just too damn bad?

Ugh.

Acting weaker than she was simply wasn't in her. All the harmless flirting was causing a serious side effect that she wasn't at all prepared for. Her furry side was getting beyond agitated. Sheila's fingertips itched with the need to flex her claws. Her gums burned and Sheila had to bite her tongue to keep the snarl from slipping past her lips.

Leo was just being a good guy. Of course, he would fall for the simpering helpless female routine. Then again, it wasn't like the little Chipmunk Shifter was putting it on or anything. Al was a total dick. She felt like an idiot for thinking bad thoughts about the female.

The woman's mate had been acting like a jerk to her, and in public, too. Leo was doing what she herself was about to. Of course, she probably would've just upended his beer over his head, and maybe had Thor, or one of the boys, drag him outside.

Leo's way was probably better. Not that she'd tell the arrogant pussy all that. Her head turned at the deep, resonating chuckle coming from her mat—*er*, from Leo. Dammit, that four letter word floated through her head again.

Mate.

Marilyn laughed too, and Sheila realized again, the tiny woman wasn't entirely unattractive. That fact only pissed off her Dire Wolf just a little bit more.

"Oh, wow. Thank you, Leo. I think Al is going to

be better now. He wasn't always this way. That Dust is affecting his attitude, and well, I have to believe he is not a bad man," she said.

"I promise, Marilyn, I'm not," Al walked over, looking contrite. "I won't do that stuff no more. It's just I've been under pressure lately with lay-offs at the job and all. I know I was wrong. I am sorry," the Donkey Shifter said, and he looked pretty damn ashamed.

Serves him right.

"Al, if you feel you are hitting a hard spot, and the counselor isn't working, I want you to call me at that number, too. I know places that can help you," Leo said.

The fact he was being helpful, and not judging the man anymore, was just astounding to Sheila. She still wanted to kick Al's ass, but maybe Leo's way was better.

Interesting cop. Decent Shifter. Good man.

"Thank you so much. It was really nice of you, stepping in like that. You're a real hero. You too, Sheila," Marilyn said and waved goodbye.

Sheila watched Marilyn and Al move some stools down. Al was looking suitably apologetic and offered Marilyn a soft smile. Sheila still thought Marilyn should bop him in the nose for all that name calling, and maybe she would. But ultimately, it was not her business. If Marilyn wanted to give him a chance, that was her right. All she knew was Leo had done well.

"Hey."

"Speak of the devil," she murmured, catching Leo's unerring gaze as he focused on her.

She schooled herself not to react. Not visibly, anyway. Keeping a tight lid on her emotions, even the somersaults her stomach did whenever the big man's eyes locked onto hers, was getting to be second nature. Sheila adopted a bored faced, careful to loosen her clenched jaw and ignore her suddenly dry mouth. She couldn't speak. Not yet.

Awareness flared to life, little sparks of electricity, like lightning, flitted across her skin wherever his golden gaze landed. Right then, Leo the Lion was focused on her face, bringing a warm, possibly horrific, blush to her cheeks. Damn her redheaded complexion. It was tough on her vanity, being pale as milk with outrageously bright locks. She'd been teased mercilessly as a cub and had to learn to fight at a very young age.

Sheila might be good at pretending disinterested, but on the inside, she was building steam like a volcano ready to blow. Now and then, Leo's gaze would drop, sweeping up and down her body in a slow, steady move that made her pulse race and her panties wet. It had been sixteen months since Sheila had last felt the touch of a man. A long, dry spell, for sure. And Leo was not just any man. He was hers.

No. NO. NO!

"What time are you finished?" he drawled the question like no born and raised Jersey boy should be able to.

She closed her eyes, willed her body to stop its telltale trembling. Leo leaned closer, inhaled her scent and she knew he was getting a whiff of the millions of pheromones coming off her.

Shit. Shit. SHIT.

"Closing time. Like always, detective."

"Will you meet me then?"

"Nope."

"Why not?"

"Can't you take no for an answer, cop?"

"From you? Nope," he retorted, giving her back her own words.

Damn, he was cute. And he knew it too. She shook her head, tossing her hair behind her shoulder as she grabbed some disinfecting wipes to clean the same spot on the bar she'd wiped a hundred times in the last ten minutes.

"Why do you insist on doing this?" he asked, voice betraying nothing of the heated emotion she saw in his eyes.

"Tending the bar? It's my job, officer."

"When are you going to admit the truth?"

"You just won't quit, will you, pussycat?" she asked, sucking air behind her teeth.

"Pussycat? Only for you, Sheila," he growled, and the deep, rumble resonated throughout her body, sending chills racing down her spine.

She could almost imagine what it would be like to hear him whisper naughty, delicious things in her ear. In the dark. With their clothes off. And nothing at all between their hot, writhing, bodies. Good Gods, she needed a drink.

"You know, I never took you for a coward," Leo casually remarked, and his smirk was really starting to irritate her.

"Excuse me?" Sheila snapped.

"Are you ready to talk about us, yet?"

"There is no *us*, and what do you mean, calling me a coward?!"

"Tell me you aren't running scared, little Wolf," Leo murmured.

His rumbly growl grew even deeper as he threaded his fingers through his golden locks and pushed them back, away from his handsome face. He could have been a movie star, she mused. That sound he was making had her inner beastie panting and rolling over, belly up. Her Wolf yipped and howled, wanting to get closer to him.

Hot boy. Sexy cop. Wonder if he takes those handcuffs home?

No. NO. NO!

Have some self-respect.

"Look, you might be some hotshot detective, but you better be careful throwing words like that around me," she growled.

"What words? Coward? I'm just calling it like I see it. And what I see is a beautiful, tough as nails she-Wolf running away from the very thing she should run towards."

"What's that, huh? You? Ha!"

"Your fate, little Wolf. You're ten kinds of sexy, Sheila Rand, and that dominant Wolf inside you is hot as fuck. But you run scared every time you see me—"

"I don't know what you're talking about, *detective*," she snarled, angry at the fact he read her so well.

"Leo. My name is Leo," he growled, and for the

first time she caught his Lion peeking at her through his glowing gold eyes.

Sheila bit her tongue to stop herself from moaning in response. He was just so big, looming over her, larger than life and a million times hotter than the sun. When had he come behind the bar, anyway? She inhaled his spicy musk, loving the mix of fur and man

Wanna roll around in that scent. Cover my skin with it. Let everyone around me know who I belong to—grrrrr.

No. I belong to myself.

"I am talking about us, *mate*," he continued, snapping her out of her inner argument with her Wolf.

"I am not your mate."

"The hell you're not," he growled, eyes flashing their frustration.

This was it. The time he finally acted like the jerk she knew he was. But as the seconds ticked by, Sheila realized he would not behave the way she expected him to. Not here. Not now. Maybe never.

She couldn't just check off a neat little box that said *alpha asshole* and be on her way, like she'd done with other males over the years. Leo did something she'd never witnessed in a male other than her cousin before.

Control.

Leo turned off his innate machismo and grinned lazily instead.

"You know you're mine, little Wolf. Why are you so scared of admitting it?"

"First of all, my Wolf is not little, and second, I'm not afraid of a damn thing."

Sheila glared at the smug Lion Shifter. She did her best to ignore the attraction sizzling between them. It wasn't easy with his immovable stare, the tension that vibrated from his powerful body, and the slight flare of his predator's nostrils as he picked up on the heightened state of her emotions.

He was so close. But not close enough. Fucker wanted her to make the first move, but she wouldn't. Even if it killed her, Sheila was going to hold her ground. She would not give in. Not one single inch.

"Hey, detective," Phoenix greeted Leo, nodding at Sheila.

Her Pack mate sauntered over and took the seat Leo had vacated, eyes wide at the two of them standing so close to one another. He probably had no idea he was busting in on a battle of wills between Sheila and the Lion. Then again, the wily Wolf might know exactly what he was doing.

"Phoenix," Leo replied, eyes still glued to Sheila.

"I was hoping you had some time for me. I've just

installed a new *Draco Fortis* system on the grounds here, and wanted to go over it with you when you have the chance?"

"Sounds like a good idea, Phoenix. When were you thinking?" Leo answered.

Sheila wanted to turn her back on him, but the damn pussycat was holding her gaze. He had it locked on his, and fuck him if he thought she would break first. She would never admit how close she was to climbing up his body and claiming the sexy man's lips in front of the whole damn bar. She flinched, her elbow sent a bottle crashing to the floor and shards of glass flew up, slicing her calf.

Shit.

"Sheila," Leo growled, lunging forward, to look at her cut. It was already healing, and she really could not have his hands on her right now.

"I'm fine," she snapped, stepping back to grab the broom.

He looked pissed, but she ignored him and swept up the busted fragments, tossing them into the trash. Sheila just wasn't cut out for mates. Having a mate meant having cubs, and Gods knew she wasn't the least bit maternal.

How could she be? Growing up in an MC meant a shit ton of time spent on the road, and zero chance of a typical childhood. Even by Shifter standards. She just wasn't a good risk for a male like him—one who'd undoubtedly want cubs.

Gulp.

Lots of little red and golden-haired cubs. She could just see him now, letting them climb all over him like a jungle gym. It was enough to make her ovaries work double time.

Grrr.

Her Wolf growled and snapped inside her. Furious with Sheila for not claiming him, and their future babies, already. To her randy wee beastie, the sooner she got knocked up by the powerful male, the better. Leo was good mate material. He was strong and powerful. He'd make an excellent protector. And then there was the little bitty fact that the man was positively freaking gorgeous, too. Add to that already winning combination, the determination he'd already shown her, and, dammit it all to hell, the lawful Lion was the perfect candidate for a mate. He was more appealing by the second, which, of course, scared the shit out of Sheila.

Dammit.

Leo was right. She was a coward. Her admiration for him, her physical attraction to him, and the crack in her determination to stay away from him, all grew by the second. The big pussycat didn't need to know any of that. He was already conceited.

So, what if she was fiercely attracted to him? There was no shame in that. Any Shifter worth his salt could scent her arousal. And if they couldn't, well, the constant damp state of her panties whenever he was near was proof enough. Not to mention, the mountain of dead batteries in her bedside trash can, all triple As, like the ones that fit inside her vibrator.

Sigh.

Maybe she should just jump him and get it over with?

About damn time, agreed her Wolf.

Mine.

CHAPTER 4

"Leo, are you paying attention?" George tried to get his attention as Leo sipped his coffee.

It was just the way he liked it, stronger than his father's second—a big, badass brawler who was Beta of the Blue Valley Pride—and hot as his *soon to be* mate. Fuck. He couldn't go two minutes without thinking of her. That feisty female had blown him off again last night.

He felt as though he'd made some headway with her, which was always good in his book. Slow and steady. That was Leo's new motto. His campaign to win over the beautiful redhead involved spending most evenings at the bar she and her Pack mates owned, admiring from afar, and engaging whenever she was near.

Serious Moonlight had drawn plenty of attention from locals and out of towners, Shifters, and humans alike. Imagine, an honest to fuck roadhouse in South Jersey. It was a risky idea, but so far, so good.

Leo saw the appeal. The place offered unique amusements, such as local entertainment, which was mostly live music, excellent fare, and craft alcohol and beer from local microbreweries. And of course, there was the view. Every single one of the Pack was an eleven in their own right. Straight or not, Leo recognized good looks, and the Dire Wolf MC had it in spades.

Of course, Leo was only interested in one of them. Still, it didn't hurt their bottom line any that the owners and operators of *Serious Moonlight* were all perfect physical specimens. All of them were fit, attractive, and their MC status gave them an air of mystery and intrigue many found irresistible.

Leo appreciated a nice motorcycle, even if he was more into his Vette. Whenever he saw Sheila atop her Softail, his pants grew uncomfortably tight. The little Wolf was a total boner inducer. He wanted her so damn badly. More with each growing day, and not just cause of her perfect ass, and sumptuous tits.

He wanted to know all about her. Found himself

wondering what she liked and didn't like. Hell, he even drove to the city to research rare breeds in the library at the Shifter Council of NYC for information on Dire Wolves. He only found the basics, but he would take what he could get. Beggars and choosers, and all that.

They were very elusive creatures—large, prehistoric species of Wolf, extinct in the wild, but still around in their Shifter cousins. He counted himself twice lucky that he would be fated to have one as a mate. Not that he'd care if Sheila was a Wolf, Wildebeest, or Walrus. He just wanted her.

"Leo, I said the elders want an answer to their requests. Otherwise, they're calling for an open challenge to the leadership of the Pride."

"George, I'll tell you what I told them at the circle the other night. Back the fuck off. I need time."

Leo's mind went back to the elder's circle he'd walked into a few nights ago. The Lionesses had gathered, as they were permitted to, under the King's laws, and had presented him with some otherwise unknown quandaries. It seemed Leo's father was no longer seeing audiences nor was he answering his correspondence.

Leo had asked for time to investigate, and he left right away to talk to the old man only to be turned away at the door. He'd had to leave a message with Montgomery, his father's valet, and still had yet to hear from him. The King was absent, and that was not a good look for the Pride. But even worse, Leo was worried about his father. Absentee dad or not, Donovan Crowley deserved his loyalty, and Leo was determined to give it.

Fuck.

"You know the laws, Leo," George said.

"Of course, I fucking do. I'm a cop, George. I study laws. I enforce them," he growled, turning on his heel and pacing. Fuck. He was agitated.

"You are still single. If you don't choose a mate, your claim to the throne will be questioned. Look, the elders are willing to give you first choice at the crown, but they want you to meet with the unmated females this week," his cousin told him.

"I know what they said, George. I was there."

How old was his cousin, anyway? Twenty-one, twenty-two? Whatever. Leo was not about to spill the entire story of why he was still unmated. It was neither his, nor the circle's business. He needed to talk to his father. To clear up this whole disastrous matter. The sooner, the better.

"I have a mate. I won't meet with the pride females. My mate is just not ready to accept me yet," he admitted, grimacing at the sting those words caused. "She requires patience, and I will give it to her."

"What? You have to meet with them, Leo! It's the only way to stall them till Uncle D snaps out of whatever funk he's in. It's not like it's cheating. You have no claiming mark, Leo," he pointed out, unhelpfully.

Would anyone really miss him if we snapped his neck and tossed him in the woods?

The Lion's question was a good one, but the answer was an unfortunate yes. Leo would have to watch the ambitious younger male. Good thing his Aunt Patricia, who was also George's mother, and all his female cousins, the real movers, and shakers behind *Eat Well Live Proud*, the hunters of the Blue Valley Pride and so on and so forth, had his back in so far as assuming his rightful role as his father's only son and heir.

"I will get to it in due time," Leo replied.

He left the younger Lion sitting in his car and sped away down the highway. Traveling just under the speed limit, of course. The sight of George's face still sputtering inside his vehicle grew smaller in his rearview mirror as Leo drove away.

Twenty-minutes later, he found himself outside of *Serious Moonlight*. Again.

Fucking pathetic.

Just grab the female, hoist her over your shoulder, take her home, and bite her, for fuck's sake. She will thank us later.

No. She really wouldn't, and Leo had to count to three just to keep the gold from showing in his eyes. He was only going to grab some food. Just a bite, he told himself.

Brock Laurent, the Beta of the Dire Wolf Pack, was an outstanding chef. His dishes constantly surprised Leo. But the truth was, he would have kept coming back, even if they only served peanuts. Maybe he really was pathetic.

Grrrr.

Leo was standing beside his Vette, chest rumbling way too loudly. A couple of humans passing told him he left his engine on, to which he nodded and pretended to shut the car off. Fuck. He needed to control himself. He should not be this riled over one tiny, albeit feisty, redheaded woman.

Sheila.

Her name began as a whisper inside his mind. The animal within him stood up, waiting to catch a glimpse. His hunter's instinct ever ready, ever waiting. The whisper built up in speed and momentum. Louder and faster until his beast roared the two-syllable moniker inside his mind's eye.

Sheila.

SHEILA.

SHEILAAA!

Rrrroooaaaar!

Control, he needed control. But it was difficult, and he was getting antsy. The animal had waited, albeit impatiently, for Leo to stake his claim. Lion didn't understand what was taking so long. In the wild, a dominant male pursued the female until he claimed her. Fast, simple, boom. But Leo was playing a different sort of game.

Truth was, he wasn't playing at all with his intended mate. Sheila was more than just a roll in the hay, *er*, grass, or whatever the fucking metaphor was. It didn't matter. She was no casual fling. She was everything.

Leo would pounce when he was good and ready and not a moment before. Even now, his beast demanded he give chase. He pressed his human side, demanding he actively pursue his claim of the sexy she-Wolf. She was his fated mate. It was destiny, after all.

She might not be ready for what Leo really

wanted, but the she-Wolf could handle lunch. Hell, she could handle anything. His mouth salivated at the thought of grilled wild-caught King salmon with a side of spicy candied bacon cooked Brussel sprouts.

Grrrrr.

His stomach growled. Or was that his Lion? Whatever. The meal was Leo's favorite. Brock was a fucking magician in the kitchen. He did wonderful things to fish, meat, even vegetables. Any person—human, Shifter, or whatever—could and did readily appreciate the man's efforts.

Brock was a culinary genius. He made the best grilled steaks, monster-sized burgers, ribs, and chops to die for. But his salmon. Fucking. Perfection. The man's salmon was better than beef, or even chocolate, as far as Leo was concerned. And that was saying something.

Serious Moonlight's menu was small, but perfectly executed. Quality over quantity. And because he was a proud member of the Blue Valley Pride, Leo had met with Brock, and he'd gotten the ornery Pack Beta to sign with *Eat Well Live Proud.* They were taking on smaller accounts now. And why shouldn't they? Plenty of caterers, restauranteurs, and people in the food industry were clamoring for better products.

EWLP could deliver what they wanted. They boasted the finest quality meat, poultry, and fish available. Fresh from the range, ranch, or sea, directly to the table. The fish import business was just one of the Pride's latest endeavors on top of the meats they already dealt in.

Leo's cousin, Ariella Golden, was in charge of new client acquisitions. The Wild Fish division was currently on the hunt for some, and Leo was hoping she could drop by to catch Brock's ear. EWLP was the Pride's top enterprise, and Ariella was a very savvy Lioness.

Even if George was her brother.

George had obviously been shorted in the whole genes department. Maybe his Aunt Patricia had been stepping out on her mate, or something. He thanked his lucky stars there were no shared genetics there. The Goldens were not blood related, though he called them cousins.

His Aunt Patricia was no relative of either of his parents. She was his late mother's best friend from childhood, and their families were very close. He supposed he was lucky. To be fair, George really didn't have a shot at standing out.

He had four older sisters, and each one of them

was phenomenal at something. Poor George was just average. Leo supposed he had time. A little bit of it, anyway. After all, Aunt Patricia had only forbidden her daughters to mail George to Saskatchewan when he was a cub. He was a man now, and he thought he saw Ariella checking the rates of international shipping for live animals the other day. No, it was not business related.

Leo smiled. Memories of life with the Pride had been coming back to him in bits and pieces. More so over the last week. Ever since he'd been forced to think about his father and visit with the elder circle. He had to admit, he missed some of his Lioness cousins' shenanigans. Pride life was never dull, he'd give them that.

Of course, he stayed in touch as much as his job allowed. He was still, technically, the Prince of the Blue Valley Pride. He also sat on the board for *Eat Well Live Proud*, holding the most shares of any Pride member, just under his father. Duty and responsibility were a key part of his makeup. Before he exited his car, Leo pushed all thoughts of Blue Valley Pride to the back of his mind. Sure, the elders had given him an ultimatum.

"Leo Crowley, you will either announce your mate by the week's end or this council will seize rule of the Pride as

your father is unfit and until we can find a formal chal-lenger for the title," Ruth Cunningham had stepped forward and made the announcement on behalf of the circle.

It was all he could do not to Shift and go after those haughty females after she'd made that pronouncement. How dare they! The elders had gone too far this time. He'd told them to back off, let him try to fix this. They reluctantly agreed to give him a week, and he intended to use every second of the time he'd won to try to sort it all out. So far, things were not looking well.

First, he still hadn't reached his father. Second, he already had a mate and the idea of looking at the Pride females parading through the palace was downright distasteful on several levels. Not to mention it was horribly offensive and sexist. Third, good manners aside, those old biddies needed to be taken down a notch or three.

Leo had no intention of being bullied into making any announcement or proclamation, and he sure as fuck was not pretending to choose a mate from a bunch of women who probably did not want to be there. Leo had a mate. His Lion wanted no other.

And he was not about to rush her, either. Despite

what the little she-Wolf thought, Sheila Rand was his one and only—his absolute fated mate. His Lion had felt it the moment he laid eyes on the sexy, fire-kissed female. His beast paced angrily inside his mind's eyes.

Right, he needed food. First, he'd eat. Then he could think through his next move. At least he could sate one of his appetites. The bar's pink neon sign was lit, though it appeared much duller in the daylight. Still, it made him grin.

Brock might be gifted when it came to Leo's favorite cut of Pacific caught chinook salmon, but Sheila was a certifiable marketing genius. She'd come up with the design and plans for the logo for the Dire Wolf Pack's bar and roadhouse herself. Something her cousin and Alpha, Derrick, had told him. So many hidden talents. And he wanted to discover them all.

Grrrr.

Both his stomach and his Lion grumbled hungrily. The beast was salivating for a Lion's portion of the perfectly cooked fish—the scents of hickory and applewood smoke wafted over to him on the breeze. He knew every flaky pink morsel would be seasoned to perfection, a veri-table delight for his senses. He had it at least three times a week, and each time, it was outstanding.

But there was another, even more appetizing fragrance on the air. Like sweet cherry wine and habanero heat. Summer breezes, and winter fires. Sugary spice, and more tempting contradictions. It could only be her.

Mate.

Leo sucked in a breath, his Lion's tongue tasting the air, savoring each hint of her. His sexy, reluctant little Wolf. That was a misnomer, of course. He'd glimpsed Sheila's animal once, and the beast was enormous, magnificent, fucking perfect.

Dark, red fur, she stood as tall as a small horse. He had wanted to change with her so desperately, but before he could move, she'd appeared back in her skin. Naked and glorious, chin high as she leveled him with one of her patented, *I dare you* looks. Leo held her gaze that day. He didn't know how, but he managed it. Used his hand to bring himself to oblivion that night to the memory of his ten second glance at her perfect, ripe breasts, and the red curls that shielded her sex from his hungry gaze.

Fuck, her image was burned into his brain, and Leo would do anything for another glimpse of her soft, pale skin. And there went his boner. Fucking hell. He sucked in a breath of air and could have cursed himself for catching her fragrance again. That sure as hell would not do a thing to relieve his hard on. No hope for him now. He followed the heady scent hanging in the air, marking the way like a lighted trail straight to its heavenly source.

Spicy sweetness.

That was Sheila. Only she could combine those two contradictory flavors and make them work. Like honey and cayenne, caramel and salt, whiskey, and chocolate—all that but more. Her flavor held all those notes and yet, there was something else. Something elusive.

She'd made him a shot one night, called it a *wake-up call*. Sassy little Wolf said he might as well try it since he sure as fuck needed one. Damn, she was amazing. The drink too. She'd made it with cherry moonshine with a concentrated dollop of iced espresso, in a habanero sugar rimmed glass with crushed cacao nibs floating on top. Fuckin' hell, that innocent looking motherfucker had burned going down, but it had been worth it. Best damn shot he'd ever tasted. And it left him wanting more. More of the drink, and more of Sheila Rand.

She'd barely glanced his way as he walked into the bar, and yet she called to him. Tempted him, like a fish hooked with a single lure, her scent, the sway of her hips as she moved unhurriedly about her business, even the curl in red hair—all of it, *all of her*, pulled him forward before he even realized he was walking towards her.

She made his Lion chuff and his pulse race even from across the large room. She was here, and that was all that mattered. Just a few yards away. His mate. The only woman who'd ever made his blood buzz in anticipation. His muscles tensed at the ready. Even his heart thundered like a freight train inside his chest. Leo needed to be near her, to touch her.

Now. Now. Right now.

Sheila.

Her name whispered through his mind. She'd been giving him the cold shoulder for weeks, but he kept coming back. Waiting patiently for her to see reason. He'd figured that in time the pull of their matebond would grow too strong for her to resist. It was there now, a living, breathing thing, weak and sickly though from neglect, but they would fix that. The second she said yes.

So far though, his plan was an utter fucking failure. The she-Wolf had proven marvelously resilient. Not exactly great for his self-confidence. He believed his patience would be key. But that didn't mean the ugly mug known as self-doubt didn't pop up every now and again.

What if Sheila really was not interested? What if she found fault with him as a prospective mate? Maybe she didn't like the way he looked. Or smelled. Or the fact he was a Cat.

No way. We are fucking awesome, his inner beast chuffed.

And true, the animal had a point. Lions were one of the fiercest predators in the land. And Leo was also honest, loyal, and handsome if he did say so himself. Obviously, he had no shortage of ego, but what could he say? Cats were King. And so was Leo.

Literally.

He'd gone too far last night, calling her a coward. Leo regretted his choice of words. Maybe his plan to wait her out was a little cowardly. And maybe he'd been projecting. Shit. He should apologize. Sheila was strong and dominant. She would respect strength, not weakness. Apologizing was not weak, it took a strong man to admit he was wrong.

He could show her strength, reveal himself as the Prince of the Blue Valley Pride, but he had a feeling that wouldn't impress her much. It wasn't a secret. Not exactly. He just wasn't sure how she'd react. The fact she wasn't too thrilled with him to begin with fucking chafed. He didn't want to use his position to gain her respect or admiration.

His Lion chuffed and snarled. The beast was being pulled in two directions. One, towards his mate. The other towards his Pride. Leo had a duty to fix whatever was going on at the Pride, and to see his father. He was a problem solver at heart.

But his heart was the reason he was still here. He did not want to go without speaking to Sheila. He straightened his back, waited for the server to seat him in his usual spot. His eyes continued to hunt for Sheila. She'd walked to the back a few moments ago and was nowhere in sight.

"Your usual, Leo?" the waitress asked with a wide grin.

"Sure, Kelly, thanks.," he replied respectfully.

The waitress was a Wolf from the Macconwood Pack. She'd been a little too friendly, but he was good at shutting that kind of thing down politely. With a shrug of her shoulders, she led the way to his table and left to grab him a cold iced tea.

Where are you, little Wolf?

The predator in him was riled. But that was to be expected when a male stalked his female. This was natural. It was the most primal chase of all, pursuing his mate. Leo stilled, looked up, and saw her coming up from the basement.

Beautiful.

Stunned, he merely watched Sheila, in her badass ripped jeans and tank top with all her curves on blatant display, wearing a pair of leather boots with big steel toes and two-inch heel in the back. They weren't *fuck me* boots, but Leo was changing his mind on what he thought about feminine footwear and quick.

He'd never gone for this kind of woman before, but everything about Sheila Rand turned him on. She was a match to his kerosene. And every time she refused to acknowledge the building lust between them, he wanted to pull her against his body and see if she was really as immune as she claimed. Fuck, he wanted her.

He knew she wanted him too. Could smell her arousal, despite the words she spouted. His Lion was a beast, but Leo was not that kind of monster. He would never force or finagle his way into her tight as fuck jeans. Leo was going to have to wait for Sheila to ask him. He was not, by nature, patient. But he would wait. Even if it killed him.

Today, he'd put in his paperwork for some overdue vacation time from his job with the Blue

Valley Police Department. He'd locked his service weapon and badge in his safe at home, cleaned out the fridge, and packed a few things in his duffel bag.

It felt good to be wearing a pair of jeans and a simple cotton t-shirt. Much different from his usual day-to-day clothing. Typically, he wore a suit and tie, tailored to fit his larger than average frame. Perhaps his new attire would win him some points with his reluctant mate.

His little Wolf was definitely a leather and denim fan. As a member of an MC, Sheila's usual attire was enough to make his Lion go cross-eyed with lust. Followed directly by an intense jealousy and fierce possessive streak. The animal wanted her for himself only.

Possessive? Yep. But that was Shifters for you. Until he claimed her, his Lion was bound to be pretty fucking proprietorial. The wide, heavy bar top made a loud thud as she swung it open, carrying a case of something or other in her arms. He watched her carry her heavy load, knowing she needed no help. Yeah, she grunted and groaned, made like her arms were wobbly, but that was for the humans. To hide her supernatural strength from them.

Leo watched her, the patient hunter, and

breathed in her hot spice and honey sweetness. He was going to miss this the next few days. Fuck, he was going to miss her. No, she never talked to him unless he initiated the conversation, but still. Being near her helped soothe his animal. If nothing else, it was going to be hard on his sanity, being away.

"Salmon plate, Leo?" Kelly asked and he nodded.

She was asking him something else but couldn't hear her. All his attention was on his mate's sweet, glorious heart-shaped ass as she rounded the bar and bent over to retrieve something from the floor. That ass was one of the many subjects of Leo's dreams lately. Especially the way it filled out the tight ripped up denim. Holy fuck, two slits under her ass had the bottoms of her cheeks coming out. The smooth, pale skin making him wild.

His dick pounded, balls tightened, and fuck, when was the last time he wore those jeans? The denim was thick and stiff, and currently strangling his dick. Fucking hell. He looked around and quickly readjusted himself.

A few customers had noticed Sheila, too. All males. All staring at her assets appreciatively. Leo had to bite his tongue to hide his snarl. He was going to fucking burn those pants—as soon as he got them off her hot little body.

Holy fuck.

"Leo? Sides?" Kelly repeated, snapping her fingers in his face.

"The usual."

"Okay—"

"Uh, Kelly? Can you ask Ms. Rand to join me for a second?" he asked.

"What? Sure," she replied, looking at her notepad.

He was still watching Sheila, and almost swallowed his tongue. Red hair down and loose in a messy tangle that told him she'd been out riding. He loved her hair. It was sexy and wild, like her. The black cotton tank top she wore hugged her impossibly curvy frame, dipping low in front to reveal the most excellent cleavage he'd ever seen. And that meant others could see it, too. Other unmated males were right now staring at the precious treasure that was his mate's sublime body.

Hell. No.

Fuck.

What was wrong with him? He'd been coming here for months, knowing she was his, but had never acted this way. It was enough to set his Lion to roaring. As if finally sensing him, Sheila's entire body stilled. She turned and inhaled, whipped around to where he was sitting. Her red lips pulled back in a snarl. She looked ferocious, spitting mad, and hot as fuck, with her hair whirling around her face and her electric blue eyes flashing like lightning. She walked over to him, graceful and sleek, like the huntress she was.

"What do you want?" she snapped.

Leo opened his mouth to speak, then closed it. Eyes narrowed, he took a step closer, wondering at the increase in the pulse at the base of her neck. She wasn't repulsed, as she often pretended to be in his presence. The sharp scent of her arousal reached him, and Leo's beast chuffed.

Fuck waiting.

Before he could stop himself, he stood up, hands reaching out, and he captured her wrists gently, *always gently*, but firmly, too. Sheila's blue eyes widened, and he pulled her closer to him, close, so close, right until she was smashed up against his chest. His usual table was a closed off booth, and because it was early, there were only a few people inside. No one near them, though. It was why he liked that table. Against the wall, a perfect view of the room, and no one could see him.

"What are you—"

"Shhh," he whispered, leaning down, giving her plenty of warning, ample time to push away.

Sheila swallowed, gaze trained on his lips. She licked hers, anticipating what he was about to do, and fuck control, he just lost his. Leo pressed his lips against her closed mouth.

He ghosted over hers at first, testing, teasing, until he felt her surrender with a deep, beautiful moan. He wrapped his arms around her body, binding her to him, licking the seam of her lips with his tongue, begging entry.

Fuck yes. He could have roared aloud in victory when his sexy little Wolf finally opened for him, meeting his kiss with a need that matched his own. The blood in his veins turned to molten lava with the strength of his desire. Passion flared between them, igniting fast and furious like rocket fuel and a spark.

She felt so good right there. Better than good. She felt perfect. In his arms. Kissing him back like he was the only man in the world. Sheila clung to him, nails piercing through the thin cotton of his shirt.

Grrrr.

Yes, the beast liked that. Liked her marking him with her claws, like that she was leaning on him, taking strength from his body. Her arms wound around his neck and she held on all the while kissing him, and kissing him, and fuck, yes, kissing him some more.

No more games, no more hiding. This was raw need. Sheila's mouth opened wider for him, her tongue tangling with his in a battle for dominance, but neither would give in. Was she all sweet and submissive? Maybe for a second, but then his little Wolf was hot and demanding. She parted her lips, angling her head and forcing him to follow, ruining his shirt with her claws, and making his dick hard with the way her tongue drove deep inside his mouth.

Leo opened his eyes. He needed to see her, needed to know this was really happening. Of course, hers were already open, the electric blue glowing with her Wolf. Sheila grinned wickedly. Wrestling with him. Maybe for dominance, or maybe pure pleasure. Hell, maybe both. All he knew was she was pure fire in his arms, giving as good as she got. Nobody had ever kissed him like Sheila Rand. No one ever would.

Fuck. Leo was man enough to admit she was making him weak-kneed, but he'd never let her fall. Never ever. It was his job to hold her up, his pleasure to be the only man to bring that lust-glazed look to her eyes. He stroked and teased her tongue with his, reveling at the feel of her nipples biting through their shirts. The feel of those two hardened pebbles aroused him all the more. From the sounds she was making, Sheila felt it too. Leo purred, a satisfied sound deep in his chest, swallowing her moans greedily.

Her hands released his shirt and ran down his back, over his hips, and his ass. She was a true queen, taking pleasure in his body, giving only what she wanted to. Fucking perfect for the King of the beasts. Leo's cock pulsed inside his pants, a steady tattoo slowly rising in tempo and potency.

Pulse. Pulse. PULSE.

He wanted more. Needed more. Wanted everything.

"Mmm," she groaned, still trapped in their kiss as he lifted her clear off the ground.

He walked with her in his arms, out of view, to the office next to Derrick's which they used for breaks, or whatever, backing her into the wall. Never once did his lips leave hers. He pinned her there with his body, shielding her from the still open door while he kicked it shut. All the while, he was devouring her mouth, sating his soul, losing himself to the heady intoxication that came with kissing Sheila Rand.

Plump lips caressed his while her long tongue drove him crazy. Her spicy flavor burst on his tongue. Today was pineapples, but those habanero peppers still stung beneath that sweetness.

Sugar and spice, and so fucking nice. Leo's hands squeezed her ass, and Sheila rewarded him with a hiss, clutching at his shoulders while he rocked his hips into the apex of her thighs. She squeezed him with her legs wrapped around his waist, grinding her hot core against him. He could no longer contain his growl.

He wanted her. Needed her. Here. Now.

A jolt of desire spiked through his blood. She was his mate. His. Mate. He was going to claim her. Here. Now. He didn't know or care what else was going on. All that mattered was Sheila, all he cared about was her, and that she never stopped kissing him.

"What the fuck is going on here?" a man—*no*, a Wolf, a *soon to be dead* Wolf, bellowed from behind them.

Leo turned his head, lips pulled back. The fucker had slammed open the door to the office, and Leo took exception to that. He loosed a mighty roar, like the beast he was. Dropping Sheila carefully to her feet, he turned, keeping her behind him as his claws extended from his fingertips and fangs descended from his gums.

He was ready for battle at a moment's notice. He was a Prince. A Lion. And this was his mate. His vision was red from the sheer strength of his anger at being interrupted. He'd take care of this.

Sheila tried to sidestep him, but Leo tucked her behind him protectively, as a good mate would. He had to shield her from harm. It was his duty. But did she appreciate it? No! Of course not. His sassy little Wolf was pounding on his back, yelling something at him. He could not hear, the blood was still roaring in his ears, but he moved when she started kicking, albeit reluctantly.

"No! Bad pussy! Heel! Sit! Where's a fucking water gun when you need one?" she yelled.

"Fuck, Leo! Sheila, you alright?" Derrick Rand growled.

"*Ohmygawd*, Derrick! You are cockblocking your cousin," Lucy mock screamed.

The tiny, yet very pregnant female, pushed into the now cramped office, giggling as she did, and was eyeing Leo and Sheila like a sorta disapproving-approving big sister. Then, she was pushing her big Alpha mate back, and Leo finally realized what he'd been doing, and with who.

Holy. Fuck.

"Ow!"

Leo ducked his head to stop Sheila from beating on it. But he could not blame her. he was equal parts frustrated and confused. Yes, he wanted her like no other, but claiming his mate in a cramped office within ear range of who knew how many people was not his ideal.

"Bad kitty!" Sheila raged and continued slapping him on the shoulder.

"Please stop hitting me, and put those away," he whispered.

"What? Sorry. Oh, shit," she muttered, clearing her throat as she tucked her fantastic bra-covered breasts back inside her tank top.

"Lucy, that overgrown house cat is mauling my cousin in the middle of the goddamn day in my bar!" Derrick pleaded with his wife, who'd just smacked him in his head.

"Housecat? Really," she hissed. "You have a problem with Cats, do you? Well, good luck seeing this pussy's pussy ever again! You flea-bitten hound dog," she raged, and pushed away from him.

"Fuck, kitten. I didn't mean that. I'm sorry!"

Derrick was quickly trying to backtrack, and Leo couldn't blame him. Even if he thought it slightly hilarious to see the big bad Alpha groveling at his five foot nothing mates feet.

Good luck earning her forgiveness, buddy. A feline scorned...

"Ouch! What did I do?" Leo asked after getting another whack from Sheila.

"I don't know, you used your Lion magic to make my brain stop working or something—"

"Lion magic? Really? Just admit it. We're mates. You want me and I want you, dammit—"

A shrill whistle filtered through the air and every Shifter in the entire bar covered their ears and whimpered. Especially the four that were trapped inside the office.

"That's enough," Lucy growled, ceasing that horrible noise.

"Okay, okay. Derrick, I am an adult. Thanks for your concern. Lucy, my cousin is a butt hole, but thank you for putting up with him. And you," Sheila said, glaring at Leo as she stepped out from behind him. "I don't know what to say to you, but honestly, Derrick, Leo and I are good here."

She turned her blue eyes on him, narrowing them angrily. Then she exhaled and made an impatient face, like he was doing—oh, yeah the growling.

He should probably stop snarling at the man in his own establishment.

"Sorry," Leo said, voice still husky with his beast.

Leo turned to Sheila to see if she approved, but that redhead was not easy to please. Still, it would be fun trying, he mused. Sure, Derrick was her Alpha and her cousin, a big fucking Dire Wolf too, but his Lion seemed pretty sure he could take him.

Wait. What? No, this isn't right. Derrick is a friend.

Leo shook his head, trying to clear out some of the noise. Sheila stood next to him, talking to Lucy in a low murmur. He was too riled up to relax, and as if she knew and understood, the sexy little she-Wolf pressed her side close to his, allowing him to place his hand on the small of her back.

Just like that, he was calm. Like magic. The faintest touch of her skin soothed his savage beast long enough to stop his grumbling. Then, she went and placed her small hand on his stomach, a sort of half embrace, and the damn Cat inside him started purring.

"I still don't know what's going on," Derrick mumbled.

"Oh, honey, when we get home, I will tell you all about the birds and bees. Though, considering you're the one that gave me this freaking forty-pound basketball under I've been hiding beneath my shirt, you should know all about it," Lucy grumbled.

"TMI, Lucy," Sheila groaned, and Leo smiled at her silliness. He liked her playful. It was just another side to the woman he wanted to know more about.

"Anyway, you two can go now. I'm fine. This was all kind of, um, unexpected," Sheila said by way of explanation and shrugged her shoulders.

"Oh, don't you two worry. We understand. We have to be going anyway," Lucy answered and embowed her mate to get him moving.

"Ooof! Seriously? Fine cuz, but next time find a fucking room, not inside my bar, or the Pack house," Derrick grumbled.

"Hush! Bye Sheila! See you later, Leo!"

"Dammit, Lucy, you pinched me, and now you're gonna pay," the Alpha Dire Wolf bent down and lifted his pregnant mate off the floor like she weighed nothing at all.

He spun her around until she was giggling and kicking like mad, before taking off with her for the Pack house. Leo and Sheila watched them for a moment, and he was already dreaming of the day Sheila looked at him like that. With love and trust glowing in her pretty eyes.

Someday.

"Oh, hell. Well, I guess I better tell the boys to steer clear of the Pack house for a few hours," she mumbled and shot off a text on her cell phone.

"So," Leo began, watching Sheila's cutesy little frown as she sent that message to her Pack mates.

"So, what?"

"You kissed me," he said, not bothering to hide his grin.

"Oh, bullshit! You kissed me. I was just reacting."

"No, no," he replied, shaking his head. "You kissed me, Sheila, and I want you to admit it."

"Oh, for fuc—you know what? Fine. I kissed you. What do you want, a cookie or a sticker or something?"

"No. I want lunch. With you. Right now."

CHAPTER 5

Sheila huffed out a breath and sat down at the booth with him. Leo the lunatic Lion.

You mean Leo the luscious, lip-smacking, long-tongued, lengthy if the bulge in his pants can be trusted, loquacious because yes, she had heard the man speak, limber, lithe, lusty, and lucky sonovabitch who made her panties wet, her heart race, and her she-Wolf howl like a banshee.

Shit.

She couldn't think straight. That kiss had certainly thrown her for a loop. Loopy for a certain loveable Lion. Dammit to hell. Sheila was turning into Motherfucking Goose with all this rhyming and alliteration.

Grrrr.

She'd vowed to steer clear of the man, but here she was, sitting in a cozy little booth with him. After she'd spent the last fifteen minutes making out and letting him feel her up like they were a couple of horny teenagers. The man had moves. She would give him that. And yeah, maybe this was long overdue. Sheila listened to him order, and with surprising ease, she gave herself permission to enjoy this opportunity to just eat lunch with the man.

Kelly was staring, but one sharp look from her, and the female yelped and hustled to the kitchen. Good thing too. Sheila did not need an active audience. She was simply going to eat with the man. An idea that was surprisingly appealing to her.

True, she'd been actively avoiding the big ol' pussycat ever since she'd gotten his scent. A fated mate. Her. She could not believe it. What were the Fates thinking? Pairing her up at all, never mind the fact he was a Cat Shifter.

She grinned and shook her head. She'd tried to keep her distance, hoping she'd gotten it wrong and the by the book detective wasn't really hers. But there was no chance of that now. This was no mistake. Fear turned her stomach until she felt queasy. That kiss, that wonderful kiss, had definitely pulled the plug on any hope she'd been holding onto that he was not her mate.

Gulp.

So, yeah, she'd agreed to lunch. Maybe they could come up with a viable solution for this thing. Some kind of temporary fix, or something that wouldn't end in ruin and heartbreak for the two of them. Also, as a little bonus for herself, maybe Sheila could spend part of this lunch date covertly studying his new look a little.

Tight jeans. Big muscles. Hot, hot man.

She had to admit, Leo the Lion looked good as hell in regular clothing. She'd only ever seen him in suits and ties. Yes, he looked good in those too, but something about a man in a threadbare t-shirt and tight jeans that molded to his powerful frame, showing off his carved muscles and the sheer size of him to the best of their ability, really whetted her appetite.

Sheila's Wolf approved. Her human side was having one heck of a hard time keeping her eyes and hands to herself. She pinched her leg under the table and shook her head.

What the hell am I doing? Eating lunch with this arrogant male who thinks he can sweep me off my feet just because he threw on some blue jeans!

Hell. No. Stay strong, Sheila. Do not give in. This is how girls get got!

Her she-Wolf snapped her jaws in annoyance at Sheila's wayward thoughts. According to her other half, this big ol' pussycat was most definitely her mate, and her inner bitch thought it was about time Sheila started acting like it.

Roll over and assume the position.

Fuck that.

Yes, please.

Not what I meant, Wolf.

Sheila growled softly, but Leo's attention snapped to her. Pussycat had really good hearing. Good eyes. Good mouth. Hot body.

The better to listen, see, eat, and fuck you with...

I'm the big bad Wolf here, not him.

Potato, potahto.

Sheila had just about had it with her inner Wolf. She didn't want a mate. Not now. Not ever. And definitely not him. Right?

Not that there was anything wrong with Leo. He was a good man, honest, hardworking, with a moral compass that seemed to pass most Shifters. Plus, he seemed genuinely interested in more than getting into her pants. Or he usually did.

What was up with him, anyway? This was probably the longest he'd gone without pinning her with that golden stare of his. Just the thought made her shiver in anticipation. He had the thickest, longest eyelashes she'd ever seen on a boy. Dark too, despite his blond hair. There was just something about that long, unblinking gaze that melted her in certain spots. Not that she would tell him that.

But for some reason, Leo was not looking at her at all. He'd already ordered but was still looking over the menu. What the actual fuck?

He's not going to just sit there and ignore me. That's my shtick.

Sheila wiggled in her seat. Next, she fluffed her hair. Then she licked her lips. Finally, she adjusted her *tatas* in her bra, dipping her shirt low enough to flash him. But the bastard still didn't look up. Not a peep. Not one fucking glance.

She glared at him with her lips pursed and eyes narrowed. She tapped the table with her long, hot pink painted fingernails. Nail polish was her one vice when it came to expensive grooming habits. It was a weakness of sorts.

Her mama had always told her material things would weigh down her soul. Best to keep the load light when you lived on the road. But things were different now. Sheila had a permanent place to lay her head, and finally she could indulge.

So, maybe she went a little wild with the old one-click button. Thank fuck for Prime delivery options. Her first online shopping expedition landed her a professional quality manicure set complete with all the tools and instructions she'd needed to care for her supernaturally enhanced nails. That meant only the best stainless steel files and clippers—the kind zoologists used for predators.

Of course, she'd added a dozen top quality polishes to go with it. She liked the stuff so much, she now boasted over two hundred premium bottles of paint in every shade, from *daffodil yellow* to the *hot crush pink* she was wearing.

Thor, the Dire Wolf Pack Enforcer, and total sweetie on the inside, had merely grunted as he'd lugged the brown cardboard box full of goodies to her bedroom door. Phoenix had laughed, Brock too. Their teasing had grated on her nerves, but it stopped right after they'd both woken up to aqua-colored nails on their feet and hands. The hard to get off kind. Neither of those boys had anything further to say on the subject.

So, what if she spent an entire month's wages on the stuff? A girl had to have some fun now and then.

Why the hell shouldn't it be on something that made the rough and tumble Dire Wolf Shifter feel pretty? It might have shocked her Pack mates, but there was more than one side to Sheila. Besides, she didn't have to explain herself to anyone.

Especially not this usually prim and proper police officer. Who did he think he was, wearing sexy jeans and a t-shirt, messing with her very staid view of him? He was supposed to be a stuffed shirt. For fuck's sake, this was silly. Truth was Leo filled out anything he wore to perfection with that hard, muscular body and ruggedly handsome face of his.

He was hot as sin and the bastard knew it. Usually, he was the one begging for attention, not her. Sheila raised an eyebrow. Yes, he was hot, but so was she in a curvy girl, badass kind of way. Being good-looking was kind of mother nature's way of ensuring survival of their species. Not that all Shifters were graced with pretty faces, but hers was more than okay.

Her red hair had mellowed from the flaming days of her youth to a darker, more sultry shade of auburn. Her blue eyes were still big and bright, framed in long dark lashes. She had an okay nose, a little bigger than she would have liked, but whatever. Nicer than average lips. And her body, while a bit chubbier than most Shifter females, was still good to look at, and even better to touch.

She was not embarrassed by her size in any way, shape, or form. Sheila had long ago made peace with the softness of her belly. Her long legs, which made it easier to ride her Harley, firm breasts, and squeezable butt more than made up for it in her opinion. Yes, she had a couple of belly rolls, but fuck it, a girl had to eat.

She didn't believe salads and celery counted all that much when it came to meals. Sheila's Wolf was a carnivore, and right then, this meat-eater was getting angrier by the second. It annoyed her that Leo wasn't looking at her. The man who claimed to be wildly in lust with her was calmly perusing the menu, in the midst of all her rapping. He didn't even flinch when she raked her nails, scoring the hard wood of the table.

Oops.

Derrick was gonna be pissed. Sheila shrugged one shoulder up. She would deal with him later. The damned pussycat was going too far this time. Why was he even bothering with the menu? He'd already chosen the grilled King salmon with Brock's spicy cilantro sauce. It was the detective's favorite dish. He typically paired it with a cold micro-brewed IPA or, when he was on duty, a tall glass of iced tea with a slice of lemon.

She blushed at the fact that she knew so much about the man. Okay, so maybe she kinda, sorta spied on the big pussy whenever he came in. Which was often enough.

Cause he's ours, her Wolf supplied.

Whatever.

Sheila wasn't stupid or blind. Yes, she noticed him. She'd have to be dead not to. He was just so big. Massive really. With wide shoulders and rippling muscles cording his tall frame. He walked with the slow, self-assured swagger of a Cat who knew he was hell on women no matter how old or young.

Damn females practically drooled at the mere sight of him. All of them stopped to admire and stare whenever he came to *Serious Moonlight.* It was all Sheila could do not to unleash her beast and smack down on those bitches.

Mine.

The enormous animal inside her paced back and forth on that metaphysical plane where she resided, while Sheila was in her human skin. Her Wolf's agitation was enough to make her start picking at her nails.

Fuck no.

She liked that polish too much to chip it. It was just that she felt uneasy. She'd never had her Dire Wolf so pissed at her human side. The two of them were usually completely simpatico. But not lately. Not since he showed up on her radar.

Grrr.

Sheila mentally gave her she-Wolf the finger and stuck her tongue out for good measure. It was just too damn bad. She might not be able to fight this whole fated mates thing forever, but she wasn't claiming him. It just wouldn't be fair to him or to herself.

Sheila didn't want to face those demons just yet. She'd much rather busy herself staring at his chiseled features while he wasted time reading today's specials. She snorted at the thought. Whatever. It was his time to waste, she supposed, but sooner or later, she'd have to get back to work. Might as well enjoy the scenery.

She'd never gone for pretty boys, but Leo was definitely that, in a strictly macho way, of course. Sheila couldn't have abided anything less. Her personality was just too damn strong. It was a turnoff for most men she knew, Shifters too, to have a woman be so dominant. So far, Leo didn't seem bothered. Time would tell, she supposed, that is, if she were to give it to him.

Maybe she would, Leo was a hottie. Leave it to the Fates to send her a man after her own heart's design. She had a thing for faces, and his was near perfect. Bodies were one thing, but if Sheila couldn't swoon at a man's face, he wasn't worth her time. Leo was worth it.

His nose was straight and long, but it didn't dominate his face. Still, it was nice, with no sign of ever being broken. Unlike several of her Pack mates. He had a broad forehead, and thick eyebrows two shades darker than his light gold hair. Her fingers itched to run through the smattering of stubble along his square jaw and back to those full lips she'd nibbled on just minutes ago.

His face was good and honest. Okay, fine. She liked it. Very much.

Her curiosity about Leo grew stronger by the second. This was the first time she'd been next to him for so long. Minutes, but they were ticking by so slowly, she felt like hours had passed. His hair was getting long, she mused. The ends were starting to curl around his neck and hang over his forehead. He was usually neater than that. Staid and proper, like the lawman he was.

Nice, she thought. Sexy, too. She'd have something to hold on to now, she thought, picturing him settling those massive shoulders between her thighs, lapping at her sex with his long tongue. Fuck, yes. Nothing like a Big Cat licking between a girl's legs, in Sheila's opinion. Leo would be good too, she could tell. He'd have her screaming his name, gasping for air.

Eeep!

Had she lost her mind? Sheila clenched her thighs tight on the wave of moisture that drenched her panties. Daydreaming about smexy times with the big pussy was not okay. Shit. She'd been just a second too slow to react. The scent of her arousal had already drifted across the table to Leo's extremely sensitive nostrils. His chest rumbled and gaze finally met hers, glowing gold with his beast.

"You know, we can postpone lunch," he growled, his voice deep and sexy as fuck. "—until after I've eaten."

Sheila's mouth went dry at the barely veiled innuendo. Her sex throbbed and pulse raced. She could think of a dozen different ways to get them both to her room in under five minutes so they could continue their, *er*, conversation in private. She shook her head and went with annoyance instead.

"Fuck off, kitty," she returned.

"Anytime you want, little Wolf," he replied with a smirk.

Sheila signaled for Kelly.

"Can you tell Brock to hurry up with our order? I have to get back to work," she grumbled.

"Sure thing, Sheila," the young woman said, and giggled when Leo looked at her, smiling.

"What?" she spat, glaring at him.

"Impatient."

"You usually have your food ten minutes after sitting down, and we've been sitting here in silence for fifteen."

Leo grinned at that, and Sheila felt her cheeks burn.

"What?" she demanded.

"You watch me when I come in."

"You come in everyday, Leo."

His response was to grin even wider. The damn pussycat was not even trying to hide his pleasure. So what? She let one little fact she'd picked up about him slip. Big farting deal.

"I don't have to be a detective to keep track of customers."

"True, little Wolf, but you are keeping track of me

and that's a win in my book. Maybe I'm wearing you down," he teased.

"Shut up." Sheila snorted. "Okay, so what's with the outfit?"

Leo looked down at his clothes, then back at her, eyebrow raised.

"You never wear jeans or t-shirts," she pointed out.

It was bad enough seeing him looking so good in his work clothes, but having him sit next to her smelling all good like freshly laundered cotton was making her mouth water. Sheila had a thing about soap, too. Had always loved the clean scent growing up. It was one she readily welcomed, especially after what was sometimes days on the road.

"I'm officially on vacation," he replied and interrupted her train of thought.

"So, what are you doing here?"

"Well, I came to see you because I have to leave—"

"You're leaving?" she asked, stunned by how hard that hit.

Sheila should not care if Leo left town for a few days on vacation, right? Shouldn't bother her one bit. And yet.

"I'm gonna be gone for a few days, and I wanted to say goodbye—"

"Oh," she whispered.

"But after that kiss, there is no way in hell I can just leave now."

"That didn't mean anything," she lied.

"Lie. But I won't argue with you, Sheila. Anyway, I have a proposition for you. If you're not chicken, that is."

"Oh, you didn't just call me chicken."

Grrr.

"Hey, Leo, Sheila," Brock greeted them.

He sauntered out of the kitchen with their lunches in hand and placed them on the table.

"Damn girl, easy on the growling. We have a lot of *normals* in here this afternoon."

"Oh, don't mind Sheila, Brock," Leo inserted. "I might have taunted her a little."

"Oh, yeah?"

"Well, I may have called her a chicken."

"No way! Ha! Sheila a chicken? Damn Leo, you must want your ass handed to you sideways," Brock replied and laughed.

"Is that so?" Leo asked, his eyes dancing with mischief.

"She's pretty tough, *for a girl.*" the Beta added.

"Gods, save me from arrogant men," she mumbled, and felt herself getting angrier by the second.

It was bad enough she let herself get roped into having lunch with a damn feline, but now she had to take shit from her Beta, too? What the hell?

"I wasn't exactly calling Sheila out. You see, Brock, I have a little situation going on within my Pride right now. I could use Sheila's help, but I understand if she's not comfortable entering an all-feline community."

"What?!" she sputtered.

"I see," Brock answered Leo, talking like she wasn't even there.

"I suppose it might be intimidating for a she-Wolf. What seems to be the problem anyway, Leo? Can I help?"

That dirty, lowdown, ass-munching traitor.

"The fuck?" Sheila snarled at her Beta and the Lion.

The two of them ignored her, chatting away like the old biddies they were about to become, once she was done slicing their balls off. Holy hell. She needed to calm down. There was no reason for her to be this riled. Only, she was.

Relax. They can take their stupid taunts and shove them up their furry butt holes.

"Thanks Brock. Appreciate the offer. I don't know who I can trust back home. It's been a while and there's been a troublesome development. You see, the King's health is bad, and the elders are looking to replace him. I need Sheila here to act as my mate while I go home to the Pride for a few days to investigate."

"Why?" she asked, curious now.

"Lions are all about breeding. When word gets out that an unmated, breeding age male is around, I won't be able to get anything done. Every family with an eligible female will be shoving them at me. I'll be drowning in unwed Lionesses, some of whom will be in heat, and I need a way to effectively fend them off, preferably without insulting anyone."

"A whole Pride of horny Lionesses, huh? That seems like a good problem to have," Brock replied, enjoying Sheila's discomfort.

Lionesses prowling around my mate? Fuck. No. Grrr.

Crap. Now was not the time to go all possessive. She was supposed to remain separate and aloof to Leo's charms. She couldn't go strutting around pretending to be mated to the man.

"You would think that, but I need to focus on the

King. Problem is with Lionesses in heat, and me still unmated, my Cat will feel a biological imperative to service those females, and well, I don't have the time—"

"Don't have the time?" she growled, deep and low.

Two-timing tomcat.

"I have a duty to my Pride, Sheila, and I am asking you to help me root out whatever is going on there by running interference for me. It would be a big help. And I will owe you a favor," he said, sweetening the deal.

"Damn, Leo, Pride politics sound intense," Brock interrupted her thoughts.

His easy going tone belied the intelligence she knew he possessed. He was the Beta for a reason. The man had an unending supply of patience and understanding.

Prick.

"So, Sheila," he addressed her. "Are you afraid to play a Lion's mate?"

"It's not that simple, Brock," she sputtered, still on the fence.

What did he know about it, anyway? She didn't tell anyone that Leo really was hers. How could she just pretend? The Lion knew damn well they were fated mates, and being in such close proximity would drive her nuts.

She'd find herself good and claimed before the weekend was finished. Maybe that was his plan. The dirty rat!

"Well, I suppose I could find some other woman to help me out. Maybe Kelly, our waitress, wouldn't mind pretending to be my mate while I investigate things. That will cause a significant delay, of course, while I teach her what she needs to know about Pride life. I'll also have to mark her with my scent," he continued despite her growing growl.

"I was really hoping your Pack mate here would find it in her heart to help me out, Brock, but if you could just call Kelly over here—"

Leo spoke with just the right amount of inflection to suggest he was really understanding, though presumably put out by her rejection.

"Now, wait a minute—" Sheila was positively incensed at the idea that she was not honoring her Pack's obligations. Okay, there was the itty bitty little fact that the idea of him marking anyone but her with his scent was turning her Dire Wolf into a homicidal maniac.

"You know, I don't see why you won't help a friend of ours, Sheila. That isn't like you," Brock interrupted. "Or is the good detective here right in thinking you're afraid of tangling with a couple of Cats? After all, Lucy whooped your ass at arm wrestling the other night."

"I let her win! You know, I did," she replied, shocked he would stoop so low.

"Sure you did, honey." Leo agreed condescendingly. "Now about Kelly?"

It was obvious he was just placating her about the arm wrestling thing, and that was bad enough. But then to ask for their waitress to act as his mate? No way was that going to fly with her or her she-Wolf.

The nerve of that milk-lapping jerk!

Anger coursed through her veins, and some other green-eyed emotion she'd rather not admit. That big pussy might have laid out this trap for her like an angler dangling a worm on a hook, but at least she recognized it. Too bad, idiot she was, Sheila was grabbing onto the damn thing faster than a hot knife sliced through butter.

"So, if I come home with you and chase those females away, you owe me a favor, right?"

"Yes," he replied, tensing a little.

"You will do anything I say?"

Leo's eyebrows furrowed as he thought about the implication, but she saw something click right before he nodded. There was no going back now. If she did this for him, Sheila could tell him to leave her alone. She could remove the temptation to be subservient to a man and get on with her life.

It was the perfect plan.

"Fine. I'm in," she said smugly.

Leo eyed her suspiciously, and Brock chuckled as he walked away. He might be bigger than her, but she was smarter.

Wily little Wolf.

"So, when do we leave?" she asked nonchalantly.

"How fast can you pack?"

CHAPTER 6

Leo was smiling like the Cat who got the canary, and he didn't care who knew it. His tousled hair was blowing in the warm breeze, and he was tapping his thumbs in time to the classic rock blaring from his high quality sound system. He didn't have a care in the world.

Bastard.

Sheila huffed silently in the passenger seat, wondering if she had really gotten the better end of this deal. She watched him maneuver his slick car expertly and cursed herself for admiring the sleek classic sports car. But she couldn't help it. The Corvette was gorgeous, much like the man driving it.

Golden boy opened his lips and sang a few bars

of a familiar and pleasant rock ballad. Covertly, Sheila sighed, relishing the deep timbre of his voice. He sounded good. Singing was something she couldn't do on a motorcycle. Nope. That kind of thing resulted in a mouthful of flies. Nothing Sheila wanted to experience, for sure. She pictured Leo on the back of her bike and bit her bottom lip. Seeing him in jeans for the first time had put him in an entirely different perspective.

Racing down the highway in his Corvette, windows open, rock music blaring—Leo was hot as fuck. His Alpha attitude would probably keep him from letting her drive his sexy ass car, but damn, if he was up for it, she would take him for a ride. He'd look good sitting on her bike, those big arms of his snug around her middle and his muscular thighs wrapped around hers.

Oooh la la.

Sheila was getting all hot and bothered just thinking about it. She was getting to see a side of him she hadn't known existed and all in a short space of time. It was unnerving.

Exciting.

Frightening.

All of the above.

Shivers raced up and down her spine as the

Corvette zipped down the lane. Leo drove past other cars like a big Cat cutting through the jungle, taking turns like a motherfucking pro. She admired the car and his handling of it. Never pictured him in the low slung, sexy as hell sports car. He usually drove a staid sedan. But that was his work vehicle. Detective Crowley was a rule-following kind of guy. The kind she'd typically avoid. But here he was, chipping away at walls and breaking down barriers.

Chip. Chip. CHIP.

This wilder side of him was making it more difficult for her to keep her resolve. He turned his head and winked at her, using his signal to exit off the highway. Her hands were itching to get hold of his vintage teak steering wheel—and no that was not a euphemism. She wanted to feel the powerful *vroom* of the rebuilt and boosted horsepower engine Leo had installed. Right then, that machine was positively singing beneath the hood. Sheila appreciated the sound.

It was a good, strong rumble that did not interfere with the stereo. In fact, it enhanced it. The leather bucket seats hugged her curvy frame, and she had plenty of room to stretch her long legs. Good car. Good man. Sexy, too.

Sheila bit her lip, hoping to hide her grin of

excitement each time he expertly shifted gears. His maneuvers were smooth, while remaining sharp, on point, and fast. Only a maniac or a Shifter would drive like that. She bit her lip as her pulse raced.

Excited as she might be about his choice of automobile, it didn't change the facts. Sheila needed to keep a level head, else she might lose herself to this man. Hell, she was still trying to figure out how she wound up in his admittedly awesome Corvette Stingray with her saddle bags packed and snug behind her.

What was she thinking agreeing to play his mate? And for his Pride no less. Shifters would sniff out a lie, but he already knew that. There were ways to get around lying, of course, but she didn't expect the detective to employ such means. Surely, he wouldn't use these circumstances to press his suit. Hell, if he even thought about it, she'd just have to show him that Wolves had claws too.

What did he think of her giant beastie? She refused to give in to the unease that threatened to creep up. She was used to intimidating others with her animal. It was hell on relationships, but she was not ashamed of her animal. Her she-Wolf was a thing of motherfucking beauty. With thick red fur and the same electric blue eyes she had in her human form, her prehistoric animal was roughly the size of a small horse and ten times as strong.

Over eight-hundred pounds of pure muscle lived inside of her and her animal radiated energy, loyalty, and the primal instinct to protect what was hers. Those things and more drove Sheila's actions. The strongest at the moment was the need to claim her mate. The Wolf wanted it. Desperately.

It was her human side who was not as sure. Sex was easy. She'd have no problem getting down and dirty with the golden-eyed cop. It was the rest of it that was complicated.

She exhaled slowly and concentrated on the yellow stripe running down the black pavement as it zipped past her window. Only fifteen minutes from the roadhouse to the Blue Valley Pride, but it felt longer. She was surprised to learn the woods behind *Serious Moonlight* eventually led to the woods owned and protected by Leo's Pride.

The trees opened up to a low, grass covered valley that was visible just behind the *Eat Well Live Proud* headquarters, which was, of course, also owned and operated by the Blue Valley Pride. She looked at their large stately sign and snorted. She much preferred pink neon to the gold block letters, but she supposed it wouldn't have made sense there.

Leo drove past it, eventually turning into a beautiful large gate.

Blue Valley Homes was scrawled across the wrought iron in big gold letters. It was an entire community just for the Pride, she realized. After he punched a few numbers into a keypad and swiped a card, the gate opened. Leo pressed the gas pedal and drove straight to the largest home in the entire complex. It was an enormous sprawling ranch with columns and statues outside.

Sheila had never seen anything quite like it. It was huge, not to mention fancy. Like one of those ridiculously expensive homes, television dramas of the 1980s and 90s loved to flaunt. Might as well hang a sign up that read *millionaire inside*, she thought, and snorted at the imagery. She balked, realizing Leo was parking right outside the opulent mansion. This couldn't be Leo's childhood home, could it?

Sheila swallowed hard and tried to calm her nerves. Noise from a large koi pond out front caught her attention. He had a fountain. His own fountain. And, of course, the shrubs and lawn were all trimmed to immaculate perfection. Though, in her opinion, Sheila always thought those tallish bushes seemed trimmed to look like dildos, for whatever odd reason. Maybe a secret landscaper joke, or something.

"Are you okay?" Leo asked, eyes intent as he waited for her to answer.

The driveway was laid with expensive pavers. Each one had a symbol in the middle, but she couldn't make it out from inside the car. The smell of fresh cut grass filtered in through the open windows and it helped settle her anxiety. What the fuck were they doing there? She turned to him.

"I thought we were going to your childhood home?"

"We are. This is it," he answered, hopping out of the car, and opening the door for her.

His face was grim as he walked around to her door. Once opened, he didn't bother to hide the fact he was eyeing Sheila up and down with a certain familiar glitter in his amber gaze. She had to admit she loved the way he looked at her. Had hated those minutes in the bar when he'd steadily ignored her. She'd never had a man pay so much attention to her before. Usually it was her saucy mouth that earned shocked stares, not so much the rest of her.

She'd changed into a pair of fairly new, un-ripped, black jeans in an effort to look presentable. She paired the tight-fitting bottoms with a cream-colored peasant blouse. The thin, gauzy material was fun and flirty, and it felt soft against her skin. She'd always been hypersensitive to clothing. Even her leather cut was lined with a special breathable cotton blend that her skin didn't object to. She'd applied some mascara and lip gloss, but that was as far as she took the makeup thing. She didn't like the way it felt.

Leo's golden stare reached her eyes, and suddenly she wished he'd look away. Goosebumps broke out on her arms and a tiny, almost unnoticeable shudder sped through her. She felt exposed and vulnerable. Maybe it was the clothes. Hell, she'd never felt so soft and feminine. She'd thought she maintained her edge with her carefully broken in leather boots and her hair hanging in loose waves down her back, but she'd been wrong.

She was completely undone, and it made her want to lash out, to hit something, to grab the man and kiss him for all she was worth. Fuck. She was in a tornado of emotions. She wasn't finished with one before another threatened to sweep her away. Her hair blew around her face with the breeze and she was grateful for the respite. It allowed her to break eye contact without losing face.

She usually wore her thick red tresses in a ponytail or braid. Harleys were made for that sort of thing. Tied up hair, little makeup, tough denim, and leather on her body. She didn't mind it, either. The badass she-Wolf in her might not like to admit it, but she was almost scared of how exposed she felt in front of him just then. Leo was looking at her with heat and approval in his stare, and she was shocked at how much she liked it. She wondered what his eyes would express if he saw her nude—*when he saw her nude.* Her mouth went dry, and she licked her lips. Leo followed the small movement of her tongue with rapt desire clear in his honeyed gaze. Her heart squeezed inside her chest.

"If I didn't tell you earlier, you look beautiful," he murmured, and she heard the truth in his words.

Sexy, sexy male. Mine.

Uncertainty made her tremble. She knew what fated mates were. Was aware what they meant to other Shifters. But her kind was different. Her parents had proved that. A quick affair that led to her birth. Absentee parents. No idea who or what her father and his real family were or if they cared. Sheila had long ago made peace with the fact she wasn't cut out for family life. It just wasn't in her genetic makeup, no matter that her body wanted more from Leo. More of those sultry looks and dynamite kisses, like the one they'd shared earlier that afternoon.

It wouldn't be fair to either of them. Her mind understood that, but her heart didn't care. That reckless muscle wanted her to throw caution to the wind. Heat and desire vibrated from his powerful body in steady, constant waves as he leaned closer to where she leaned against the car, stroking, and teasing her with promises of better things to come. Hopefully her. His emotions seemed to wrap around her. Lust, desire, absolute certainty that she belonged to him, and more, so much more. She wished she had a tenth of his resolve.

Her Dire Wolf whined, the animal wanting to get closer to him. To mark herself with his scent, his energy, until every one of her senses was filled with only Leo. Both sides of her, Wolf, and human, were completely focused on the man. Awareness buzzed around her like bumble bees swarming their hive.

"Sheila," he whispered her name, his body hovering so close, but still not touching.

She could feel the tentative pulse of their barely there *matebond*. That tie that urged and called her to claim him as her own, to solidify what the Fates had decreed eons ago. Want became demand, and need became essential. It rose more and more with each passing moment.

No.

Sheila fought against it. She knew better. Knew from her own mother that she wasn't made for permanent things. Her dame rode with Derrick's mother, the older Alpha fem, and her band of twelve Dire Wolf widows. They'd claimed their own Pack and had formed an MC decades ago. Though Sheila's mother had never married, she still rode with them.

Her so-called mate had been married to another when Denise Rand had met him. She'd never lied to her daughter, told her all about the one night of passion she'd shared with him. That was, of course, when Sheila had been conceived. The she-Wolf had left the next day. The call of the road was too strong for her to stick around and watch while he stayed with his family.

At least, that was the way she'd described it. Aunt Mabel, Derrick's mother, had welcomed her sister into her Pack no questions asked. Together, they'd traveled the North and South American continents from Alaska to Cape Horn, and back again, over the past forty years. Dire Wolves aged slower than normal Shifters. Their lifetimes lasted a bit longer.

Sheila was only thirty-two years old. She had plenty of time left. Plenty of time to disappoint Leo. To prove she was not good enough for the golden boy. It was that thought that scared the shit out of her.

"Did I mention you look good enough to eat?" Leo remarked, shaking her from her unpleasant daydreams.

"After all that salmon, I can't believe you'd have any room," she joked.

"Aww, little Wolf, I always have room for you," he promised, eyes flashing heat.

Leo stepped closer. He was crowding her with his big body. She gasped, not quite liking the fact that he was above her since he was so damn tall. His gorgeous face broke out in a smile as he continued to reach and reach behind her, until she realized he was trying to move around her to get to her bags.

"Nice trick," she said.

"Thanks. I always liked that I could reach the trunk through the back seat. Handy if anyone ever tried to stuff me in there."

"You? In the trunk of this thing? You barely fit behind the wheel."

Leo frowned, pretending to be affronted, and

Sheila responded with an unladylike snort. Next, he grinned, and her heart went crazy.

Bum-bum bum-bum.

"You know," he said and straightened to his full, glorious height. "I had them customize the car to accommodate my greater size."

"Yeah?" Sheila cleared her throat. "Must have taken years," she teased. "Seriously, though. It's a sweet ride. No wonder you take such good care of it and don't use it for work."

"My work car is different. Needs to blend in. This is special," he confided with an edge to his voice that went straight to her core. "When something is made specially for me, little Wolf, I treat it with the utmost respect and care."

"Yeah?"

"Yessss," he hissed.

His eyes glittered like yellow diamonds and Sheila felt an echoing tremble rack her soul. Beautiful, dangerous man. He was doing things to her heart she hadn't counted on. Scary things.

"I cherish the things I'm lucky to have in my life."

"You still talking about your car?"

"You tell me, little Wolf. And when you're ready, I'll prove it to you."

He backed up a step and she immediately missed

his heat. His Lion blinked back at her from behind thick lashes. He could mesmerize her with that slow, unblinking stare. The realization stung.

Golden boy. Dangerous beast. Sexy, handsome man.

"Come on, let's go inside."

Sheila tucked a lock of hair behind her ear and stepped carefully beside him. She wasn't sure what just happened, but it felt like his Lion had announced his claim on her, and her Wolf really fucking liked it. She tried to shake the feeling that something big was about to happen. Something that was going to change her life irrevocably.

Fuck it.

Sheila narrowed her eyes. She was no coward and she sure as shit wasn't going to back away from a challenge. She focused instead on the man next to her, and the heat emanating from his powerful body. It warmed her, chasing away the chill she didn't even realize she'd felt.

Spring was strange like that. The winds blew hot and cold with no rhyme or reason. Kind of like her emotions, she frowned. That wasn't entirely true. Sheila knew how she felt about Leo. She just didn't know if she would ever be ready to share it with him.

He's our mate, her she-Wolf, insisted. But Sheila still had her reservations.

She wasn't mate material. Anyone could see that. He was calm and steady where she was riotous and loud. They couldn't possibly mesh together. It would not work.

Yes. It will.

"You ready?"

Leo cocked his head to the side, his steady gaze unwavering as he waited for her response. It touched her somewhere deep that he seemed to understand her trepidations. Sheila played it off like it was no big deal, rolling her eyes and sashaying past the big pussy.

He's the pussy?

Her Wolf seemed to have it out for her today, so Sheila just kept on as if the animal wasn't having a dig at her. There was no point in fighting all the time. Leo opened the front door—apparently, he did have a key.

Inside, the sprawling mansion was even more stunning than the exterior. Every inch of it seemed to sparkle and shine brighter than a new penny. Fucking Lions loved their gold. Sheila's eyes widened as she took in the gleaming marble floors in the hallways that gave way to an enormous round living room with not one, but two huge fireplaces and thick, plush carpeting covering every inch.

There were two large sectional couches that faced each other in that same circular pattern, with a large round marble coffee table in the center. Everything was beautiful, but it all seemed so clinical to her. Maybe Cats were different from Wolves in that respect.

All the Pack and Clan houses she'd ever been in were filled with several members of that Shifter group. There was always noise, mess, and signs of life. But not here. This was super classy, and yet, where was the heart?

This was not the typical middle or even upper class home she'd expected of Leo Crowley. Perhaps she should have done some more homework on the good detective. Still, it surprised her to find not one single Lion on the premises.

"It's, uh, nice."

She raised an eyebrow, but he didn't respond. The immaculate entryway and living room area were just one section of the imposing structure. It reeked of money and class, but she could sense from his grim expression that all was not right in this house.

Hell, she was running through the entire myriad

of emotions herself, just standing there and taking it all in. Paintings hung on the walls, huge carved bookshelves with what had to be first editions covered one enormous section of space, there were glass curios with what looked like ancient relics, dozens of awards, and some historical photographs on display. She'd never been one for pomp and circumstance, but she couldn't help but wonder if she should remove her leather boots. Maybe she should take off her socks, too.

"This place is like a museum," she said, and he grunted his reply.

Money had never been a big deal to her, but this place reeked of it. What the hell did Leo say his family did for a living, anyway? That's right, he didn't. She'd assumed he had something to do with that export company. Maybe his dad was the CEO or something.

"What?" Leo asked and turned around when he realized she wasn't following him down the hall.

"Is this really where you grew up?"

"Sheila, there are some things we haven't discussed," he began, but the sound of footfalls speeding closer had Leo's attention.

Sheila turned when she saw a man in a three-piece suit come rushing up to him, head bowed, neck bared. What the hell was going on?

"You're here early," the older man gasped and dropped to his knees.

"Montgomery, please, stand up. You know, you don't have to do that," Leo replied, and offered the man a hand to help him stand up.

The Lion refused. He shook his head, insisting on staying in that strange, bowed position for a full three beats before slowly rising. Still, he would not meet Leo's gaze.

"I knew you would be back. I told the King, you would not leave us," Montgomery took Leo's hand and pressed it to his forehead, bowing in subjugation.

"How is he?" asked Leo.

"As good as can be expected, sir."

What the hell? OMG. Wait—was that a blush spreading across Mr. Law and Order's face? Sheila would have laughed if she wasn't so confused.

"Um, Leo? What's with him?"

"I am sorry, sir, I did not see your, *uh*, friend. Shall I make up a guest room?" Montgomery rose to his feet, looking anxiously at Sheila.

"No, Montgomery, that won't be necessary. This is my mate. Sheila, meet Montgomery, he's been the caretaker of the Blue Valley Pride house for as long as I can remember."

"Longer, sir. My father was the caretaker before me, and his before him," he said with an air of pride that had nothing to do with him being a Lion Shifter.

Montgomery leaned in just a fraction, and Sheila thought she saw him sniff. Weird. He looked confused, but turned before she could gauge his reaction. Surely, the Pride was not prejudiced against mixed species matings? But who knew? Maybe they were. Montgomery's eyes flashed briefly, before he turned his attention to Leo.

"Apologies, sire. I had no idea you were mated," the man replied.

"Is there a problem, Montgomery?" Leo's quiet question held an air of authority that sent shivers of excitement rippling through Sheila's body. She always did like a man with a little bit of bite to him.

Grrr.

"No, of course not, sir."

"Good, then you will see to my mate's needs while we are in residence."

He stated the fact without a single doubt in his voice, and that made Sheila's stomach clench and her sex moisten. Her body recognized her mate, and the following desire was only natural. Especially when he spoke about her like that.

So hot.

Of course, her rational brain's reaction was something entirely of its own making. She'd agreed to play Leo's mate through this thing, but she wasn't prepared for the thrill that zipped through her at his proclamation or his ready defense of her.

"Sire, um, she's a Wolf," the man mumbled, confusion evident in his face.

"Yes, Montgomery. Sheila is a *Dire Wolf*, and she is also *my mate*," Leo growled with authority ringing in his tone. Sheila watched as the man backed up a step, eyes locked on the floor.

"Yes, sir," he returned.

"No worries, Montgomery. I trust you will act accordingly. Now, I will see us to my room, and after we are settled, we shall go see the King."

"As you say, sir."

Sheila followed Leo quietly as she tried to make sense of that little exchange. Leo had seemed stiff and unlike himself. In fact, the further he stepped into the sprawling Pride house, the less she recognized the serious detective.

She watched him maneuver down the long hallway carefully and with purpose. His back straight, head high, confidence bubbled over like water from a boiling kettle. He was just this side of conceited.

Fuck, he was cute. Sexy and with an air of authority that called to her wilder side. Would he be bossy in bed? Would he try to tell Sheila what to do? Maybe even spank her if she was naughty.

Yes, please.

She swallowed loudly. If she didn't get her hormones under control, she was going to jump him the second they were behind closed doors. She just couldn't help it. Lying and pretense didn't sit well with her, she might as well just admit that she wanted him. Really wanted him.

Standing up, lying down, on his knees, on a train, on a plane—she didn't give a fuck where. The only thing that mattered was Leo. He could have all her fucks. Every. Single. One.

Mine.

Sheila shook her head. Wolves did not always experience a heat cycle, but because of the nature of Dire Wolves, and their rarity, her kind did. Sheila had never experienced it, but there was no other explanation. It was the only thing that made sense. Too much time with her fated mate, and her primal instincts were bound to kick in.

Her eyes roamed over him from head to toe as they made their way to his room. The unfamiliar jeans and t-shirt revealed a side of him she wasn't ready for. A human side perhaps. It was so easy to dismiss him as nothing but a big ol' pussycat, but not when he wore soft cotton that clung to his every muscle and outlined his rock hard abs.

He stopped at a set of intricately carved wooden doors and raised his hand in the air. Leo hesitated, almost as if he was afraid to touch it. But it wasn't fear, it was resignation on his face. She frowned. Why should he look like that?

Her Wolf whined inside of her, and Sheila was caught unawares by the need to comfort him. Again she tried to stem her instincts, to ignore them, and she focused on the beautiful doors instead. She recognized images in the wood. A full moon, a lion's head, a crest of some sort, and other symbols that were lovely yet unfamiliar. Running her pink polished fingers over the smooth surface, she stopped and looked up. Amber eyes glittered at her in the dimly lit hall.

"What does this mean?" Sheila traced one symbol that looked like a series of circles, starting with a small center, and growing larger with each ring until it spanned two of her hands.

"That is the symbol for greatness. My mother had it carved on my door when I was born."

"Why?"

"Because she had high hopes for me, Sheila."

"Why? Who are you?" she repeated.

"You know who I am."

"I don't think I do. What are we really doing here, Leo? Who are you really?"

Leo frowned, and it was the first time she saw no humor in the big, golden man's gaze. She wanted to erase that severe expression, replace it with something lighter, something good. And that scared the shit out of her.

"Come inside, little Wolf," Leo replied, eyes begging for something she was not sure she could give.

"Come inside," he repeated. "And I'll tell you everything."

Sheila nodded, and she walked into the room, knowing everything she had ever thought in her entire life was about to change. Leo was important. He was big. He had secrets.

And Sheila wanted them all.

CHAPTER 7

L eo growled softly. His Lion snapped his jaws inside his mind's eye. The beast was on edge. He'd been that way since the second he'd stepped over the threshold of his ancestral home.

Five generations of Crowleys had lived and ruled under this roof. Five Lion Kings born within these walls. Inside the Palace was duty, obligation, resignation, and responsibility.

I am not ready yet.

Leo had his own life to live. His own mate to claim. A career waiting for him. This was not his time to rule. Not yet.

His grandfather had ruled for sixty years. His father had sat on the throne for only half that. Of course, after his mother's death, his father had experienced a tremendous suffering. Their people had expected a slight change, but not this. Something was wrong.

For the King, the pain of losing a mate was unimaginable, but Leo would never have anticipated this. The Palace was empty. The King absent. For his father, the mighty Donovan Crowley, to simply give up, was completely out of character. All Leo's detective's instincts were on high alert. He saw red flags everywhere. Something was not right. Not at all. The Pride house, or the Palace as it was sometimes called, used to be teaming with Lions. Now, it was empty. A cold shell of what it used to be.

The elders should have told him this when he'd gone to the circle. They'd kept this from him. When he'd visited his father that night, he'd assumed it was empty simply because of the late hour. Kings needed their subjects. Alpha's needed their Pack. And Primus' needed their Lions.

Having his lions around would give the King's beast something to care about, rather than dwell on the loss of his mate. This isolation was poison.

Yes, Leo had been angry at their ridiculous demands regarding his mate. As if they could force him to claim some unwitting female in order to inherit the throne from his father. That was just a little too pushy, in Leo's opinion. They'd wanted him to choose from a list of females they'd already vetted. As if.

He'd surprised them with his demand to back off. George, too. Only when he'd told his cousin he had already found his fated mate had the younger Lion finally shut up. It was not a lie. Not in the least. Sheila Rand was the only one for him. He knew that for truth. The she-Wolf was beyond his wildest dreams in so far as beauty and personality. His perfect companion. The one person in the universe who understood and completed him.

It didn't hurt she was the sexiest little thing he'd ever seen with those cornflower blue eyes of hers, that shiny red hair, and her killer body. She was more than enough to tame his inner Lion. Thoughts of her constantly filled his mind. Hell, he wanted her all the time, even when he should think about other things. Like the Pride and his father's health. He couldn't help it. The Lion wanted to claim his mate.

Roarrrr.

At the very least, he planned on kissing her the second he got inside his room. Leo couldn't wait to take that sassy little mouth under his again. That small taste he had of her at the bar wasn't nearly enough to satisfy his hunger. He wanted it all, but only when she was ready. A kiss would have to be enough.

The hesitation he felt coming from her both hurt and confused him, but he tried to understand. He was a patient man. Unusual for Shifters, but not for him. Trained as a detective, he understood the importance of timing. Raised as a Prince, he also knew it was necessary, and rewarding, to be compassionate with others.

Sheila would be his. There was no doubt in his mind. He just had to wait. Things were complicated and messy right then, but Leo would convince her soon enough to take the plunge. He had other things to do while she figured out for herself that he was a Lion of his word.

Leo needed to explain it to her. All of it. The fact his father was the King, that he was actually the Prince of the Blue Valley Pride might be a tough pill to swallow.

Shit.

He was nervous. Then there were the circumstances he was there to investigate. And finally, the real reason he needed her with him. Not because he wanted to trick the elders, but because she brought his Lion peace and purpose.

Mine.

He followed her inside the room, eyes riveted to the fiery redhead as she turned to face him. Everything about her commanded his attention.

Beautiful, strong, sexy woman.

"Spill."

Sheila tapped her booted foot against the gleaming marble floors of his bedroom. She should have looked out of place among all the riches, but she didn't. Not in the least. Sheila belonged there. With him.

He looked around and tried to see it from her perspective. He knew Sheila was not materialistic. But this world, though far removed from his daily life, was still his. Leo was royalty, whether he wanted to be or not was inconsequential. But his mate had grown up on the open road. Literally. She'd been loving every moment of her wild and free existence, riding her Harley from town to town since she could sit on one.

What if his sassy little mate was not happy with him? What if the road called to her once more?

Easy peasy. She goes, we follow.

His Lion was right. The Big Cat had provided the only possible answer. Leo would follow Sheila Rand out on the open road, and off into the sunset each and every time. No contest. He would follow the woman he loved anywhere.

Fuck. I do love her.

The knowledge hit him hard enough that the room seemed to spin out of focus. He'd only just put a name to the feelings he'd been having. How would he feel once they consummated their mating? The thought sent a shiver down his spine, but it wasn't of fear. Not at all. That slight tremor was wholly born of anticipation.

"Well?"

"This is where I was born. I haven't lived here in a while, but my father still does."

"Your father? What is this place?"

"It's the Pride house, some call it the Palace."

"Okay," she murmured, a frown on her pretty face.

Leo did not like that. He wanted her to smile. Wanted to be the one to make her smile. Her blue eyes widened as he stalked her across the room, and Sheila froze. She knew better than to turn her back on him—hunter, predator, beast.

Smart, sassy, little Wolf. Go ahead and run from me. I'll catch you.

"You trying to distract me, pussycat?" she asked, eyes narrowed as she took a tentative step to the left.

She could do that, but he would cut her off with a single bound to the side. Just imagining her tight little body snug against his made Leo feel ten times frisky.

Yes. Do that, his Lion urged.

Already his cock throbbed, and his heart went wild inside his chest for the sweet, spicy Sheila. The beautiful she-Wolf who called to his Lion. Yes, she belonged to him, and he to her. Claiming her would only increase the desire he felt, and that idea was getting more appealing by the second.

"Come here," he said in a gravelly voice thick with his Lion.

"No."

"Scared of a Lion?"

"I'm not afraid of you," she replied, narrowing those beautiful baby blues. "You're nothing but a big pussy."

"The only pussy in this room is right there, soaking in sweet honey, begging for me to take a lick. Mine," he growled the word, breathing in deep, his chest vibrating with need.

Sheila bit back a moan and he growled deeper. Her eyes glowed bright with her Wolf as he backed her up into the wall.

So close. So hot. So mine.

"Wait," she whispered, and he stilled. He would do anything for her. Anything at all.

"Explain. Now."

Was it wrong that he liked the fact he'd reduced her to one-word sentences? Maybe, but who cared? She was cute when she was pretending to be outraged. He could scent her reciprocal desire, and it was making him hungry. The notes of an old eighties classic rock song filtered through his brain, though Leo changed the lyrics a bit.

Hungry. Hungry. I'm hungry for the Wolf.

"Are you afraid of the big bad Cat, little Wolf?"

"First of all, it's the big bad Wolf. You are just an overgrown tabby," she replied, poking him in the chest with her hot pink painted fingernail, scoring the cotton tee he'd worn just for her.

Damn.

She was so fucking hot. Soft, feminine, vulnerable on one hand, and completely fucking badass and in control on the other. Standing there in her jeans, those shit-kicking leather boots, and that see-through gauzy top. Leo rubbed his body on her, meeting her gaze, the predator in him gaining satisfaction as she stood her ground.

A challenge.

Yes, but a good one. Win or lose, he still wins.

Whoever came out on top, Leo would still consider it a victory. His muscles tensed, ready to pounce on a moment's notice. He needed her fiery lips against his, had to taste that spicy sweet flavor that was all her.

Roarrrr.

He swallowed her surprised gasp, mashing his mouth to hers, and finally, he tasted the fire from its source. Her lips were plump and soft, exactly right for savoring.

Leo was drunk on kissing her. Her contradiction of flavors burst on his tongue. First spicy, then sweet. Always provocative. Stimulating. Tempting him to sin. The taste of her stamped itself on his brain, like a permanent tattoo he never wanted to erase or forget.

Just having her in his arms changed the course of his life forever. Fuck. It wasn't enough. Never enough. He wanted more. Needed more. Never had he felt such desire for a woman. He was desperate to have her naked in his bed, writhing beneath his touch, buried balls deep, coating her walls with his cum, filling her to the brim.

"Leo," she said his name, and ran her nails down his back until she lifted his shirt and touched his skin.

His already hard cock grew even harder. The thick length throbbed and pulsed, threatening to burst the seam of his jeans. He would've gone with fucking sweatpants if he'd known his body would have such a severe reaction to her. Leo groaned as her hands found him through the denim, and he wrapped his arms around her curvy frame.

He fucking loved the feel of this woman's body pressed against him. Her drool-worthy curves filled his searching hands. She was perfect for him. Perfect size. Height. Everything.

Leo was big all over, especially those parts that mattered most, hands, tongue, cock, and heart. He needed a woman who could take all of him in stride. Sheila could do more than that. She was the ultimate match for him. Unsurpassed by any other female. She topped them all. A true mate who could take on every inch of his powerful frame.

Mine.

Kissing, touching, squeezing her in his bedroom made everything better. He didn't forget why he was there, but for a little while, Leo could push it all aside. Sheila was everything to him. But he would not claim her until she asked him to. She was much too important to him and his future to fuck things up by acting like an unlicked cub.

He had her in his arms, and that alone was worth celebrating. For months she'd been fighting him, but not here. Not now. Finally, Leo could savor his mate. He lifted her onto the edge of his dresser, and Sheila immediately brought her legs up and around his waist. She tangled her hands in his hair while he lifted her shirt high, and then off, revealing a pink lace demi-bra, barely large enough to contain her. His lips twitched and his breathing increased. He wanted her, ached for her.

"Beautiful," he growled, then dipped his head.

"Leo," she moaned his name as he brushed soft kisses on the bits of flesh that were revealed to him.

"So soft," he growled and lifted his head, meeting her eyes as his hands traced the tops of her breast.

Her blue eyes seemed to glow, and he knew it was her she-Wolf joining them. His own animal approved and rose to meet his mate. Leo's chest vibrated with a low, rumbling growl as he slowly caressed the delicate skin of her ample breasts with his work-roughened fingertips. This was dangerous. Touching her like this was pure madness.

But he couldn't stop. He wouldn't. Not unless she said to. He pulled the fabric down gently, allowing her ripe nipples to spill out. Leo couldn't contain his groan. So pretty and pink. Her tip-tilted breasts were perfect for his hands and lips, and he traced them *oh so carefully.*

Slow and steady.

He wanted this to be better than good. He wanted to raise her temperature to match her fiery sass. Leo growled at the apt description. The redheaded seductress was just that. Fire and sass, mixed with a little bit of sugar just for him. Together they'd break bad, raise hell, see the stars, and bring mountains to their knees with the height of their passion.

At the very least, he'd make sure she never thought of him as a pussy again.

"Leo," she moaned his name again, arching her back, offering him better access to her succulent body.

Only a fool would refuse, and Leo was far from that. This was what he'd wanted, what he'd been chasing for weeks. Sheila's willing submission to his desire, her need for his touch. It was what he craved, what his beast demanded, but that wasn't all. He wanted more from the sexy she-Wolf.

He didn't just want her ready, willing, and waiting, he wanted her panting, begging, and demanding. He wanted her to feel the same way he felt about her. He'd been lusting after her like mad. Ever since he'd first laid eyes on her, but it was more than that. Leo was head over heels for the little Wolf. He wouldn't rest until she felt the same.

"Tell me what you want, baby," he growled and nipped her earlobe between his teeth as his hands made short work of her bra.

Finally, completely freed from their confines, Leo took both her gorgeous breasts in his large hands. He kneaded the supple mounds, pushing them together, and tweaking her nipples with his thumbs and forefingers.

All the better for him to kiss, lick, and suck each plentiful bud and that valley between. Visions of sliding his cock between the two mounds had him growling almost nonstop.

"More," she demanded, gripping his hair, and pulling his head closer.

He did not disappoint. He couldn't. He sought her pleasure as if it were his own. She might be one sassy little Wolf, but in this, in the bed, *or* dresser, Leo was the maestro and she, his orchestra. He would coax her to symphonic precipices until they both tumbled off together into sheer bliss. His beast would accept nothing less. Nothing, save her utter and complete surrender to the pleasure he dealt.

"Bed now," she said, and shoved against his chest.

The blue fire flashing in her eyes had a direct and almost painful effect on Leo's cock. His member, already swollen in his need, throbbed painfully in the strict confines of his pants. Fuck, he needed her.

Sex was important to Shifters. It was necessary. An outlet, a means of expression, not taken lightly, and yet indulged in sometimes a little too haphazardly, in his opinion. Because of his status, Leo was not one to take women into his bed lightly.

Hell yes, sex was fun, but no youthful experimentation, none of the meaningless unions of his past, nope, not a fucking one could have prepared him for his reaction to having his mate shove him down hard onto the mattress while she stripped for him. Leo almost swallowed his tongue whole.

"Ffuucckk, Sheila," he growled.

Leo's eyes bulged as Sheila kicked off her leather boots. She winked at him, wiggling her tight jeans and panties down and over her ample hips, kicking them off after her boots. She stood there in all her naked glory, proud and sexy as sin. Then she unzipped his jeans and ripped them clean off his legs. Leaving him naked and standing up, tall and straight as a fucking May pole.

"I've been waiting for this for a long time, detective. You better not let me down," she growled the words, eyes flashing blue fire.

Leo hardly made a sound before she was already jumping on top of him. Fierce, proud, gorgeous woman.

My woman.

"Mine," he growled the possessive word as he caught her delicious body.

If he thought he had seduced her, he was wrong. Sheila Rand was not one to be manipulated into anyone's bed. She chose him, here and now, and the feeling was the best kind of high. Only to be super-seded by the bliss he was bound to feel when he finally claimed the sassy little Wolf as his own.

Automatically, she wound her arms around him, lips going to his neck for a biting kiss that made him shudder. His hands reached between them, dipping between her slick folds. So fucking hot and wet for him. Perfect.

He was grateful his quick Shifter reflexes allowed him to catch his feisty female before she could land. Hot, naked flesh felt like heaven against his skin. Even better was the wicked smile on her face as she held herself just out of reach before mashing her lips to his.

Leo's heart hammered in his chest like a herd of

wild horses, his gums ached, and fangs threatened to lengthen. He was holding on to his Lion by a thread. The heady scent of her arousal made him salivate as he strummed her clit with his thumb, testing to see if she could take him.

Leo was big, and he would not risk hurting her. Sheila moaned, twirling her tongue with his as he fingered her with two thick digits. Her legs were wide as she sat astride him, her sex tight and wet. She felt so good, squeezing his fingers with every thrust and withdraw.

So sexy, hot, and wet for him. Good girl.

Her hips rocked against him, and Leo's cock ached to replace his hand. He was completely invested in this, in her. Needed her hotter, wetter. His cock slid up behind her ass and he kneaded one globe with his other hand, while fucking her with his fingers. He fucking loved her response to him. She moaned and moved, letting him know exactly where she wanted it, how hard, and how fast. They devoured each other with their lips.

Fuck.

Desire bubbling over, Leo waited for the first signs of her orgasm to hit. He was ready, and he wanted to feel her squeeze his fingers tight before he swapped them out for his dick. Hell, he wanted it all.

Wanted to bathe in her sweet scent. Get her juices all over him. Coat her walls with his cum. Wanted to taste her cream right from the source.

Some stereotypes were true. Cats liked cream, and this pussy sure as fuck did. He was dying to lick her. Wanted to bury his head between her luscious thighs and swallow down every drop.

Later.

Yep, that sounded like a plan to his Lion. He wanted all of that and more of her. Wanted to take his time to enjoy every smooth inch of her soft, smooth, delectable flesh, but his mate had other ideas. Just when she almost came, Sheila backed off his hand, taking hold of his more than ready cock. Leo hissed. Fuck, she was killing him.

She took his hard length, placed him at her slick entrance. She held him there, her wet pussy dripping, kissing the tip of his dick. But she waited, eyes flashing blue fire at Leo. His balls tightened as he held her gaze.

Fuck, she was so sexy, and she held all the cards. Literally, held him by the dick. Her predator's gaze unblinking, and dammit all to hell, Leo was desperate for her to sink down and swallow him deep inside her heat.

Why the fuck wasn't she moving?

The Lion clawed at him, but it was obvious she wasn't ready. Not yet, and fight though his beast did, Leo held himself still. Sheila looked him in the eye, making sure she had his attention before she spoke.

Fuck, she has more than that, he thought.

"No biting, Leo. Promise me. Sex only. Fucking only. No claiming. Or we stop, right now. Agreed?" she asked, her voice husky with need.

He wanted to roar and demand, but fuck, she had him good. Sheila raked one hand down his chest, not hard enough to break skin, but definitely hard enough to rouse his beast.

"Sheila," he started, unable to do anything while she held his cock in her firm hand.

"Agreed?" she asked again, dropping a fraction of a centimeter onto his pulsating shaft.

Ffuckk. So tight. So hot.

Leo was going to go permanently cross-eyed if the woman didn't finish, but he wasn't hard of hearing. He'd already promised himself he would not claim her until she asked. It was going to be hard, but so what? The best things in life did not come easily, and he already had plans to make his mate work for it. Puns intended.

"No biting. I understand, but it will never ever be just fucking. Not with you, *mate*,"

His growled words ended on a groan as Sheila impaled herself on his cock. Sinking down hard, she swerved her hips and took him even deeper inside of her incomparable heat. Sexy little Wolf, she'd rendered him speechless with her body.

Roarrrr.

Leo's Lion threatened to burst forth as his mate's tight pussy sheathed his cock, covering him with her heated, wet flesh. He growled aloud as her molten walls stroked and squeezed his steel length.

"Oh fuck, Leo. You feel so good," she murmured and rocked her hips.

His little Wolf growled low in her throat as she rocked slowly along his thick length. She wanted control, but Leo couldn't not move. He simply could not be an impassive party to this poignant culmination. For weeks, he'd dreamed about this. Days, hours, minutes that seemed to stretch into eternity just picturing the moment he finally had Sheila Rand in his arms.

Finally, his waiting was over. The little Wolf wanted no strings, but she had no idea what this meant to him. He had her now, and he wasn't letting go. Sitting up straighter, he moved with her, thrusting upwards to meet her downward grinds with sharp, precise motions. They marked the time with a rhythm all their own, the steady thudding of the mattress music to his sensitive ears.

Sheila was glorious, a thing of pure beauty. Her tight channel stroked him good and hard. Deep, so deep—he moved within her sex, stroking her like he was born to. Leo had never felt anything like this, had never loved anyone like her.

"Sheila," he growled her name, holding her head behind her neck and crashed his mouth to hers.

He had to kiss her again. Just couldn't stop himself from kissing this woman. She was everything he'd ever wanted and never realized. A conundrum of opposing actions and ideas. She didn't want to be mated, and yet she lay claim to his heart with every swivel and slide of her luscious body. She kissed him like she was born to, but still refused his claim.

Not yet.

That was the key phrase. Her eyes locked onto his, and Leo felt his Lion's growl answer the call he saw there. If he tried, he'd see the tentative bonds of their mating growing stronger. Those magical ties that bound every fated mate together existed even now. This consummation solidified theirs just a fraction more. She might not want to face it just yet, but they belonged to one another like they never would to anyone else.

Leo was as sure of that as he was the sun would set each night and rise again the next day. Awash in that star's fiery rays, his Sheila practically glowed in the golden-hued beams that filtered down from the skylight above them. He was mesmerized by her beauty. She was a goddess.

Woman. Warrior. Mate. Fierce Dire Wolf.

Her flame-kissed hair swirled around her shoulders, the deep red color more pronounced against her flawless ivory skin. Sweat beads dotted her forehead and her body was slick with it. Sheila panted and moved with increased vigor, taking him deep, riding him hard, and fuck, if he didn't hold on tight. Leo's heart squeezed, ready to explode with the strength of his feelings. The muscle tightened almost painfully inside his chest.

He always used to laugh whenever he'd heard people described as having the *heart of a lion.* What normal man or woman could know a Lion's heart? What Shifter, for that matter? But Leo knew. At least, he did now.

He had been unprepared for the powerful wave of emotion that started with that muscle housed inside his chest. Right then, it beat with the strength of his thousand pound beast, filled to overflowing with all the love he had to give this fiercely beautiful woman who rode him so expertly.

Sheila's mouth opened in a soundless scream. She raised her arms high over her head, rocking her hips in time with his thrusts with all the grace and fire of a Valkyrie charging into battle. Untamed and dazzling, she reached for him and crashed her mouth to his, controlling the kiss, and in turn, the pace of their fucking. Each tug on his tongue seemed to echo all the way down to his cock. It was marvelous, poignant, and so fucking hot he almost came right then.

How did this happen? When did she become the master in this exchange?

He didn't give a fuck as long as she kept moving. Her sweet, succulent pussy squeezed and sucked his cock, bringing him to heights he'd never imagined. Sheila moaned in her pleasure, and he felt her pulse and ripple around him. Her walls tightened, gripping him like a velvet vise. She rocked her hips harder, faster. Leo grunted with the effort. He was close, so close, but she needed to come first. He still had that much control.

"Faster," she ground out, her movements

becoming more and more erratic and disjointed as her orgasm neared.

"Sheila."

"Leo," she panted.

He understood what she needed. He grabbed her waist, nipping her lower lip between his teeth, he held her in place until she opened wide and allowed his tongue entry. If they were going to fall apart together, he wanted his mouth on hers. He wanted every single one of her groans and gasps. They were his, dammit. Leo lifted his sweet mate and dropped her down hard, impaling her on his cock.

Up, down, grind, swerve, harder, faster, again, and again.

"Yes," she moaned, and this time she nipped his bottom lip between her sharp teeth.

Leo growled. His Lion loved that little bite, wanted her to break the skin, mark him, claim him. He pumped his hips, thrusting upwards and into her faster and harder from underneath her sweet body. Together, they moved, grunted, and rocked. He kneaded the flesh of her plump ass. Loving the way her globes filled his large hands.

Sheila clawed at his shoulders as the pressure built and became almost overwhelming for her. His Lion hissed inside of him, encouraging him to strengthen his mate's pleasure. He dipped his head, releasing her lips so that she could moan as he licked and sucked on her neck, teasing the spot he would one day mark with his claiming bite. Hopefully sooner than later.

With one hand still on her waist, directing her movements, the other spread her cheeks apart. Sheila growled and tensed as he teased the sensitive, puckered skin surrounding her forbidden hole before finally testing the thing itself. Steadily he continued to increase the speed of his thrusts, swallowing down her moans, one after the other greedily as he slipped one thick digit inside her tight, trembling orifice. Leo had found it. Her breaking point. That edge she needed in order to completely surrender to the pleasure only he could deliver.

"Mine," he roared the possessive word, and tasted victory in that moment when her orgasm claimed her.

Pride filled him as Sheila threw her head back, howling out loud in her ecstasy. He'd done that. He'd brought her there. That was, of course, his last coherent thought as her pussy clenched around his cock, squeezing him tight while her forbidden hole did the same, tightening around his finger.

She continued to howl her release, her nails

scratching at his shoulders, and finally he let his own magnificent climax take him. Leo roared. Loudly. He came long and hard, coating her walls with his seed and marking her with his scent.

"Mine," he said, despite his fangs.

The words would have to suffice in calming the beast when all he wanted to do was bite down and claim her.

Mine.

CHAPTER 8

*H*oly. *Deliciousness.*

Sheila blinked slowly. A wide grin cracked her face as she stretched her well used body. She throbbed and ached in places she'd forgotten she had. She was exhausted, deliciously so.

Good dream. Sexy.

The ache in her muscles was a good ache. A welcomed one. Who knew a pussycat had moves like that? Speaking of, where was he? Sheila shot up like a rocket and looked around. His scent was everywhere. That thick, spicy masculine musk was in the sheets, the pillows, on her skin. That was no dream.

Oh. My. Gods.

Sheila had done the dirty with Leo the Lion. Holy. Fucking. Hell. She'd *made the beast with two backs, knocked boots, shook the sheets, got down and dirty, shtupped, rutted, balled, boinked, bumped uglies, got laid, got lucky*—no matter how you said it, she did it and done it with the pussycat.

Slightly panicked, she realized Leo was gone. Well, at least she did not have to face him first thing. Squashing the tiny bubble of disappointment that threatened to rise, she got out of bed and made her way to the connected bathroom.

"Is that a bidet?" she murmured, shaking her head as she took care of her business, trying to wrap her mind around what had happened during the night.

And with Leo. Her pretend nemesis.

So much for keeping him at arm's length. She'd actually jumped him. And hot damn, the man was a monster in the sack. He'd truly matched her every inch of the way. She washed her hands and face, looking in the mirror at her reflection.

For the first time in like ever, Sheila looked content. Happy. Satisfied. And she was. Imagine that? She ran her hands along her neck, but he hadn't betrayed her. True to his word. no claiming bite marred her skin.

Sheila did not want to dwell on the feeling of disappointment that sprung up on her suddenly. Instead, she looked around the ornate bathroom and opened the door to the bedroom. He had not returned, her Wolf hearing would have told her if he had.

This space was just as fine and expensively decorated as the rest of the huge house. Not what she imagined Leo's childhood home would look like. He was a detective, so she'd pictured normal, middle-class suburbia for the pussycat. Not this Palace, which was also the dwelling place of the Lion Pride's current King.

Sooo…. what did that make him? Was he the son of an Enforcer? A Guard? Whatever the fuck these pussies had for hierarchy? She really didn't know a thing about Prides. Maybe he was involved or related to the head honcho, somehow?

It was sort of bizarre they had an actual King, but whatever. To each his own. She'd been in such a fury of hormones last night, her body and emotions both went haywire, and Sheila had gotten none of the answers she needed. But he sure made her feel good last night.

Yes sirree. Really, really good. Grrrrr.

Grabbing her cell, Sheila balked at how many hours had passed since they'd arrived, and she'd basically attacked Leo. Had she really slept that long? Sure looked like it. But in her defense, she'd had the best sex of her entire life, so yeah. Some good, all through the night, sleep time was well earned. Seriously, she had never come so long or so hard with anyone ever before.

And you won't with anyone else. He is ours. Mate.

OMG. Can you just let me enjoy this? Sheila growled at her Wolf's inner bitchiness.

From what she knew of mates, the need to consummate their relationship, to lay claim with fang and claw, would only grow until they finally went through with it. Afterwards, there would be even more amazing sex. That's how it went with Shifters.

Sniff. Insta-lust. Sex. More sex. Claiming marks. Then even more sex.

Not bad, if you didn't mind the whole out-of-control lusty sexy times, followed by bitey claiming marks, then forever stuck together, and finally, the almost always pregnant thing. Hell, even swollen like a cantaloupe, there was still the sex, right? At least, according to Lucy. She'd already told Sheila, with way too much TMI than any cousin-in-law should share, that sex with her mate got better every single time they did it.

But it was not the need to be with him that scared Sheila. It wasn't the sex. Or even the pain of the bite marks, and sometimes clawing, that went along with claiming your mate. Sheila would stick like glue to someone she was loyal too. After all, she'd stuck with Derrick and her Pack since she was a teenager.

But the possibility of motherhood, being an actual mom to a fragile, needy little cub—that scared the shit out of her. And for good reasons. Sheila had no real parental role models. Derrick was about as close to having a parent as she came.

What if she sucked at it? She loved her mother, but the woman was no kind of actual parent. Sheila had grown up with the other cubs, hanging around the graybeards of her old MC when the others went with their moms and dads. Those old Wolves had been patient when it was called for, and stern, too, when she needed it. She earned diplomas on the road. Got her real education from life. And any milestones were achieved with and witnessed by her cousin and friends.

When she left the Pack of her birth to follow the Pack of her heart, Sheila felt positive she'd made the right decision. Being the only female was tough, but she liked having a bunch of honorary brothers. They had her back, and she had theirs. Her Pack mates were loyal and tightknit, but not exactly demonstrative about their feelings.

Fuck.

Sheila would make a terrible mother. But even acknowledging her greatest fear didn't stop her body from reacting to the mere idea of being with Leo. Wearing his bite mark. Bearing his young.

Shit.

Her heart started pounding, and pulse raced up just thinking about the big, sexy Lion. Where was he, anyway? She grabbed the sheet and inhaled, breathing in his musky scent. Want, need, longing filled her. She missed him. Even though it had only been a few hours, she missed him. Her Wolf whined, beast in agreement.

It was sort of like nature's way of ensuring destiny didn't fuck things up. That attraction, that never ending need to be with him. Wow. She really didn't appreciate waking up to an empty room. One night of good sex, and Sheila was turning all clingy, dammit. What the heck had happened to her life? Sheila was out of control and all because of one overgrown, presently absentee, tabby.

The fucker.

One minute she was all aloof, handling the whole

pretense of their mating just fine with no *howdy dos* about the whole damn thing. She'd agreed to this ruse not to be near him, but so he could solve the mystery of whatever the fuck was happening here. Still, that didn't explain why one minute she was touring the sprawling mansion, and the next minute she was butt ass naked, and wrapped around the big pussy like a cheap suit.

How was that his fault? Her snarky she-Wolf seemed to laugh as she asked that question.

Fine, she admitted.

That was all on her, even if he didn't exactly resist. Leo made no secret of his desire for her from the beginning. It was flattering, but also pure biology. Fated mates and all that jazz. Whatever. Sheila knew just how to get her swerve on. So, what if she was horny? The big ol' pussycat had the goods, and he wasn't shy about using them.

They'd both had fun. It didn't have to mean more. She'd help him with his Pride's issues, then she could move on. Fuck it, he could move on too, with whomever he wanted. Find a nice Lioness to settle down with, have some cubs, live a good, settled life.

GRRRR.

Her she-Wolf was really not having any of that. She closed her eyes and shook her head. Tears welled in her eyes, and she punched the mattress. What the heck? She did not do crying. Ever.

Shit.

She wiped her face.

Goddammit.

She was crying.

Sigh.

Way to stay strong and resist the mating fever. Not. She rolled her head on her neck and then her shoulders, stopping the tears and stretching her exhausted body. Sex with Leo was better than good. It was fanfuckingtastic. But she couldn't let it happen again.

She'd almost bitten him. Then where would she be? Mated for life. And that could only be disastrous. Okay, so it was a near thing. A one off. Done and done. She had just made up her mind, sitting down on the large luxury bed as a hurricane in the form of two waspish felines came crashing into the room.

"Alright, you hussy, where is my nephew?" the older one with silver hair, and a cute as fuck pair of printed capri pants topped with a gold, off-the-shoulder blouse, demanded haughtily.

"*Oh my gah!*" The younger of the two snapped her chewing gum and pointed at Sheila. "Mom, she's a Dog!"

"What?"

Sniff.

"You're right! She does smell like a canine, doesn't she?" the older woman addressed the younger, as if Sheila wasn't even there.

"Excuse me?" Sheila asked.

She was starting to get more than annoyed with these two intruders. Not bothering to cover herself, she worked to rein in her she-Wolf, the beast definitely didn't like them, until she knew who and what they were. For all she knew, these could be Leo's relatives.

"There is no excuse for humping my nephew in his childhood bedroom without even introducing yourself to us," the older female said.

Sheila's eyebrows disappeared into her hairline as she watched the two felines lay down and settle on one of the two sofas in the bedroom. Sheesh, this room was fucking huge. Four times the size of her own bedroom at the Pack house. Still, how had she missed the gold-trimmed pieces of furniture? Probably because she was too busy attacking her mate's sumptuous body.

EEEP!

She really had to stop calling him that. She looked around again and tried to ignore the tingle of anxiety that shivered up her spine. Everything in the room was of the highest quality. Looking down at the crumpled sheets, she recognized the checked pattern of the mattress beneath it.

The Vividus was a luxury mattress upwards of fifty-fucking-grand. What the fuck kind of money did Leo have? The hand carved dresser, mirror, and chairs all reflected the same top quality craftsmanship. Like most Shifter wares, it was specialty built to withstand the antics of a growing Shifter. In Leo's case, a Lion cub.

Shifter furniture artisans responsible for pieces such as these would undoubtedly charge tens of thousands of dollars for each one. They were beautiful works of art, and they were well-cared for. The entire mansion was full of them. Everything was top of the line, cleaned and polished.

Void of Lions, though. Sheila frowned. It was odd, seeing a Pride house empty like this one.

The plush carpets were spotless, the furniture shiny. For a she-Wolf who'd slept under the stars on an old bedroll for most of her life, this place was over the top grand. It was way out of her league.

Sheila didn't react outwardly—the Lionesses would be all over her if she did—but she couldn't stem the tide of panic that welled up deep inside. She was good at keeping her crazy to herself, and she would have to do just that right now.

Once she got hold of that sneaky pussycat, she'd let it all out. What was he, anyway? Some rich flunky of the King's? How could he not tell her? She thought he was just a detective, and that had been bad enough, but finding out he was rich too.

Ugh.

Sheila did not belong here. This place was top shelf, and she was more a dollar drafts kind of gal. She didn't want an audience for this little breakdown she was having. Did not want to reveal too much to these two strange Lionesses. That would be incredibly foolish, and Sheila was not that.

Nope.

She needed to think. She needed to know more about their agenda, at the very least. The two felines watched her with that same steady glare of house cats, and Sheila's Wolf snarled. Should they prove to be enemies, her animal wasn't opposed to using them both as chew toys.

Grrr.

"What I want to know is what was that hair-brained nephew of mine thinking bringing a Dog inside the Palace?"

"Well, she has good boobs, Mom," the younger said, and Sheila looked down.

Shifters were usually comfortable with nudity, and Sheila was no different. The fact they called their Pride house a Palace was something only a fucking Cat would do—haughty little shits.

"Thanks. I need to shower," she told the females, who seemed perfectly fine just lounging around.

She needed answers, but her pussycat ran away. It was a sneaky move. Definitely not straightlaced, and she didn't know whether to be angry or proud of him. Leo always followed the rules, as far as she knew. It was kind of sexy to see a mischievous side of him. OMG, she really was sick. How could him hightailing it out of there turn her on?

"Easy there, Spot," the younger Lioness said, sniffing the air and picking up on the effect Sheila's naughty thoughts had on her body. "We don't swing that way."

"I swing a lot of ways actually, but incest is not my thing. Seems like my nephew has finally been having some fun with—say, just who are you, anyway?" the older Lioness asked.

"Yeah, what's your name, Doggy?"

"Okay, first, I'm a Dire Wolf Shifter, not a Dog, so you're going to want to watch it with the insults or you two kitties are going to lose your tails," Sheila replied.

She turned away from the bathroom door to face them, naked as a jaybird. The two blonde-haired females slunk further into Leo's sofas and eyed her with casual interest. Nothing icky, eyes on her face, but they definitely knew something she didn't. Best to make friends, she decided.

Lounging lazily like the haughty felines they were, Sheila wondered just why they had presumed to simply walk in. Were these relatives allies of Leo? They were definitely nosey. Sheila reached for her jeans and top. She did not do confrontations naked —unless they were with Leo.

"A Dire Wolf, huh? That's kinda cool, but you didn't answer the other question. *Who* are you?"

"Second," Sheila continued, as if she hadn't been interrupted. "You don't get to just walk in here. Not anymore. And you certainly don't get to snap questions at me."

"And why not?"

"Because," Sheila continued as she turned around and entered the bathroom, closing the door unhurriedly. "I'm Leo's mate."

"Holy butt-sniffers!" the younger woman squeaked and practically choked on her bubblegum.

"Ariella, I don't know about you, but I like her," the woman with silver streaks threaded through her stylishly short blonde locks said loud enough for Sheila to hear her with the bathroom door closed.

Yay, Sheila! She smirked and turned on the shower. Sixteen minutes later, she was cleaned, and dressed in fresh jeans and a t-shirt. Sheila opened the door to see the two Lionesses still there.

"You clean up nice," the younger one said.

"Gee, thanks," Sheila said, rolling her eyes.

"Well, since you are Leo's mate, I figured we'd stick around for formal introductions. I'm Leo's Aunt Patricia. Guess that makes me your auntie, too. This here is one of my daughters. Ariella, stand up and say hi."

"Hi," Ariella said once she stopped choking. She grinned wickedly, and peaked at her mother.

"George is going to shit himself."

"Ariella! Don't talk about your brother like that. He is though, isn't he!" Auntie Pat said, smirking before she laughed wickedly.

"You see, my little brother Georgie has been lining up all the eligible Lionesses for Leo to choose his mate. In fact, they should be parading through the Palace interviewing room in about an hour," Ariella informed her.

"Oh, really?" Sheila growled.

"Yes, really," added Aunt Patricia. "Forgive me, but how do we know you're actually his mate?"

"Surely, you can scent what happened in here?"

"Sex is sex, dear. But where is your mating mark?"

"My Pack prefers to hold all claiming ceremonies for the night of the full moon," Sheila replied.

It wasn't a lie exactly. Dire Wolves did prefer to mate by moonlight. Afterwards, the ritual of the claiming tattoo would take place in sight of the Pack. Odd, she did not really think of them as an MC now, since they'd retired. But some shit was bone deep. In fact, she grabbed her cell phone and shot off a text to Brock. The bastard owed her one after that shit he pulled in the bar yesterday.

"So, you know, the full moon is tonight, you know," Ariella supplied, and Sheila's heart immediately started beating overtime.

Hmm.

She wondered if Leo would mind getting a tattoo. She hadn't noticed one on him earlier. His wide shoulders and broad chest would be perfect in her opinion, and with those muscles, he'd only look hotter with a bit of ink.

Whoa.

That would only be an option if Sheila was thinking about making this mating real, and she was far from doing that. Her emotions were all over the place, but her Wolf was consistent. She wanted Leo to be hers, regardless of her human fears.

"You ladies up for a ride?" she remarked casually when she was feeling anything but.

"You're changing the subject," Aunt Patricia said.

"Yep. You pussies riding with me? Or are you a couple of scaredy cats too timid to follow a badass Wolf?" Sheila baited them, sliding her boots on, and tugging her hair into a low ponytail.

"What kind of ride?" Ariella asked.

Just then, the sound of a couple of Harley's revving their engines echoed in the room. Ariella bounded over to a row of long curtains lining the wall. She pulled a switch, revealing double, glass terrace doors. Sheila gasped her surprise before Ariella opened said doors, that led out to a stone patio leading to a path that split off to different areas of the massive yard. One path went to the side of the Palace, to a fence the other side of which sat her ride.

Wowza.

Leo had a fucking terrace in his bedroom. This man was way too good at hiding bits and pieces of himself from her. Some goody-two shoes he was turning out to be! It was like he was leading this whole double life. Leo was a bad boy! And that just made her she-Wolf swoon and sigh dreamily over the big puffed up pussy, for fuck's sake.

Just think of the midnight runs! We could find our fur together and come right to bed.

Sheila rolled her eyes at her canine's imagination.

"Well, ladies? What do you say? Want to burn some rubber with a couple of Dire Wolves?" she asked, and the two Lionesses looked at each other, mischievous grins on their faces before joining her on the patio.

"We talkin' tires, or other kinds of rubber?" Aunt Patricia asked and wagged her eyebrows.

OMG. The older Lioness had just made a condom joke. Ha! Sheila snorted.

The woman was old enough to be her mother, but hey, Sheila wasn't judging. People had sex because it felt good. Sex was fun. Sheila was not going to hold her suggestive and hilarious questions against her. That Lioness was funny as fuck.

"Just a ride on a Harley, Auntie P," she said and winked.

"Oh pooh! Well, I suppose I could be persuaded. I'll take the big, bald one," she purred.

"Um, Sheila?"

"Yeah, Ari?"

"Who are these guys?" Ariella asked and blinked slowly as she took in Thor, Brock, and Weylin.

The latter was riding Sheila's custom pink, and black painted Harley Softail Convertible. She watched her Pack mate pull up to the fence along the side of the rock wall that partially closed off the garden and opened to the field and forests behind. Fucking place was amazing, she thought while admiring the view.

The back of the property seemed to begin as a manicured lawn with all the customary entertaining doodads that crazy rich people always seemed to have in their yards. There was a large swimming pool, a fountain, a gazebo, tennis courts, and a huge grassy lawn. Maybe that's why these Lions called it a Palace.

There had to be some good explanation for why her Leo lived with the King of the Pride. She swallowed hard and pushed the thought away. She wasn't ready to hear her own ideas on that situation, much less whatever these two Lionesses had to say about it.

Sheila eyed the high rock wall separating the property from the small side road where her Pack mates were currently idling on their bikes. She could clear that on her two legs. No problem. A sharp whistle reached her ears, and she turned to see Brock signaling to her. Right. The Beta had a kitchen to run, and it was almost lunchtime. Sheila's pulse raced as she got closer to her motorcycle. Her blood hummed with the need to ride.

"Those are my Pack mates," she finally answered, noticing Ariella's still and unblinking stare. The Lioness had her golden gaze on Brock, and the Wolf seemed unwilling or unable to break eye contact.

Hmm. That's interesting.

She'd save her curiosity for another time, though. Right then, Sheila had better things to do. Like maybe get herself away from the weird situation she found herself in so she could mull it over.

Grrr.

Her she-Wolf was not happy about this at all. But she shut down her animal with a sharp command. Her human side was in control, and she had some thinking to do.

Relax, she told the beast.

She needed to beat it, even if just for a minute or thirty. Not like she'd run out on the big ol' pussycat without telling him. Not now that she'd let him in. Sheila couldn't walk away cold if she tried. And for once, she did not want to try.

Also interesting.

It had only been a few days since she'd jumped on the back of her Harley and cruised the open road, but she could use the clarity right about now. There was something about miles of black asphalt that allowed Sheila to just think.

Oddly enough, that sweet moment of peace she got whenever she went out for a ride, no matter how long or short, was even sweeter now that she had a permanent place to land. For a she-Wolf who'd never had a room, much less a home of her own, that was something alright.

But was she really destined to live in a Palace? The thought stuck in her throat like an un-popped piece of popcorn.

Shit.

She didn't want to have those thoughts. Not when she was still feeling so good after her sexy little romp with Leo between his silky sheets. Fuck, they were probably real silk she realized with an unsteady breath. Her fingers itched to get ahold of his hot and hard body once again, but for now she'd settle for gripping the handlebars of her bike.

She'd had Weylin repaint the trim a few months ago. It kind of went with her nails now, and their logo. She grinned excitedly at the hot pink lines and flames that covered the custom body of her ride. The other two boys were on their own rides. Brock on his FXSTB Night Train and Thor on his VRSCA V-Rod. All three Harleys gleamed in the setting sun and the men on them with their leather cuts and dark helmets looked pretty dang good, even if they were her family.

"Well, ladies? Let's go!" Sheila laughed and took off for the wall at a run with the two felines right behind her.

"Hey there, Sheila girl. Dang, you stink like Cat —*ouch!*" Weylin rubbed his arm where she'd punched him.

"Shit, Sheila, you know I bruise easily!" he complained.

"Oh, shut up, you big baby. Now, scoot out of the way, I'm driving. Ladies, this here is Weylin. He's just a grunt," she teased despite his scowl. "That's Brock. He's our Pack Beta. And that giant over there is Thor, our Enforcer. Guys, this is Aunt Patricia and Ariella. They want to go for a ride, what say you?" Sheila asked grandly and grinned wickedly as the humor left her Pack mates' faces.

"Ma'am, I'd be happy to take you for a ride," Thor said and offered his hand to Aunt Patricia, who slapped it away.

"I can get on myself, big guy. You just keep this thing straight, and I'll hold on to the good parts," she replied and grinned wickedly. With a throaty little purr, the older Lioness mounted behind the big man.

"Ooof!"

Thor's eyes bulged out of his head, and he actually squeaked as the feline wrapped herself around him and clung like a vise. She nipped his ear, and Thor revved his engine, taking off like a bat out of hell.

"Mom!" Ariella blushed as she gingerly got on the seat behind Brock.

Sheila pretended not to listen as the Dire Wolf Beta instructed her to scooch on closer. He handed her his helmet, turning to latch it carefully beneath her chin before telling the little kitty to put her arms around his waist. The lust in the air was pretty hard to miss, but Sheila was much too worried about herself to tease her Beta about it just yet.

Very interesting.

It seemed like it was open season on the DWMC. She supposed Cats and Dogs could get along if circumstances were right. Maybe this was a sign of some sort.

Fuck it.

Sheila might not be able to stop fate, but she'd go down swinging. That was a guarantee.

"Let's ride," she said before taking off with Weylin clinging to the seat and cursing for all he was worth.

Sheila's laughter was swallowed by the wind as she sped away from the Blue Valley Pride, and from Leo. Her she-Wolf growled and snapped until she reassured the beast she'd be returning within the hour.

Make it fast.

Grrrr.

CHAPTER 9

Leo squeezed his father's hand and looked into the older man's sightless eyes. It's not that he was blind, the Lion King had perfect vision. And yet, he knew his father was not seeing him.

It was as if he was somewhere else, locked away inside his mind. The old King seemed caught in his past somehow and judging from his expression and the occasional moan that escaped his thin lips, it was not a pleasant experience.

"Car! Car!" Donovan Crowley repeated the nickname he'd given Leo's mother a long time ago.

It struck a chord deep within Leo as his father called out for his mate over and over again. Caroline Crowley, Leo's mother, was a human woman, a *normal*, as their kind referred to them. Fate had dealt his parents quite the hand, but it all worked out. His human mother fell in love and got mated to the Lion King of Blue Valley.

Their story was legendary in a time when prejudice and hatred for humans had run rampant among Shifters. Things had settled down some, but there was always that fear of being discovered to make human supernatural pairings uncomfortable. The Pride had not wanted to allow such a mating. But his father had not backed down an inch. Donovan had claimed his human bride, and the massive Lion had torn down every doubter in his Pride.

Leo knew the tale well. He'd cut his teeth on it. Hell, he was in awe of them both. His parents had succeeded despite the naysayers from the Pride. Leo was proud of them and of his heritage. It saddened him that Leo didn't know his father that well anymore. They'd drifted apart over the years. It was a hard truth.

Still, he loved the man. Respected him. But this frail shell of a man was not the father he knew. It was not the King he remembered.

"I'm going to figure this out, Dad," he whispered into his father's ear, and kissed his withered cheek.

The old man turned with a speed Leo didn't expect. Hell, he didn't think his father still had it in him. Hope sparked deep inside his chest. His father clutched his arm, and when he finally spoke, Leo saw the cloudy white film of disease leave his eyes and the golden amber of his Lion leaked through.

"Car! It's Car," he growled.

"Dad? No, Dad, it's Leo. Mom is gone. I'm sorry, Dad, but she's gone."

"Caroline? Gone? No, no!"

His father released his hold on Leo's arm and clutched his head. The once mighty King rocked back and forth, sobbing in his hands. He muttered to himself, and Leo noted the cloudiness had returned to his eyes. His heart nearly broke at the sight.

Something was not right. How did a once robust King suddenly turn into this? It was unnatural, but Leo was too close to the situation to see it clearly. Damn. He needed Sheila. She could help him. Both his Lion and human sides were at peace when she was near. He needed his mate. Now.

"My Prince? What are you doing here?" Montgomery entered the room with a wheeled cart filled with food and his grandmother's tea service.

Leo's cousin George was hot on his heels. His Lion growled, and both men stopped in their tracks. He didn't want them to witness his father's weakness, but he was helpless to stop them. Montgomery was a trusted attendant and George was being groomed to fill the position of advisor once Leo ascended the throne.

Fuck.

Dread filled him. He wasn't ready. Not yet. He nodded his head, and both men moved cautiously into his father's room. He had to keep level to find the truth.

"Leo, it's good you are here. Please, come into the interview room and we will begin—"

"I told you, do not discuss those things in here," Montgomery hissed, surprising Leo and George.

"Excuse me, but what do you have to say on the matter?" George responded.

"Oh, sorry, I was just thinking of the King. He needs his rest. Excuse me," the man said and continued to prepare the tea.

"Okay," George replied, eyes wide. "Well, Leo, there are a few items on your agenda you need to see to immediately. Maybe something that will cure whatever ails you," the younger Lion said and wagged his eyebrows.

Unfortunately, Leo was in no mood for games. His father was worse off than he'd thought.

"George, I want to speak to the Pride healer. Now," Leo grumbled, turning back to cup his father's neck, pressing his forehead to his sire's in a show of deep affection and respect felines were known for before heading out of the room.

"Now? Why? He isn't going to say anything new, you know," the younger man replied, trailing after him, and looking puzzled.

Leo turned around and barked an order to Montgomery. The older man stopped what he was doing and followed George, though he did not look happy about it. Well, wasn't that too fucking bad?

"George, Montgomery, when the two of you entered my father's room, did you show him the proper respect befitting your King?"

"What?" George sputtered.

"Pardon, sire?" Montgomery balked.

Leo's Lion growled deep inside of him, the sound filling his stomach and chest until it reverberated throughout the tiny hall between rooms. Leo wasn't King yet, but he was the strongest Lion there. Immediately, George and Montgomery dropped to their knees, baring their throats under the heavy weight of his dominance.

Both males averted their gazes, neither daring to look at Leo with his Lion so close to the surface. It was a good thing. A smart thing to do. Leo felt raw and angry. His beast wouldn't like the challenge their direct stares would pose.

Still, he did not like feeling this out of control. It was unbefitting a man of his station, and Leo was all about the rules.

"I apologize, sir," George replied.

His voice sounded strained under the force of Leo's alpha Lion's will. That sort of power was inherent in certain Shifters. Wielded by those who would lead, the alpha gene was inherited, but that extra bit of Pride magic was only granted to those few chosen strong enough to be Kings. The Crowley family bred such Shifters and George would do well to remember that. What it all meant was fairly simple. Leo was not to be fucked with.

It was clear some members of the Pride had forgotten that one little thing. Leo would have to correct that. He'd been gone too long, but he was not going to make that mistake again. Leo pressed his will on them for just a moment longer, then he released his hold.

They stayed on the ground, unsure of what to do next. His Lion gleaned satisfaction from their submission. Sick? Maybe. But he was a predator, a dominant, a born Primus. It was his natural power and position within the Pride. His due if you will.

"Thank you, sir. May I tend my duties now?" Montgomery gestured to the door where Leo's father waited.

"My father is still the King, Montgomery. That means you, and everyone else, needs to afford him the respect he is due at all times. Is that understood?" Leo asked, barely holding onto his beast.

Power pulsed through him, and it was all he could do to fight his Lion's urge to dominate these others into the ground.

They are of our Pride, he reminded his Lion. Finally, the regal animal relented.

"Yes, of course," Montgomery spoke with his forehead still pressed to the cold, hard marble floor.

Guilty for his bullying tactics, Leo nodded for him to rise. The man had been around forever. He had always been overeager to please, and exceedingly efficient in his duties.

But Montgomery had always made him a tad uncomfortable, even when Leo was just a cub. His mother had told him about Montgomery's family's history, and stories of the Clover males and the fact they had been employed in the Palace for just as long as a Crowley had reigned. Those stories softened Leo's point of view.

The man simply took his job seriously. Nothing

wrong with that. In fact, Leo could relate. How many cases had he brought home with him over the years? His supervisors had one constant reprimand, and that was for the number of hours in overtime Leo worked in his search to bring justice to the people he served and to hunt down any criminal who dared transpire in his territory.

Hell, he'd stopped reporting those long overtime hours years ago. He didn't care about the money. He had plenty. It was the thought of leaving a case unsolved that haunted him.

"Of course," George gasped. "I know Uncle Donovan is our King. Look, Leo, I am sorry, I just got excited. I have a surprise, that's all."

Leo lessened his Alpha will, and George rose hesitantly from the floor. His eyes were still averted, and Leo realized he was being an ass.

"Okay. Sorry, bro, I'm just tense. Get the healer anyway, and I'll meet you in the interview room," he growled, and walked away from his sputtering younger cousin.

It seemed like George was always upset about something or other. Leo didn't give a rat's ass at the moment. His cousin was an adult, he could handle his own problems. Right then, he had his own Lion to worry about. The animal was on edge.

In fact, he was seriously pissed at Leo, and not because he wouldn't let him snack on those two less dominant males. Heck, those Lions were not even on his radar at the moment. No, the beast inside him was angry at Leo for leaving their den with Sheila still asleep. His animal was livid he had not claimed his mate.

He was still reeling from the fact that Sheila had taken the reins from him almost immediately after he'd instigated a kiss. Sexy little she-Wolf had stripped her clothes, then his, teasing him with glimpses of her pale, silky smooth flesh. She was the hottest thing he'd ever seen.

His cock hardened at the memory of her delightful sexual aggression. She was so damn confident, so sublimely seductive with her ivory skin, sapphire eyes, and that mane of wild red hair. He was positively enamored of her. Leo swallowed, clearing his throat. He could admit it to himself.

He loved her. He was in love with her. The feelings were right there, and dammit, they felt good. It was just a shock. He knew he adored her, cared for her, and wanted her. Hell, he worshipped the feisty woman, or he wanted to, but she hadn't given him the opportunity yet.

Next time.

Next time, Leo would have his fill of her the way he'd dreamed about. He'd start with that sassy little mouth of hers. It made him smirk when he thought of her kickass comebacks. She was so damn cute.

Yeah, he'd start with that mouth of hers alright. Kissing Sheila was like trying to hold on to the wind. She was everywhere at once, filling his senses and haunting his dreams. Wild, untamed, and fucking glorious. He'd claim that spitfire's mouth with his alright. Then, he'd leave a trail of kisses down her smooth neck until he could savor the plump berries that tipped each of her splendid breasts.

He'd lick and nibble his way further still to the curve of her belly, over the flare of her hips, to that delicate smooth skin of her inner thighs. Finally, he'd find paradise in between those gorgeous legs of hers. Her short-cropped auburn curls hid the passage to absolute glory that Leo was destined to claim as his alone. Just thinking about her made his dick hard and his mouth water. He wanted his little Wolf with him.

Here. Now. Always.

Roarrrr.

Leo really needed to calm his beast before the Lion claimed her without permission, and he'd already promised to do no such thing. Some alpha

Shifters ruled with big shows of strength, but Leo had always appreciated a quieter, more subtle approach. Reining in his beast was difficult, but he would wrestle his Lion down every single time if it brought him closer to his ultimate goal. And of course, that was claiming Sheila.

His Dire Wolf mate had made her position clear. She would help him with his mission to solve the source of his Pride's issues, but she wasn't sticking around forever. Or so she thought. Little did she know he had no intention of letting her go.

The sound of motors revving got his attention, but he was needed in the interview room. Besides, he'd left her snug in his bedroom. He would join her as soon as he finished with the Pride. First, he'd have Montgomery cook them a few porterhouses as a late lunch. He'd feed her, make love to her, then he'd bring up their future. That sounded like a helluva plan to him.

His Lion would never be satisfied until she was truly claimed. Difficult with her insistence that this thing between them was temporary. He just had to get her to change her mind about mating him. Shouldn't be too hard.

Yeah right.

He entered the King's interview room and immediately went on high alert. This was where he would conduct Pride business acting in his father's stead, where the King normally sat to hear his Pride's concerns, and to rule on things that needed ruling on. Apparently, stuff had been left to slide this past month and there were many issues that needed his attention.

Leo stopped short at the sight awaiting him inside. What fresh hell was this? No less than a dozen Lionesses stood in a line, each of them with what looked like a file folder in hand.

Fucking George.

He snarled. Were those resumes? He bit off his growl, noting the shocked gold stares eyeing him like some prize. Leo straightened his shoulders, grateful he'd donned his at home uniform. The navy blue suit with the Crowley crest on his cuff links acknowledged his position. It also happened to be one of his favorites with a thin pin strip and a silk shirt underneath. He'd foregone his usual tie but wore the medallion of his station. A thick gold chain with a single Lion claw hanging from it.

Should he need to shift, it would be both large and strong enough to withstand the power behind his change. And if that younger cousin of his didn't watch himself, Leo was sure to go all fierce and furry on his ass. Maybe take a bite out of the cheeky male's hide.

Fuckface.

He had already told George no to the whole Lioness thing. Leo raised an eyebrow as he sought his cousin. Ah. There he was. George tried to herd the females into a line, swatting down the hairs on the back of his neck that were undoubtedly standing up because of Leo. He was pissed.

What was his idiot cousin up to now? He took out his phone and shot a text to Sheila, wondering if she was up. He asked her to respond the minute she woke.

Dammit.

He missed her. Yes, he needed her too. Not for the reason he told her. Not to dissuade these griping females. He needed her to settle his animal, to make him feel whole—because fuck knew she did.

Beautiful, tempting, sassy seductress.

"Leo! Excellent, sit down and meet the most eligible females the Pride has to offer!"

The females stood at attention. Some he knew from when he was a cub, others he did not recognize. They were all dressed up, like this was some kind of pageant, and George, the idiot, had the nerve to smile at him. Leo was going to murder him.

Grrrr.

"George, I asked you to bring the healer to me," he said instead.

"Um, yes. I called, but he is delivering a set of cubs right now. I assured him you would be fine for a few hours. Besides you have other things to tend to, my Prince," George whispered and nodded to the first female in line.

She was wearing an expensive suit that showed off her best assets. She had her blonde hair piled on her head in some sophisticated, and painful looking updo. Her nails were neatly trimmed and polished a staid beige color. She was attractive, sophisticated, a bit boring, truth be told.

The blonde woman flashed him a toothy grin, and Leo nodded politely. His Lion snapped and spit in revulsion. The beast wanted nothing to do with this or the other tawny-haired females. This was exactly the type of female he'd thought he would end up with when he was just a cub. But not him. Not now.

Adult Leo found his tastes ran much different from Leo the cub. What he really liked was dazzling redheads with hot pink nail polish. Sexy biker chicks in leather and ripped jeans. One in particular with bright blue eyes, skin pale as milky, and a Harley between her legs when he couldn't be.

Yessssss.

"George, when did you notice my father started feeling ill?" he asked, ignoring the female.

"What? Oh, I don't know. He has not been himself since Aunt Caroline passed away, but he didn't start showing these signs till a few months ago, I think."

"I see. And had his habits changed?"

"Really, Leo, I don't know. Look, you should at least hear them out," George said and tilted his head. Leo noted a group of older Lionesses had entered the room from the other side.

Fuck.

All of them were elders. He knew well that the females of any Lion Pride were the backbone. Even in the wild, the females were the hunters, the providers. They had the numbers and the strength, but a male was King. It was simply their way.

After the circle he'd attended a few days ago, Leo had expected some backlash, but even he could not have predicted this. The four Lionesses included Maribel Clover, Ruth Cunningham, Margaret Donner, and Evangeline Mayers, all present and accounted for.

These Shifter females were cunning, sharp, and determined hunters. Strong despite their silver hair and the signs of age on their once unlined faces. Leo's father had allowed the elders to have a say in the way things were done within the Blue Valley Pride by listening to their council on more than one occasion. He would not undo all of his father's work, but that didn't mean he would go into this blindly.

Leo had spent years as a detective, he knew better than to trust people's motives. Especially when they had their own agendas. These women would not approve of Leo's announcement that he'd found a mate without their counsel. For one thing, his mate was not a female of their choosing. For another, she was not a Lioness.

Either way, they were going to be pissed. Something that would have worried younger Leo, but again, not now. Neither the elders nor the Pride would have a say in his choice of mate. He noted several of the females George had gathered for this introduction belonged to these Lioness' immediate families.

Well, fuck me again.

There was just no graceful way out of this. He had to do his duty and at least allow them to present themselves. George was still smiling, idiot that he was. He nodded his head at the Lionesses once more, knowing full well Leo was not happy.

"The way I see it, cousin, this is the way our Pride has always conducted such things. You have a duty, you know."

"I have found my mate, George. This will not change that."

"Maybe you're wrong," insisted the younger male.

Leo growled unhappily. Of course, he wasn't wrong. His Lion chuffed and snorted. He would not be happy about it, and he sure as fuck wasn't changing his mind, but there were rules, and he had to at least appear willing. He had a protocol to follow.

Leo sat in his father's chair and nodded for the first woman to present herself. He would pretend to listen, and maybe he would find out just what the fuck was going on here.

"This is Taylor DeBlume," George said, smiling at the first boring blonde.

Leo huffed out a sigh. It was going to be a long morning.

CHAPTER 10

"You are so right, Mom. Leo picked good."

Ariella giggled and fluffed her hair as they stumbled through the front doors of the Palace. They were all a little windblown, but no worse for wear. Besides, that ride had given Sheila exactly what she needed. Time to clear her head.

"Ladies! What are you doing here?" Montgomery sputtered at them.

His eyes raced wildly as he looked back and forth from one female to the other as if their presence were somehow blackening the polished floors. Sheila did not know what the fuck was wrong with this guy, but she wiped her feet on the rug, for fuck's sake.

"Look, it's cool, Monty. I wiped my feet," Sheila told him straight out.

She winked and opened the door wider, lifting each of her leather-booted feet into the air and holding her black and hot pink helmet under one arm.

"Montgomery, why do you always look like that?" Aunt Patricia asked and narrowed her eyes at the man. "You know, I've been trying to get in to see Donovan for weeks now! What is going on, anyway?'

"You should not be here, madam. Your presence is unwanted," he growled the words between clenched teeth.

"Whoa, tone it down there skippy. I don't think Leo will like you talking to her that way," Sheila growled. "I sure as fuck don't."

"How does he look, Mom?" Ariella asked.

"Oh, like someone farted right in his face," Aunt Patricia barked out a laugh that even a Dire Wolf could be proud of.

The two drunken kitties giggled, and Aunt Patricia leaned heavily on the wall. Okay, so, maybe Sheila shouldn't have stopped at Serious Moonlight with Leo's aunt and cousin for a couple of pitchers of mimosas. Of course, those had turned into margueritas, and from there it was shots all around. And it wasn't even dinner time!

Sheila bit her lip guiltily. But what a time they'd had. Sigh. She recalled Aunt Patricia's bar-top dancing while guzzling a bottle of eighty proof tequila like a motherfucking champ. It took Thor and Brock both to get her down. Shifter metabolism was such that alcohol burned off within minutes and by the time she left, she was not even buzzed. Ariella and Patricia were, but that's because they were still drinking.

Her stomach fluttered. The butterflies inside waking up now that she was closer to him. She'd expected to feel better, less anxious, once she'd hopped on her Harley with her Pack mates and her two new friends, but truthfully, that familiar calm she'd sought had proven elusive. Her she-Wolf had been seriously pissed at her for leaving Leo. She'd done her best to shake it off. Had some drinks, checked in with her Pack mates, and talked to some friendly customers. Including a certain Ass and his mate.

"Hey! It's you? Where is that amazing man of yours?" asked the Chipmunk Shifter Leo had rescued a few days ago.

"He's working, how are you?" Sheila had replied to the

one and looked from her to where her mate was standing with one hand on her waist in a protective and possessive gesture. Sheila approved.

"We're good, never better," she'd returned with a twinkle in her eyes.

"Ma'am," the Donkey Shifter, Al, nodded at her and whispered something in his mate's ear that had her blushing like a schoolgirl.

"Um, we better go. Tell him, thanks again for me," the woman winked and left with her mate wrapped around her.

Sheila had felt a pang of jealousy as she watched the pair hurry on through the crowd. Probably on their way home, together. There was something about mates and being Shifters that meant when things were good, sexy fun times often ensued. Sheila could get used to an arrangement like that. But it was more than sex that appealed to her. Leo was simply perfect.

He was outrageously handsome, had an impeccable moral compass, was good to talk to, and possessed an air of power and strength that her Wolf wholeheartedly approved of. He was her ideal everything. How could she ever measure up? And, as if that wasn't bad enough, her new buddies had spilled the beans in a very bad way.

"You know, you're gonna make one helluva queen," Aunt Patricia *slurred her words after she'd tipped off the bar when she'd finished the first bottle of tequila. The woman had taken a header into the unwilling arms of one particularly unhappy Pack Enforcer.*

"For fuck's sake," Thor had muttered and glared at Sheila. Still, he was gentleman enough to drive them home after.

"My bad," she'd apologized to her Pack mate, but she was more concerned with what the Lioness had just said.

"The old Palace could use a little livening up. We haven't had any fun since Caroline passed. Leo's mother was one helluva queen, I tell you, and Donovan was so in love with that woman. She was my best friend. You're a lucky Dog, Sheila! The Crowleys are good Cats. Ha! A lucky Dog! That works even better cause you're a canine! Ha ha ha!" The matronly feline had snorted and laughed at her own jokes.

A few more shots, a couple of dances, and some indirect questions were all it took for Sheila to get the truth about Leo Crowley from the mouth of that swaggeriffic feline, Aunt Patricia. And when she finally pieced it all together, Sheila was fucking furious.

That lying, no good butt-sniffin' mother-humper!

Grrr, even her she-Wolf was pissed.

Sheila had not been prepared for that little tidbit of information he'd been holding back. Talk about a shock. He lied. After her initial fury had settled, Sheila was pissed to discover the real reason she'd stayed away much longer than she'd intended when she'd taken off earlier. Hurt flared up inside of her and fear.

Yes.

That's right. Sheila was afraid. What did a foul-mouthed ex-biker Wolf know about being a queen? Fated mates or not, she didn't see this working out for either of them. No wonder the strait-laced, law-abiding pussy was so uptight.

Apparently, every one of her Pack mates, even Derrick, her Alpha and so-called cousin, had known or suspected the entire time. They'd all been privy to that tiny factoid, and no one, not even her dear mate, had bothered to tell her.

Fuckers. Each and every one of them.

And what had her cousin's reply been when she'd confronted him with the news? The dumb Alpha had gotten all snarly with her.

"So, Leo's a Prince. Big fucking deal, woman."

"But Derrick, why the fuck didn't you tell me? How am I supposed to face him now?"

"What the fuck are you on about, girl? You're no damn

slouch. We Dire Wolves have our own hierarchy as you well know, cousin, and the Rands are top fucking shelf. He's a Prince and you're already a Princess around here, so go make it official already. Claim your mate and stop your snarling."

She'd been spitting mad, but in the end, she knew Derrick was right. Her Alpha cousin was usually right. The jerk.

So, Leo was a Prince among Shifters. And not because he was charming and handsome, or because he wore a badge, or because he was a hero to Chipmunk Shifters and women everywhere. No, he was an actual, honest to goodness heir-to-the-throne Prince like in a fairytale. Sole successor to the King, and the current ruler of the Blue Valley Pride, while his father was incapacitated by illness. Her Leo. Her fated mate.

And that made her what, exactly?

A fucking idiot.

At least that was how she'd felt. Leo was a Prince, and he hadn't trusted her with that information. Hurt by his betrayal, she'd stayed out longer than she'd planned. Why hadn't he trusted her? That was the question.

Anger and pain warred with each other for dominance throughout most of the night, but

Sheila still walked away, confused and a tad annoyed.

"Sheila, I wanted to ask you at the bar but did not have the chance. Um, are all your Pack mates, uh, single?" Ariella hedged as she took off her high-heeled shoes and rubbed her feet.

"Do not do that here! Have you no decency?"

Montgomery was trying to sweep some imaginary dust and was definitely close to losing his shit for no reason that Sheila could see.

Talk about an uptight pussy.

Sheila narrowed her eyes at the man before turning to the striking, yet shy Lioness. Unlike her extroverted mother, Ariella had behaved in a more staid fashion at *Serious Moonlight*. One might have observed her actions as a sort of recon mission, instead of just hanging out. She'd chosen to nurse her margarita from her barstool with her eyes trained on a certain Pack Beta.

The finicky feline had dismissed the attention she'd garnered from other men at the roadhouse, and that had been quite a few, in Sheila's humble opinion. Brock, the object of her interest, had also behaved strangely. In fact, he'd disappeared entirely when it was time to leave, and Ariella had to ride in the sidecar they'd hooked up to Thor's bike.

Strange indeed.

"Far as I know, only Derrick has a mate," she answered the pretty Lioness.

"And you. You have a mate, don't you, Sheila?" Aunt Patricia snickered.

Sheila swallowed. She nodded and tried to stave off the feeling of dizziness that statement brought on. Holy shit. She did have a mate. A big, strong, seriously hot one, if she recalled correctly. Maybe it was time she started acting like it?

She sucked in a deep breath, suddenly needing a quick infusion of oxygen to clear her foggy brain. Crap. If she didn't know better, she'd think she was drunk. Alcohol left her system fairly quickly, as it did with most Shifters, but still. She would have passed for drunk right then. She felt unsteady on her feet, a little nauseous, and was she sweating?

Of course, she never would have ridden her bike home if she was actually intoxicated. There was just no way. Besides, Sheila was not impaired by the shots she'd thrown down with these two felines. And yet, suddenly, she found it difficult to form a coherent thought other than one, single word that kept popping in and out of her brain.

Mate. Mate. MATE.

Goosebumps broke out over her skin and her

throat felt dry. Sheila licked her lips and tried to count to ten inside her head. Anything to still the churning in her stomach and the heavy pounding of her heart. She was wobbly and tense, uncertain and clear, she felt everything and nothing all at the same time.

It had absolutely nothing at all to do with alcohol, and completely everything to do with the scowling mountain of a man who was right then stalking down the hallway towards her. Leo wore a pair of navy blue suit pants with a lighter colored silk shirt. His sleeves were rolled up, revealing powerful forearms that ended in large, long-fingered hands.

Her skin itched with need, she could almost feel those hands on her body. His tailored shirt was unbuttoned down to his navel, exposing hard muscles and scandalous inches of golden, tanned skin that she longed to touch. Sheila's body responded to the sight, heating, and readying for her fated mate. The she-Wolf inside of her growled and panted.

Her inner beast wanted her to claim and be claimed. Suddenly, she couldn't remember why she'd said no in the first place. Everything about him called to her, beckoned her to him in every single way. Desire swelled, as if the need to have him was a living thing. It grew and grew until she felt like her skin was on fire.

It itched and burned, and Sheila wanted to strip. To tear off her clothing, hell his too, but their audience prevented that. Her Wolf was a tad bit possessive when it came to sharing her man, and relatives or not, Leo's sexy body was for her eyes only.

She shivered as another powerful wave of desire swept through her. Her nipples hardened, clit throbbed, and she damn near salivated down the front of her shirt. So this was what it felt like to be in heat, she thought as her pussy dripped moisture, drenching her panties.

Her stomach clenched as he drew nearer. Leo's long legs ate up the distance between them quickly. She couldn't help but admire her leonine lover, this Lion Prince, whom the universe had decided was for her.

Mine.

Fuck.

Really, though? Was he? Could the Fates be wrong? She couldn't possibly mate a Prince.

Yes. We can, her she-Wolf insisted.

She swallowed hard and raised an eyebrow. He wasn't exactly playing the besotted lover at the moment. No, he was not happy at all. His stride was angry, less calculated than normal, and his breathing was heavy. Sheila's eyes widened as she realized something was different about him.

Oh shit.

Leo was pissed. And the giant, sexy as fuck pussycat never looked hotter.

"Where?" he growled the word at her, not even bothering to finish his sentence.

"What?" she asked, arching one eyebrow, and cocking her head to the side, fascinated by the change in him.

"It's late."

"I can tell time," she responded.

The two feline females nearby looked back and forth between Leo and Sheila with mischief glittering in their golden eyes. They reminded her of observers at a tennis tournament.

Well, fuck her sideways. Like hell was she going to be fodder for their entertainment.

"Not here," she growled, and stepped forward, hoping to get him to move this out of the hallway. But the big dumb cat thought he made a better wall than a man. "For fuck's sake, Leo, move."

"Where?" he asked again and refused to back up an inch.

"Hello, nephew," interrupted Aunt Patricia in her current drunken sing-song-y voice. "Sheila here was kind of enough to take Ariella and me out for a ride and then we had lunch, and then some drinks, and some more drinks. Then a band came, and there was dancing, and drinking —"

"Yes, she brought us to *Serious Moonlight*," Ariella supplied. "We were only gone for a few, *er*, hours. And she introduced us around."

"What are you doing?" Sheila gasped as he leaned forward, lightning quick.

Pressing his nose to her neck, Leo sucked in a deep breath. His lips were so close to her skin, she could practically feel them, but he did not touch her. Leo retreated as quickly as he'd closed in, and she was left reeling. Why hadn't he kissed her? Didn't he want to? But no, apparently not. He just breathed her in. Sheila swayed involuntarily.

Her heart was pounding in her chest, so hard he had to have heard it. Her Dire Wolf whined. The animal inside her wanted him closer. She wanted Sheila to leap into his arms, to press her lips to his, wrap her legs around his waist, and get on with the claiming already. Despite the lies and omissions, she'd missed him. Even more stunning, she wanted him. Like really wanted him.

Sheila wasn't known for her public displays of affection. She was tough as nails usually. Hell, even her Pack mates knew better than to fuck with her, but for him her Wolf went belly up. She bit her lip to keep from grinning. Hell, it was all she could do not to jump him right there in the hallway for all to see.

"Aunt Patricia, Ariella," he said, acknowledging the females.

But his gaze never left Sheila. He nodded towards the other hall.

"I had George make up extra rooms. Montgomery here will get you anything you need."

"But sir," sputtered the man.

"*Roarrrr!*"

The sound of Leo loosing his beast's roar erupted through the hallway. Every Lion in the small space looked to the ground, and Sheila's heart thumped heavily.

Sexy, powerful, hot male. My mate.

Chip. CHIP. CHIP.

"Thanks."

Aunt Patricia sniffed and giggled while keeping her eyes averted.

"Well, the sexual tension coming off you two is making my Lioness want to yowl at the moon, so you better get on that. We'll just head off to bed now, and leave you to it," Aunt Patricia replied. She winked at Sheila, then sashayed down the hall.

"Mom! Sorry," Ariella whispered and gave Sheila an apologetic smile before chasing after her mother.

"If that is all, goodnight, *sir*," Montgomery said without a glance to Sheila, who at that moment did not give a fuck.

Prince Leo nodded his head and turned around, leaving Sheila no choice but to follow. And follow him she did, noting the hard, straight line of his spine and the ripple of muscles beneath his shirt and slacks as he walked away. She recalled something funny the boys used to say and thought it fitting as she watched his fine ass walking away.

Hate to see you leave, but I love watching you go.

And boy, did she ever. Her little pussycat had quite the gluteus maximus. Sheila licked her lips and closed the door to his bedroom behind her. She watched him as he looked out the terrace doors. A Prince overlooking his Kingdom, but no, there was more to it. Something was bothering him. Something more than her staying out all day.

Right away, she wanted to comfort him, to share in his pain, to take it away, but she paused. Uncertain of the reception she'd receive. Leo opened the sliding door and allowed the evening air to rush inside the room.

It teased her sensitive nose and made her think of youthful days spent on the road. Of course, the air was cleaner here than some places she'd stayed when she was young. Better company too.

Leo moved in that liquid way Cats had about them, jogging her from her reverie, and she watched as he started removing his clothes. She swallowed down her desire for him and simply watched.

This was not a striptease. He was angry and agitated, but she couldn't help but admire him, anyway. His physique was sublime. The power rolling off him, seductive.

"You know, I never was much for museums, but I swear if I was a painter or sculptor, I'd make works of art around you, Leo Crowley, Prince of the Blue Valley Pride."

Sheila's voice had been clear, quiet, and maybe a touch whimsical. She meant every word, too. Knowing full well, he would hear the lie if she'd been fibbing at all, which she was not. He stopped and waited a beat, absorbing the hand she'd just shown him. Leo had taken a gamble by not telling her everything, and she wanted him to know she knew, and she was still here, waiting for him to own it.

This was it, she supposed. The moment of truth. Leo turned to look at her. His eyes glowed with his beast in the darkness of the night that seemed to seep in from the outdoors. He did not try to talk around the truth she'd had to learn on her own. Didn't apologize yet, either. That made her curious.

"Is that why you left?"

"You mean because you lied?"

"It wasn't a lie, little Wolf."

"Lie by omission, officer."

"I didn't mention it, because it doesn't matter," he stated.

"Well, that one little thing that doesn't matter to you is the fucking difference between night and day, Leo, You're a fucking Prince and I'm an ex-biker bartender."

"You are my mate, Sheila. After last night—"

"No. That was sex. This, this won't work," she said, gesturing between them.

Fuck. She was panicking, crying too. Tears streamed down her face. There was a difference between thinking something and saying it aloud. For fuck's sake, she was no princess. She turned around, wiping her face on the back of her hand as she grabbed her saddle bags.

"I just came back to grab my shit. I won't be able

to stick around to help you do whatever it is you're doing," she said casually, trying to play the part.

Fuck. What was she thinking? She'd honestly thought for half a minute that she could do this, but she couldn't. They were too different. Sheila hated her weakness. She was disgusted at the tears that pricked her eyes. She felt him then at her back, but she refused to face him, refused to let him see her like this.

What the fucking fuck, Sheila? You don't cry, and you don't do feelings. Ever.

"*Shhh,*" his deep gravelly voice touched a chord inside of her and she trembled with it. "Please, Sheila. I'm sorry. I am so sorry. Swear on my life, I was not lying to you. I didn't think it mattered because I never wanted the throne. I need you Sheila, please. Stay. Don't cry."

"I can't be what you want," she said and shook her head as pure misery filled her soul.

Sadness on the heels of arousal was fucking draining. She didn't know what to do. She felt tired, but mostly miserable at the thought of a life without him.

"You are the only thing I want."

"I should go."

"Don't go. Run with me. Now, tonight, please."

Leo was so vulnerable like this. So honest and unsure, and fuck, it made her fall for him just a little bit more. He wasn't the cocky Lion tonight. He was just her Leo as he dropped his forehead down till it touched the back of her head and she shivered at the contact.

"Leo—"

"Please, mate."

Sheila turned at his whispered plea. His amber eyes were so big, so focused on her. It made her feel like she was the only person in the world. The only one who mattered, well, to him, anyway. But how could that be when he was a Prince, and she was a nobody?

"You are not a nobody," he growled, and she knew she'd spoken aloud by mistake. "You are the most important thing in the whole fucking universe to me, Sheila Rand, Dire Wolf badass, most beautiful woman I have ever seen, sassy, sexy queen. I love everything about you. Now, will you run with me? Please."

"Okay," she answered, stunned by his admissions.

Leo smiled then, and it was like the sun coming out after a storm. Sheila's pulse raced as he backed up one step, and another, until he was a safe enough distance away. She noted the change in his stance, and the scent of ozone fill the air as Leo switched his skin for fur. The transformation was almost instantaneous. His powerful body accepting the shift from man to Lion in the blink of an eye.

"Beautiful," she whispered, her eyes widened with awe.

Leo stood before her majestic and proud as only a Lion could be. His mane was thick and lush, his entire body covered in golden fur that did nothing to conceal the lines of muscle and strength within him.

"But you're still just a big ol' pussy," she said and grinned at his shocked expression.

With her next breath, Sheila shredded her clothes and swapped skin for fur as she went from woman to Wolf. Together, the Dire Wolf and the Lion stalked through the night into the forest beyond the Palace. Imagining this little slice of heaven tucked away in the beautiful, quiet town of Blue Valley, New Jersey, made Sheila want to laugh.

In her Wolf form, it came out a yip, and the Lion beside her chuffed and swatted her on the rump with his long tail. She growled playfully and followed him down a path. The woods were noisy with new life. The song of Spring filled the air, and Sheila reveled in it. The woods began to thicken around them, and she felt peace the likes of which she had never known. It was a sort of meeting between two worlds. The two of them were so different, and yet, they were fated to be together.

Leo and Sheila ran and stalked each other through the acres of tall grass, and thick copses of trees, to the stream that cut between both lands. As a Dire Wolf, she was huge with reddish fur and long black claws, but Leo was even bigger still. His Lion was the largest she'd ever seen, with a thick, glossy mane of dark gold circling his head like a crown, announcing to one and all that he was meant to rule.

He was gorgeous and lethal, more than capable of protecting even a fierce Dire she-Wolf. The beast approved, and she wanted him to claim her as soon as possible. Sheila's human side agreed. Her feelings were too strong to deny, and why should she even try to?

They stretched out along the bank after playing like a couple of cubs. Sheila panted with glee, it had felt good to run. They both lapped up some of the cool water before settling beside one another. It was unusual for her to share her space with someone in this shape, but it felt natural and good.

Her Wolf was perfectly at ease with Leo. Like everything was right with the world as long as he was beside her. Then again, she always could see things a little clearer when she wore her fur. Her Pack bonds pulsed dimly and told her she was close to them. In fact, the Pack house lay just beyond the stream and the next stand of pines.

She would always be a Dire Wolf and a member of the DWMC no matter what. She didn't need Derrick to tell her that, though he had. The Pack house would also be there waiting anytime she needed it. Sheila could stand up and stop this thing with Leo right now. She could walk through those trees and go home, tell Leo to forget it, but that wasn't what she wanted.

Her eyes found the Lion's glittering gold stare, and she knew she wouldn't leave him. Not that night. Not ever. His intense gaze was focused on her, as it always was, but she didn't feel rushed or trapped. Looking through her she-Wolf's eyes, Sheila no longer saw things in terms of money, class, or circumstance of birth. She only knew one thing as truth. This Lion was her fated mate, and she wanted to claim and to be claimed by him.

Now.

Her Wolf was ready, and she decided it was about time Sheila did something about it. The full moon shone down on them from high above, and Sheila knew the time was right. Turning to face her Lion, she allowed her Wolf to recede into that plane where her beast rested until called upon, and Sheila found her skin.

Her nudity aside, she was nervous for other reasons. Tremors ran up and down her spine because tonight, she would claim her mate as her own for all time, and with any luck, he was going to claim her right back.

"Leo," she had just finished his name when he completed his shift.

"What's wrong? Are you okay?" he asked, and the concern on his handsome face warmed her.

"I'm fine," she smiled.

"Then what?"

"I think it's time we stopped playing around. I think it's time we mate, for real."

His entire body vibrated with power. The lines of muscle that corded his tall frame seemed to tremble with barely restrained intensity, and Sheila felt an echoing shiver race through her. She wanted him more than ever. She craved his touch, his kiss, his cock, his bite.

All of them. Now.

"Be sure, Sheila, because I won't be able to stop once I get my hands on you," he said.

His words made Sheila bold. She inched closer until all she could see was him. Sheila pressed her naked body to his and reached for his hands. She took them and placed them on her body with more certainty than she'd ever felt in her entire life.

"Who's asking you to stop?"

Mate.

CHAPTER 11

E*arlier that evening...*
   Mate. Mate. MATE.
Leo was about to lose his fucking mind. After he'd listened to the endless parade of Lionesses, and their overachieving mothers sing their praises, he wanted nothing more than to get the fuck out of the Palace with Sheila.

She had ignored his texts, was not in his bedroom when he went to search for her. And yes, he looked. He'd stalked out of the interview room, leaving a dozen angry Lionesses waiting, but she was gone.

His unclaimed mate was nowhere to be found, and his Lion had nearly shredded him from the inside out. He felt raw fear for a full minute till it almost crippled him. Then, after he'd regained his senses, Leo made a few phone calls.

"Yeah, she's here, man. Everything cool?" Derrick *Rand had picked up his phone on the second ring.*

"It will be," Leo *had answered.*

The Alpha of the Dire Wolf Pack had been a good friend ever since he'd introduced himself. He was someone Leo trusted. Now that he knew Sheila was safe, all he had to do was wait. And wasn't that a kick to his ego?

Most females, a whole fucking gaggle of them in just the last couple of hours, pursued Leo relentlessly. And yet, his one true and fated mate acted like he didn't fucking exist.

Sure, she enjoyed what physical pleasures he offered, but even then, she'd cut him loose. Only taking the very tip of the iceberg of what he had to give. Leo had so much feeling brewing inside of him for the woman, he was about to explode. He just needed the opportunity to show her.

Shit.

He had it bad. For a normally patient man, he'd assumed it would be easy to wait her out. After all, how long could Sheila resist the mating call? Apparently longer than his Lion. The Cat was beyond lovesick. He was agitated as fuck now that he knew she was not there, safe and sound in his den.

Any dominant male, no matter how sure of himself, was liable to lose his shit, knowing his still unclaimed female was out on the town. Even with a couple of his own Lionesses at her side, it was all he could do not to give in to his Lion and race over to get her caveman-style. As in, toss her sweet ass over his shoulder, then fuck her until she couldn't get out of bed. Sounded like a good plan to his inner animal.

Leo ran a hand over his face and worked instead. His father's illness meant a massive amount of correspondence had gone unanswered. It took him three hours to sort through it all, and he still had dozens of emails to go through.

Eat Well Live Proud, the Pride's major concern was doing very well. Their new expansions were right on the money, and he felt confident with those Lionesses, mainly his cousins Ariella, Annabella, and George running things.

The elders were another matter. Those older felines had a whole lot to say about how things were being run and not all of it was within their purview. In fact, after the parade of eligible women he was forced to sit through, they'd tried to get him to agree to hand over a percentage of the corporation for them to run.

That was a hard no, to which they'd all grumbled and complained. He'd finally had enough, and when he stood to leave, it was with one parting statement.

"Might I remind the elders that your job is to simply advise the King on the health of the Pride? You have nothing to say about our corporate interests. I am not the King yet, but when I rule the Blue Valley Pride, I shall disband this circle, as it is clear you have lost sight of your purpose. Good evening, ladies."

That had not gone over well. In fact, George had to restrain one of them almost physically after they'd been dismissed. Leo had certainly stirred up the litter box. Wasn't that just too bad for them?

The police department never put up with shit like that. He'd only been back with the Pride for a day, and he already missed his old life. Being born to rule didn't necessarily create a desire to rule. He would do his duty, always, but his mate came first. As she should.

Fuck.

He was flustered. His Lion snarled and hissed inside of him to where Leo could hardly think. The sound of motorcycles pulling up outside reached his ears, and his feet hit the marble floor before he thought about what he was going to do or say. The Lion in him snarled.

Fuck decorum. He wanted his mate. Now.

It was all he could do not to pounce the second he saw her standing in the vestibule. Sheila's eyes glowed with her Wolf as she took him in. He scented her conflicting emotions over the distance between them. He twitched with the need to go to her, to soothe and kiss away any remnants of whatever upset her. Only his will stopped him from doing so.

There was so much unsaid, and he needed her to hear him first. He wouldn't just go at her like some lovesick animal, but he wanted to. Gods, how he wanted to. She was beautiful, standing there like a siren in ripped jeans and that gauzy top.

Her windblown hair had come out of its braid. Long waves spread around her like wildfire across her creamy shoulders. One errant curl dipped into the rounded collar of her shirt, finding a home nestled between her ripe breasts, making Leo jealous of her own precious locks.

He was a fool. A lovesick fool, and he didn't give a shit who knew it. His animal was aware of others in the hall with them, but his full attention was on her. After a brief interaction, where he couldn't even recall enough words to form sentences, Leo embraced his fur and running into the night with his mate.

If hearts could burst from happiness, then his Lion's heart surely would just from having Sheila running at his side. She was magnificent with fire-kissed fur and sharp claws digging into the ground with each leaping bound they made deeper into the woods.

Her noble Dire Wolf stood almost as high as his massive Lion's head. She had long, razor-sharp claws, enormous fangs, a powerful body, and eyes as blue as when she walked on two legs. Gorgeous, formidable, and perfect.

They ran and played like the wild things they both were. Leo roared into the night sky. It was his Lion's way of telling others to be wary of encroaching on his space when he was out with his mate. He heard a few answering calls, and his beast chuffed, content because his Lions would obey.

He might not want to be King yet, but some things were beyond even a Shifter's control. When the time came, he would be ready. First things first. He had a mate to protect and to cherish. They'd shifted back into their skin as they lay side by side on the mossy bank of the stream and Sheila had just said the words he'd been longing to hear.

"Who's asking you to stop?" Sheila's voice echoed through his brain as the seductress mashed her mouth to his.

Had anything ever felt more right? Never. His Dire Wolf mate stole his breath in every way, shape, and form. Kissing her was like touching a star, she burned so hot and bright, but Leo could take it. He was made to take it, and he wanted more. He wanted all of her.

Once he had his hands on her, Leo's mind flashed to every single fantasy he'd every indulged in since the moment he'd laid eyes on the sassy little she-Wolf. But this was no fantasy. This was the real thing.

Even the taste he'd had of her before was nothing compared to the things he was going to do with her here and now, before nature, fate, and the gods themselves.

Leo pulled her down onto a soft bed of moss that lined that part of the forest's floor. The spongy greenery made up the perfect place for what he had in mind. Sheila sighed and laid back, her trust humbled him, and he dropped his forehead to hers kissing each eyelid, then moving to her slightly upturned nose, her plump lips, that stubborn chin he loved so much, and further still.

Leo sat back to better admire her beauty. He ran his hands gently over the many curves and valleys, up and down the sweet and sultry delights of her sumptuously soft flesh.

"You're so beautiful," he said, catching the slight flash of her big blue eyes.

Leo licked his lips, holding her gaze for one more beat. He noted the hitch in her breath with satisfaction as he skimmed his fingers over the peaks of her lovely, pink-tipped breasts, teasing the tiny buds until they were hardened pebbles under his hands.

"Am I?" she breathed the question.

"Yesss." His voice was raspy even to his own ears.

"Perfect, mate. Let me show you how beautiful you are," he growled and leaned down, the better to savor each pebbled nub with his lips, tongue, and teeth.

Sheila moaned aloud, the scent of her pleasure increased, and Leo growled. He suckled her sweet flesh, loving the sting as she reached up to grab hold of his hair and pulled. She was all ivory limbs and bountiful curves, acres of smooth, flawless skin for him alone to discover. She was a goddess in the forest, on a bed of moss, trembling beneath his touch.

Leo was one lucky Cat. She moaned his name,

heightening Leo's own desire as he licked a trail between her breasts down to her navel. Kissing her body was like taking a shot of honey and Tabasco laced whiskey. Sweet and fiery, and guaranteed to warm him inside and out.

His cock throbbed painfully, and Leo reached down with one hand to give himself a good, long tug. Fuck, he was like a steel rod and more than ready, but first he wanted a taste. Needed it. He'd dreamed of this, of sampling her tantalizing cream from the source plenty of times, but nothing prepared him for what he felt being so close to his goal.

His fangs descended, and Leo's beast pushed forward. He'd never hurt her, of course, teeth were just another way Shifters expressed passion. And his Lion did so enjoy a good lengthy nibble. His Shifter eyesight enabled him to see despite the darkness and what a sight.

She was glorious, completely nude, and bathed in moonlight. Sheila's plump, pink pussy lips were just ripe for the tasting. They gleamed with the evidence of her desire and his Lion purred in anticipation. All that cream, his for the taking.

Mine.

Leo moved between her legs, bending them at the

knee. He parted them, spreading them good and wide until he was face to face with those glistening copper curls and the treasure beneath. Breathing in her honeyed musk, Leo's Lion surged forward, claws tipped his hands as he carefully held her thighs wide. He had to work to push the beast aside, but eventually his Lion understood.

"This is mine," he stated, catching her eyes before opening his lips and sliding his long tongue out of his mouth and towards glory.

Fucking hell.

He groaned as her flavors burst across his tastebuds. A feast for his senses. Sugar and spice, and Leo groaned as he lapped at her.

"Yes," she moaned, and bucked her hips, but he stilled her with his hands,

"You're driving me crazy," she pleaded, and he grinned while he slowly tasted her from asshole to clit with the flat of his tongue.

"So sweet," he groaned and watched her desperation etch into her face.

It mirrored his own, but this was something he simply refused to rush. She tried to move again, but he held her still. It was his turn to dominate. Her turn to submit. And she was going to love it. He could make sure of that.

"Patience," he said, enjoying her musky taste, imprinting it on his tongue and his brain.

"To hell with patience, fuck me already," she growled.

Leo smirked, holding her thighs down. Then he dipped his head and pierced her core with his tongue, loving the frantic growl that escaped her lips as he started moving slowly, then faster, then slow again. Her moans held a mixture of satisfaction and frustration, of anticipation and desire, and he reveled in them. In his ability to bring her to this state.

He would always give her what she wanted, what she needed, but when he said, and not a moment before. Sometimes, you just had to be patient. Sheila whimpered, arching her back and wiggling her hips as much as she could under his strong hands, and finally, he relented. He let go briefly, only to replace his tongue with his fingers. He slid between her folds, stretching her channel with two thick digits. He pumped them slowly in and out of her welcoming heat.

"You taste so good, mate, so sweet and hot," he said in a voice barely recognizable.

"Leo, need you," she moaned, and he felt her walls contract around his fingers.

"What do you need, mate?"

"You. More," she pleaded with him.

What man could resist that? Especially when it was his destined mate who was asking. Fuck yeah. He was going to give her more. He was going to give her everything. His balls tightened in anticipation as he felt her shudder around him.

"I'm gonna make you come, little Wolf," he promised.

"All over my hand and in my mouth. Then I'm going to fuck this sweet pussy of yours, fill you with my seed. I'm going to have your ass, too. I'm gonna fill that tight little hole, make it good for you. You want that, don't you?" he whispered.

Sheila whimpered. His sassy little Wolf loved hearing all the naughty things he was going to do to her. She nodded her head, bucking her hips, and trying to get him to move. But Leo wasn't ready yet.

"I'm gonna take every inch of you and stamp myself on it. Make you mine, gonna bite you, mate. Going to claim you every way I can. Here, now, tonight. Tell me you want that," he growled. It was his turn to demand. She whimpered and nodded her head, her Wolf growling. His Lion chuffed and grunted. The animal was impatient to claim what was his. But first things first.

"I need the words, little Wolf."

"Yes," she mewled. "I want that. I want you. Mate."

Leo growled and his chest vibrated with the force of it. He added a third finger to her tight channel, circling her forbidden hole with his pinky. He teased and tested the tiny, puckered entrance. Licking around her tiny bundle of nerves and pressing, until finally, he had both orifices full of him. Then he latched onto her clit, giving the swollen nub long, hard pulls from his mouth.

Fuck, she tasted divine. His own personal flavor of cream.

Me-ow.

"Oh my gods!" she cried out.

"No, baby, it's just Leo. Say it. Say my name," he commanded.

"Leo. Leo. LEO!" she cried out as she fell over the edge. Both holes squeezed him while she bucked wildly in her release.

His balls tightened as her sweet pussy rippled and fluttered. He was desperate to be inside of her, filling her with his cum, claiming her in every way possible. First with his mouth, then with his cock inside her pussy, and finally he was going to claim her sweet ass. He needed to.

It was raw. It was primal. And it was meant to be.

The desire to fill her with his scent, to mark her as his, in every way, so there was never a single doubt about it, was the only thing riding him at the moment. His beast roared inside of him. She'd moved in time with his ministrations.

Sheila's head whipped from side to side. Searching for a little bit more and Leo knew instinctively what she needed. He hummed against her mouth, purring with his beast, the vibrations going from him and straight to her clit. Sheila came then with a long, hard howl, bucking wildly against his lips.

"Now, need you now, now, now," she moaned the words, and grabbed his shoulders, pulling him up her body.

Kneeling between her splayed legs, he crashed his mouth to hers in a hard kiss that forced her to taste herself on his lips. It was raw and sexy and fucking perfect. Just like she was. Sheila opened wide, both mouth and legs, tugging his hips until her wet pussy kissed the tip of his cock.

"What do you want, little Wolf?"

"Claim me as your mate, Leo. Do it now."

That was all he needed to hear. Leo pushed inside of her molten heat. His thickness stretched her walls as he slid deeper, and deeper into her tight channel until he was buried all the way to the hilt. His engorged cock pulsed and throbbed once he'd slid home, but he did not move. Not yet.

"Feels so good, mate," he grunted.

"Yes," she moaned, and her hands came down on his ass in a hard slap that stung so good.

"Fuck," he growled.

"Yes, fuck me, now," she demanded, squeezing his cheeks almost painfully, until he started moving.

"Thank the gods," she growled and slapped him again.

Leo's beast roared, the animal approving of her aggression. He grunted. The slap had smarted, but it made the pleasure that much sweeter. She had desires and as her mate he loved giving in to her needs.

His Sheila was fucking sublime. Wicked and sexy as hell, her tight pussy sheathed him perfectly. She was his other half, designed for every inch of him. She squeezed him and he moved faster, harder, deeper with every thrust.

Every inch of silken heat was like a glove wrapped tightly around him. His balls tightened, he was desperate to come, but he needed her with him. Her sex rippled and caressed his length. So fucking good, Leo had to fight to keep from spilling his seed too soon.

Did he say he was lucky before? He didn't know then just how lucky. His little Wolf was a hellion in bed, *er*, on the moss-covered ground. She wiggled and worked him so fucking good from beneath his heavy body. His Wolf could take it, she could take all of him. She murmured sexy little taunts and phrases, raked her long pink nails down his spine and nipped his earlobe between her teeth.

How the fuck had he ever looked at another woman? Everyone else paled compared to her. Together they grunted and moaned, each seeking the other's complete release. He could lose himself completely in the pleasure of his mate's body. She was so fucking incredible.

He opened his eyes, catching her lust-glazed ones and holding them there while he pumped harder. *Swivel, grind, withdraw, slam, and repeat.* Leo lifted her hips, and she wrapped her legs around his waist, allowing him to sink even deeper.

"Right there," she screamed, and he knew she was close.

"Come on, baby, come," he grunted, fucking her at a furious pace.

Her sheath tightened, their breathing increased

to rapid pants, sweat slicked their bodies. Silver moonlight bathed them both, seeming to stroke them in the magic that only mating with your fated other could bring.

"*Sheila,*" he thrusted.

"*Sheila,*" he withdrew.

"*Sheila!*" he pounded home again, saying her name like a litany to the whole fucking universe. She was his to worship, to praise, to cherish. Only his.

Mate.

"I'm gonna," she moaned, scoring the skin beneath her nails.

"Now, now, now," she cried out in ecstasy, and Leo struck.

He sunk his teeth through the soft flesh between her neck and shoulder, swallowing down her life's force, and solidifying that unbreakable bond between a Shifter and his mate. His balls tensed, and finally, Leo came deep within his mate's sweet sex.

Pain exploded on his right shoulder, followed by an even longer, harder orgasm as Sheila reciprocated the claiming bite.

Holy fuck!

That sting of pain gave him the edge he'd never knew he needed, and pleasure erupted from the very bottom of his soul until man and beast both felt it.

Roarrrr!

Still, he did not stop thrusting his hips, he fucked her through her orgasm and his, and soon she came again, longer this time. Sheila's mouth opened, and she loosed the longest, loudest howl he'd ever heard. Her blue eyes glowed with her Wolf, and his Lion rose to meet his mate. Slowly, he eased out of her, lapping at the wound, sealing it with his special Shifter's saliva.

"Mate." Sheila smiled as she tried to catch her breath, and Leo's heart pounded heavily inside his chest.

"Mate. Love. I love you, Sheila," he said as she grabbed his head and claimed his lips in a hard, poignant kiss.

His dick responded immediately to his mate's touch. Hardening as she sat up and pushed him down until he was flat on his back. Fuck, he was ready again. It would always be this way. He was insatiable for her.

"Mine," he grunted as she scratched his thighs and pushed them wide.

"My turn," she smiled as her lips closed over him, sucking him deep and down her throat. Passion flared to life and mischief twinkled in her electric blue gaze as she took him deeper.

"Oh fuck, baby, that's it. Suck me," he grunted and took hold of her head, holding her in place while he thrusted in and out of the hot, soft cavern.

He couldn't take much more without exploding, and as promising as that sounded, his Lion had other plans. He needed to fill her one more time. To mark her once more.

"Come here, baby," he said and pulled her to her knees, taking her mouth with his, "Gonna make you come, little Wolf, you want that?"

Sheila whimpered, nodding her head, and holding on to his shoulders. Leo kissed her hard, then turned her around. He eased her head down and moved in behind her. She thrust her pert ass up in the air and he growled.

In that position, she was fully exposed to him. Her virgin asshole on display, and those swollen pink pussy lips pursed as if waiting for a kiss. He could not resist placing one right there. Leo bent and dropped a hard, open-mouthed kiss on her slit, working her until more of that sweet cream flowed down her thighs. With his fingers, he worked her natural lubricant around her slit and into her asshole, easing the way for his passage. She grunted and moaned against his invasion.

"Shh, s'okay. Need you, mate. Gonna fill this

sweet ass, make it mine," he growled, noting the flare of arousal his words elicited.

More cream coated his fingers. Yes, she wanted him. Was more than ready and willing for him to take her in this way too. It was the way of Lions, and perhaps Wolves as well, he thought. Sheila's trust humbled him, her submission turned him on so fucking much. All musings left and instinct took over. He'd marked her once, but the mating wasn't done.

Leo moved closer, teasing her clit with his fingers, and massaging her asshole with his thumb. He pressed the thick digit in, moving it in and out of her tight hole, stretching, and readying it for his cock. Finally, when he thought she could take it, he nudged her hole with the head of his dick. He was big and long and needed to proceed with caution.

"So fucking sexy," he growled as she moaned and pressed back, sucking his cock deep inside.

"S'mine."

"Yes, yours," Sheila moaned.

His sexy little mate liked it when he got all possessive about her, and that was fine with him. Leo couldn't help it. She was his, and he was desperate to mark her again.

"Mine," he growled again, kneading her clit with

his fingers until she pushed all the way back, taking his cock even deeper into her sweet, heart-shaped ass.

Fuck, she was so tight, so good. Leo caged her in, holding where he needed her as he worked his thick cock back and forth, in and out of that tight hole. His passage was made slick by her own natural lubricant, but he was careful to keep it that way, rubbing her moisture on his cock and in her hole. He heard rather than felt the crackle of her bones and knew her Wolf was coming out to play.

Naughty girl. My girl. My woman. My Wolf. My Mate.

Leo squeezed her hip and pushed in deeper.

"Fuck, yes, mate. Need you," Sheila shouted and pushed back.

"I know what you need," he growled.

"Yes," she grunted.

Leo fought his orgasm back. He would not let go, not until he felt her begin to slide into the abyss of pure pleasure only a fated mate could deliver. Yes, he knew what she needed, and he would give it to her if it killed him.

Grunting and groaning, sweat poured down his back as he worked her good and steady. Strumming her clit with his hand, Leo fucked her ass until her orgasm began to rage through her. He fucked her still until her pleasure echoed through Leo as well.

"My Sheila, mine, my mate," he roared as they both tipped over the edge, slicing his fangs into her other shoulder.

He bit her again, sucking on the wound while white hot lights of ecstasy exploded behind his eyes. Hard jerks turned to slight twitches as they collapsed in a heap on top of their mossy bed. The night was silent, as if everything had just taken a deep, long breath and was holding it in. Sheila turned and cuddled into him, her face a study in satisfaction and wonder.

"Mate," he whispered and kissed her head, unable to stop the rumble of pleasure from his Lion at her cuddling.

"Mmm, mate."

She smiled, still panting, and dropped a kiss on his chest. Leo held her to him, and they dozed together as the sounds of crickets and the bubbling stream filled the night.

Finally, he thought and sighed.

Sheila was finally his and his Lion had never been more content.

CHAPTER 12

"Are you nervous?" Leo looked concerned, and Sheila couldn't help but shrug guiltily.

"I never met a King," she said.

Like duh.

What was wrong with having some issues about it? The man was royalty, even if he was sick.

"Actually, the King of a Lion Pride is no different from a Wolf Alpha," he tried to assure her, but Sheila had her reservations.

No Dire Wolf Pack had ever lived in a Palace with servants. They certainly didn't stand on cere-mony. Wolves ruled by might and loyalty. Anyone could challenge for the position, though Dire Wolves argued against that. As a mostly nomadic species, they could simply leave if they did not favor a ruling Alpha.

A challenge was a profoundly serious thing. Not at all the same as in a Pride, after Leo had told her of the elder's threats, she'd been outraged. Her own Dire Wolf was fiercely loyal to her cousin and would not tolerate anyone who dared make such flippant remarks about him. Now that Leo was her mate, he topped her list of males she was devoted to. As a result, her canine had a few choice words for the nasty bitches who dared threaten him with a challenger!

He'd assured her it was simply politics, but she was not impressed with that excuse. The haughty Lionesses needed to be taken down a notch in her opinion, but that was up to the King. The King she was about to meet. Leo's father. Her mate's dad.

Holy shit.

Her mate was a Prince, and he'd said he'd loved her last night. Fated mates were one thing, love was something else. She'd heard of couples who were mates but felt no such affection for one another. Of course, perhaps they weren't fated exactly, but she had no way of knowing that.

Did she love him? She felt strongly for Leo. Maybe she cared deeply already, but the words were hard for Sheila. Perhaps she would grow to feel love someday?

We already love him, her Wolf insisted.

One step at a time, Sheila growled back.

She'd taken the leap and mated with the Lion Prince, but she still felt that same fear deep inside of her. What if she felt trapped? It terrified her to think she could hurt him. That she would be the one to let him down. Like her mother and the man who fathered her. What if Sheila had no staying power?

"Hey, it's alright. If you'd rather not meet my father today," Leo said and rubbed her shoulders, and Sheila leaned into him.

Her sweet mate was a good and kind man, a powerful Lion Shifter, and fiercely loyal. She was truly blessed to have him, she realized.

"We're gonna be okay," she said, verging on tears.

"Of course we are," he stated, with no doubts at all evident in his words.

Knowing that, she vowed she would never hurt him. How could she? It would be like hurting herself or worse.

"Good, I'm ready," she smiled, and she meant it.

Thunder sounded and lightning flashed just outside the terrace doors. New Jersey Spring was a psychotic bitch if you asked her. Glorious one minute, and downright mean the next.

"We beat the rain back," he laughed, and she nodded.

That they had. He'd carried her back to the Palace sometime around five o'clock in the morning. Of course, she could have walked, but he'd insisted. Like a proper wedding night, he'd said, and secretly, Sheila loved it. They'd showered together and made love some more. Hunted down some food some-where in between. It was wonderful.

She loved the play of muscles across his wide shoulders and chest as he buttoned his shirt and Sheila reached up to smooth it over his back. She had never felt so cherished, loved, and content.

I've never felt so happy.

It was like a switch had gone off inside of her and suddenly all the pieces clicked into place. Last night was simply amazing. Their claiming was beyond anything she could have ever imagined. Right then, all her doubts washed away like the rain washed away the grit they'd tracked onto the terrace. She sighed.

Shelia really loved him. It welled up in her slowly, a new feeling, bright and fresh. Just like his scent, that clean grass after a storm scent that drove her

Wolf crazy with need. Her emotions grew and grew, a fountain, a pool, until they turned into a flood.

"I love you," she blurted, and turned her startled blue eyes to him.

Leo's gaze glittered with the gold of his beast. He reached for her, one hand on her waist, the other on her cheek as he lowered his mouth to hers and pressed a soft kiss there.

"I love you too, mate," he said, and tugged on her lip with his teeth.

She moaned and stepped back, looking up at him with all her feelings in her gaze.

"Let's go meet your father," she smiled and took his hand.

She'd donned the one dress she thought to pack with her. It was long and flowy, feminine, and soft in a way she never got to wear while roaming the Americas with her Pack. The sage green looked good against her pale skin and red hair, or so Lucy had told her.

Her cousin-in-law had been extremely helpful in picking out new clothes when they'd gone shopping for some maternity things for the Bobcat Shifter. Lucy was pregnant and getting bigger by the minute. Sheila snorted and stopped in her tracks.

Holy shit.

She could be pregnant, too.

Not yet, her she-Wolf spoke inside of her, and she wasn't sure if she felt relief or sadness. That alone was a wonder.

"Sheila?" Leo inquired with a raised eyebrow.

"Nothing," she said and just looked at him as his cousin George rushed to meet them.

Aunt Patricia had shown her a picture of the man on her phone, and she recognized him immediately. Like most Lions, he had tawny-colored hair, and he was big and tall, though not as massive as her mate. He had a pleasant face and green eyes she found unique. So far, all the Lions she'd met had some combination of brownish-gold eyes.

"Leo," he greeted her mate, and nodded at her respectfully.

"George."

"Sorry, I have not had the pleasure," George replied and smiled.

He might have looked at her a second too long because Leo smacked him in the back of the head.

"Ouch! She's hot. No disrespect," he said quickly, and averted his gaze to the floor.

"The name is Sheila, and you will have to forgive him, George. We are newly mated, after all," she explained with a smile in her voice.

Sheila felt that smile down to her toes. Happiness was new, but it was good, and she was really looking forward to getting used to feeling this way.

Pleasure rang through her at being able to say those words aloud with no trepidation. This might have started as a ruse to help Leo work out what was happening within his Pride, but it was real now. She'd been so caught up in her personal emotional conflicts that she'd almost forgotten about why they were there to begin with.

"Shit, you claimed the Wolf? The elders are gonna be more pissed now than ever," George whispered.

Leo smacked his cousin on the head again, this time it was followed by a similar slap from Sheila.

"Ow! I'm sorry," George mumbled his apology.

"Good job, Sheila," Leo said, and damn, but he sure looked proud of her.

"Crap, cousin, you know I think she's perfect for you," he said, rubbing his head as he walked with them and explained the day's agenda.

"Did you find the healer?" Leo asked.

"That's what I wanted to talk to you about. The schedule says the healer is supposed to check with your father once a week, but when he called me back yesterday, he was surprised."

"Oh?"

"Yeah, he said his last six appointments had been canceled. Leo, he hasn't been here in over a month and neither has the other staff. Just Montgomery."

"What? Why?" Leo asked.

"He didn't know. Just said your father canceled the appointments."

"My father has not been himself for months now. The last few weeks he's been practically incoherent. How could he cancel his appointments?"

"I don't know, Leo," George replied.

Sheila took a step closer, breathing in his scent to determine if he was telling the truth. Oddly enough, he was. Leo's amber eyes flashed with his Lion.

"Is he coming here now?" her mate asked.

"Yes. I told him to meet us at ten, it's 9:45 now."

Sheila listened to the byplay curiously. Leo was right, there was something rotten within the Pride. It was her Pride now too, and the fact that someone was fucking with it really pissed her off.

"Did you tell anyone else we were going to see the King?" he asked.

"No," replied George. "I didn't have time. It was all I could do to get dressed in time to meet you."

"Leo, I think we should hurry," she said and the hairs on the back of Sheila's neck were standing up.

She raced beside her mate, the younger Lion trailing them, and together they entered the King's rooms. Lying on the large bed was an older version of Leo and the sight brought Sheila to a hard stop. Donovan Crowley looked pained and confused, but not as much as the man hovering over him trying to force feed him from what looked like a child's medicine dropper.

"Car, Car," the King moaned, and pushed at the man's hand, but he was too weak to do much.

"Montgomery?" Leo's shocked voice seemed to spur the man into action.

"You aren't supposed to be here!" he snarled.

"Montgomery, these are my father's quarters. I have every right to be here. What are you doing to him?"

"You were supposed to choose a Lioness," he said between clenched teeth.

The man looked crazed, and he stank of fear and madness. The smell was so thick, Sheila almost choked on it.

"For what, Montgomery?" Leo asked.

"As a mate, you were supposed to choose from your own kind," he sneered.

"I see," Leo said and moved in front of Sheila, placing himself in harm's way. "But Sheila here is my fated mate," he continued, naming her so as to make her more real in the madman's eyes.

Fat chance, Sheila thought, but applauded his effort. She knew Leo was trying to get the man to put down whatever that was in his hand. She admired his tactics. Came with being a cop, she guessed.

That was so hot.

She blushed at the turn of her thoughts. Ooh, she could just picture him in his dress blues, doing a little striptease that ended with one of them bound to the bed and the other in charge.

Grrr.

"Stay back!" Montgomery waved the vial and growled.

Sheila refocused. Yikes. Here they were with a madman waving around some sort of poison, and she was thinking naughty thoughts of Leo and a pair of handcuffs.

Okay, so she was proud of him. Proud of her Prince and his chosen career. Of the bravery it took to face criminals such as this, every single day. He could've simply stayed home and lived the life of pampered royalty, but he didn't. He'd worked hard and put his life on the line to protect Shifters and normals alike.

Her she-Wolf growled low and deep inside her. Sheila never minded bending the rules before, but now that she had her own personal police officer, she vowed to be more mindful just as soon as they stopped this traitor.

"How can you rule with that Dog at your side?" Montgomery snorted and pointed at her wildly.

"She is my fated mate, surely you know what that means," Leo tried again.

"So what? Your father said he couldn't live without his fated mate, but when I got rid of your whore mother, he hung on. I had to fix his mistake, but he wouldn't die! Then I decided to get rid of him for good, so you could takeover under my and the elder's guidance but look at you! You ruined everything! I'll kill you and your slut, too!" Montgomery shouted and spittle ran down his chin.

The snarling valet turned on the three of them with his Lion bursting forth. His animal was wiry and lean, strong despite his age, but Sheila wasn't worried. She'd seen her mate's beast, and this man was no match for him. Her only worry was for the King who'd slumped onto his side, remnants of whatever that was oozing from his mouth. He must've imbibed some before they'd gotten there.

"Get back!" Leo shouted.

George dove to tackle the shifted Montgomery while still in human form, but the Lion swatted him away like a fly. Poor George crashed into the dresser. Hitting his temple on the sharp corner, he crumpled to the floor.

The big Cat roared and hissed, leaping over the bed, he crouched in front of Sheila. Before she could blink, Leo was on him. Her mate had half-Shifted. Holy hell, that was rare and spoke to his power.

His arms and legs tore through his clothes, building in bulk and muscle. His hands shifted into his beast's claws while maintaining most of his human face and biped appearance.

This sort of half-change was not something many Shifters could pull off. It required great reserves of strength, discipline, and that special supernatural power that made them what they were. Sheila watched in awe as Leo squeezed and squeezed, keeping his stance tight as he crushed the Lion's throat between his powerful arms.

His eyes locked on hers, glowing gold with his beast, and Sheila nodded for him to go ahead. This was about more than revenge for his mother's death, and for the attack on his father. It was about more than his threat against his mate. This was about a Lion King fixing a very real wrong within his Pride.

"It has to be done," she said, and with her words Leo struck, snapping the neck of the mad Lion, and tossing his carcass to the floor.

Sheila jolted across the room and gripped him in a fierce hug, ignoring the sounds of footsteps headed their way. She had her mate in her arms and reveled in the fierce way he clung to her.

"Are you alright?" he asked, and she nodded.

"Yes, you?" she returned.

Her heart was pounding, and shivers raced through her body. It was the adrenaline, but it was more too. Their *matebond* wrapped around her strongly. Through it, she felt all his love for her, as well as his anxiety over the present situation.

"Car, Car," mumbled the King, and they both rushed to his side.

"Easy, father," Leo said and checked his father over for signs of physical harm. The older Lion coughed and retched over the side of the bed, a sour stench came from the poison he vomited, and Leo wiped his face with a cloth. Sheila went to check on George.

"He'll be fine," she said, and returned to where her mate stood next to his father.

Sheila crouched down and gingerly lifted the medicine dropper. She sniffed the tube and her she-

Wolf growled. Whatever it was, it was clearly poisonous.

"What is going on in here?" Aunt Patricia's voice rang through the room as she and Ariella, along with another older man, burst through the doors. She leaped to her son's side with her daughter in tow.

"George? Donovan? Leo? What's been happening here?" the Lioness spoke a mile a minute and Sheila answered her, trying to calm her.

"Yes, George is okay, just a bump on the noggin'. Montgomery there was poisoning the King with this," she held up the dropper.

"That's a pretty big noggin', little bro," Ariella snorted at her little brother, who was moaning and groaning for all he was worth.

"*Shyaddap*, daughter. Now come on, cupcake, open your eyes," Patricia said, rocking her son in her arms.

"What is wrong with the King?" the stranger asked.

"You're the Pride healer? I'm Sheila," she began.

"Sorry," Leo said, "this is my mate, Sheila Rand. Sheila, this is Tom Royce, the Pride healer."

"Pleasure," he said and began taking the King's temperature. "So, why have you canceled my appointments with the King these last few weeks?"

"What? I haven't canceled anything," Leo growled, and Sheila placed a hand on his arm.

"I see. Well, someone has, using your seal. Now here, help me turn him over."

The healer and Leo worked together to turn the King onto his side so the man could begin an examination of his spine.

"Excuse me, gentlemen," Sheila interrupted. "Boys!" she yelled when they didn't answer.

Every pair of feline eyes locked on her, and she straightened her shoulders. Bunch of pussies! It seemed Cats really didn't like to listen, no matter how big or small they were.

"The King has been poisoned with this, I figured you might need it," Sheila said and held up the discarded medicine dropper.

"Give me that, carefully," Tom held out his hand.

"Sorry, mate," Leo mumbled.

He took her hand in his and kissed it. She could see he was riddled with worry, and she could not blame him.

"No need," she assured her mate.

Really, there wasn't any call for him to apologize. The last few minutes had been quite a lot for anyone to go through. Even Princes had their limits, she supposed.

"Thank you," Leo said once more as the healer investigated the contents.

"This is Carbofuran. It's a pesticide with the greatest acute toxicity known to man or beast, cats especially," he told them. The healer's outrage was echoed by everyone in the room.

"Farmers in Africa use that on wild lions to stop them after they've killed one of their Cattle. They lace the carcass with it and sometimes poison entire prides with the stuff," Ariella snarled, and her outrage was damn near contagious.

"In a Shifter, with our fast metabolic structure, only large doses would be lethal. If Montgomery were dosing your father daily with this amount, it would cause confusion, loss of control physically, diminished motor skills, memory loss, and eventually paralysis. Ultimately, the loss of all normal neurological function followed by death, but that would only occur after months of this torture," he explained angrily and grabbed his medical bag.

"What can you do for him?" Leo asked.

"I am going to start by hooking him up to an IV and flushing this junk out of his system. Here, hang this bag of fluids from that post," he gestured to one of the grand columns that surrounded the King's bed.

"Okay, you two got this."

Sheila squeezed Leo's hand and turned to the women who were helping George to stand.

"Can you three get some bodies in here to clean this mess? I want only the most trusted Lions," she instructed.

"Yes, *Princess*," Aunt Patricia replied with a wink and pointed to her neck.

Sheila felt her cheeks warm. Holy crap! She was blushing, and fuck it all, yes, she was now officially a Princess.

"You got it," Ariella agreed.

"Yes, ma'am," George replied.

"Sheila," Leo called her name, and she returned to his side, certain now that things would get done.

"Mate," she walked into his open arms and nuzzled his neck, thoroughly enjoying the pressure of his arms as they squeezed her to him.

"Tom says my father will be okay," he told her, and she felt his joy at the news reverberate through her as he kissed her temple.

It fucking amazed her they had gotten to this place, but here they were. Together. And she knew now, she was never letting him go. Sheila's place was right there beside her mate. She wanted to share every woe and triumph, every battle and victory—even the defeats, with him.

Equals. Lovers. Soul mates. Friends.

"Thank you so much. Gods, I love you."

"Of course. That's what mates do, pussycat," she said, and ran her hands over the remnants of his ripped shirt. "Come on, let's get your father settled."

"Are you gonna call me that all the time now?" he asked with mock anger.

"Maybe," she replied and winked saucily.

Sexy man. My very own Prince.

They spent the next few hours re-calling in the King's guard. All of them had been sent away over the last few weeks by the now dead traitor. After they disposed of Montgomery and cleaned the King's chambers, Aunt Patricia entered the bedroom and insisted she was going to stay by the King's side until the man could send her away himself.

"I might not be your aunt by blood, Leo Crowley, but I was your mother's best friend. My children are your honorary cousins and I absolutely insist you march off to your room and take care of your mate. Look at her, poor thing, she's dead on her feet!"

"What?" Sheila gasped, outraged by the notion, but then she caught the twinkle in the older woman's eye and played along.

"Yes, uh, I could use some food, a shower, maybe a rubdown," she suggested and shrugged.

Leo's protective male instincts flared, and he swept her off her feet before she could blink. His chest rumbled with his Lion. The beast within him purred as he carried her to their room, and Sheila swallowed her moan. She never knew a purr could be so sexy.

"Mate," she nipped the sensitive skin at the base of his neck and loved the tremor that ran through him.

What a lucky Dog I am!

T*hree weeks later...*

Leo entered the King's interview room with Sheila on his arm resplendent in hip-hugging denim and a soft white blouse that emphasized her womanly curves. The leather cut she wore over it sporting the DWMC patch had him drooling with the desire to strip off all her clothing, save for that one particular article.

He caught her wide-eyed stare and shrugged.

Not like he could help it. The female aroused him every second of the day. The feisty Dire Wolf snickered, and he couldn't help but pinch her right on that spectacular ass of hers. She yelped and glared back at him despite his innocent expression.

He'd spent each day going over every move Montgomery had made since before his mother's death. They'd had experts pour over his computer and found hidden emails and documents that pointed to not one, but two accomplices. Oddly enough, Montgomery's sister, a member of the elder's circle, Maribel Clover, was found innocent of any wrong doings.

Except one, of course. Sheila had been pretty pissed when she'd found out the Lioness had been pitching her daughter as a mate for Leo. A night of sweaty, panting sexy fun times and a re-claiming bite had eased his little Wolf's worries and made his Cat super fucking happy.

Montgomery's emails had named Margaret Donner as a co-conspirator against the crown, and the Pride had had her arrested. Leo had alerted the Council of Shifters, the one governing force that all Shifter groups obeyed, to come and take her away after they'd presented them with all the evidence. She did not even try to defend herself.

Apparently, she had been a childhood playmate of Donovan Crowley and had always assumed he would take her as his mate. When he'd come back from an expedition abroad with a human woman in tow, jealousy had driven her to commit the heinous actions of conspiracy to commit murder against the Queen, Caroline Crowley, and poisoning the King.

He had spent the past three weeks putting the Pride back to rights. His bosses at the police station were happy to see him take his accumulated vacation time with the promise he would return to the job soon. Something his mate was also fiercely happy about. She didn't mind being called a Princess now and then, but he could tell she longed for a little space from the dozens of Lions who once again roamed the Palace halls.

"Son!"

Leo's head shot up at the sound of the familiar bass, and he vaulted towards the throne where he'd failed to notice his father, the King was waiting for them. This was the first time Leo had seen his father resplendent in his own navy suit bearing the medals of his station since he'd come home.

Donovan Crowley looked better than ever. His father's mane of silver streaked dark blonde hair was thick and healthy once more, as was his face which had filled out over the past few days. Leo watched as his father's amber eyes glowed gold as his beast rose to meet him. He stilled and waited for the challenge, the animosity that they had both always feared would rise as a result of their dominant natures, but nothing. Nothing happened. He had to remember that those rumors were pushed onto the Pride by Montgomery and his cohorts. None of it was real.

"Son, I am so proud of you. Come here," he opened his arms and Leo went to his father and embraced him in a fierce hug with his mate beside him, tears shining in her bright blue eyes.

"I am so sorry I listened to them and let them keep us apart. Sorry I couldn't save your mother, I didn't know," the King confessed.

"That's not your fault. You trusted them. They were your Pride. I'm sorry about Mom, Dad. And I am sorry I stayed away so long," Leo wiped his face and reached for Sheila.

"Thank you, son. Ah, you've brought my new daughter to see me, welcome Sheila," the King opened his arms and embraced Sheila warmly.

"Thank you, *er*, your majesty?" she squinted, and the King laughed jovially.

"Nonsense, you must know by now we aren't that kind of Kingdom," he said and winked. "A Lion Pride is like any other Shifter group. King is our word for Alpha, that is all."

"Well, what do you know?" Sheila nodded at Leo. "I knew this guy was just an uptight butt-sniffer, and he tried to tell me he was Prince."

The King blinked slowly, then he grinned. Soon that grin turned into a full-blown belly laugh. Leo appreciated that his mate amused his dad, but an uptight butt-sniffer? Someone was getting spanked later. And he couldn't wait. In the meantime, he'd just have to remind her who she was mated to.

"Oooh! Leo," she crowed when he scooped her up and spun her around.

"What was that again, mate?"

"Okay, okay, I give," she said when he started tickling her.

"Alright, children sit down while we discuss the future," the King said and waved them towards a pair of chairs and they sat and listened.

"So, as you can see," his father said after a while. "I am quite fit to continue my rule now that we've weeded out the bad seeds. You are my heir, Leo. You and your children are destined to lead, no one and nothing can change that, but perhaps, it won't be as soon as you thought."

"I see," Leo returned.

"What are your feelings on this, son?"

"Actually," Leo turned and glanced at the current and only owner of his Lion's heart.

Sheila's lovely face was carefully blank, but she could do nothing to stem the scent of confusion from reaching his nostrils. That confusion soon turned to hope as he spoke. He knew then and there that he was about to deliver the correct answer for them both, and his chest swelled with pride.

"I am actually really glad to hear that, Dad. My mate and I won't mind having a closer relationship with you, the Pride, and *Eat Well Live Proud*, but I have a few more years left on the job, and Sheila is building a business with her Pack mates."

"So, what are you saying?" asked the King.

"I am saying that I think this arrangement works very well for all of us. What do you think, mate?"

"Yes," she answered without hesitation, "oh, yes."

"What is going on here? Donovan, you said fifteen minutes, and I've been waiting twenty!" Aunt Patricia walked into the room holding one gold-painted helmet under one arm and waving the other with her hand.

"Hiya, kiddies," she said and winked. "Tell Phoenix I am going to need some more *oomph* added to my engine," the older woman said to Sheila.

"Ah. Yes. I'm coming, dear," the King replied, and growled at the Lioness as he stood up.

George rushed over and handed him a leather vest, which he exchanged for his suit jacket. Leo looked from one to the other, his confusion growing.

"Wait, aren't you related?" Sheila asked.

"Honey, I was your mate's mom's best friend, and I am his godmother, but me and your daddy-in-law don't share any DNA, otherwise this would be too kinky even for me," Aunt Patricia replied and tossed the helmet at Leo's dad before she slapped him on the ass.

"Later, son," the King said, and the two older Shifters headed outdoors.

"Wow, I was not expecting that!" Sheila's look of astonishment matched his own, before the two of them fell into a fit of laughter. Leo growled and tossed his mate back over his shoulder.

"What are you doing?"

"I'm taking my mate down the hall to our room, where we are going to pack our suitcases and break out of this place."

"Then?"

"Then I am going to take you home and claim you on my bed."

"A bed? Now, that's kinky," she growled and swatted his ass.

Fuck, if he didn't get hard at the sharp contact. Maybe they should stay for a little? No. If they didn't leave, they'd never get out. He loved the Pride, but he was years away from taking over and he wanted to have his mate all to himself for a while yet. Just then, the scent of his mate's arousal reached his nostrils and his resolve wavered.

"Behave or else," he threatened.

"Or else what?" she teased.

"I'll just have to show you," he promised.

He entered the bedroom and stalked towards the unmade bed. Flipping her onto the soft mattress, Leo didn't hesitate to slice through her jeans and blouse, leaving her in her leather vest and lace thong.

Sheila sat up and took off the cut, tossing it onto the chair beside the headboard, her eyes never leaving him. He stroked his length beneath his pants and licked his lips. Fuck, she was so hot, her Wolf's musk and the spicy sweetness of her cream tempted him like no other.

"Mine," he growled, but he didn't move to touch. He simply watched as she wiggled and writhed on the bed.

"Yours?" she asked, and he nodded.

"Show me," she demanded.

He squeezed his hard length through his pants, liked the flash of her eyes as she watched him slowly take off his clothes. Once nude, he took his cock in his hand once more, spreading the pearl of precum over the broad head, and cupping his balls with the other hand. She was a goddess bathed in fire and light, and he loved looking at her.

She moaned as he touched himself and moved her hands down to cup her breasts and tug her nipples. She kneaded the flesh under his rapt gaze and bit her lip while her right hand snaked down her luscious body. Pulling her knees up to reveal her glistening pink lips, Sheila skimmed her fingers over her clit.

"Fuck baby, do that again," he growled, watching as she parted her slick lips and dipped her finger inside her honeypot.

Sheila moaned and slid that long, wet digit free, gliding it along her plump little nub. She circled the tiny button of her desire, faster and faster, panting as Leo stroked his cock.

"Hey, little Wolf?"

"What?" she grinned.

"You touchin' my pussy?"

"Mine," she teased and moaned, speeding up those tiny little circles as she rubbed her clit.

"I don't think so, baby, that's my pussy," he growled and let go of his dick.

Leo crawled across the mattress and kneeled at her splayed legs. He nuzzled her hand out of the way, bringing it to his mouth and licking her digits clean. Sheila mewled in response.

He knew what he wanted. Had known since he first laid eyes on his sweet and sassy little Wolf. He rubbed his thick length along her slit, torturing them both to near madness before finally he filled her with one perfectly aimed thrust.

"Leo?" she murmured.

"What, mate?" he growled, trying hard to pace himself, to make sure she came first.

"You know how you said this is your pussy?"

"Mine," he growled and pumped harder.

"Well, I think you're wrong," she said, and that got his Cat snarling and stopped his movements long enough for her to flip them both over.

Astride him and proud as any warrior, Sheila grinned wider like the wicked little Wolf she was. Her breasts thrust forward, and Leo growled as her molten heat squeezed him tightly.

"Fact is," she said, her blue eyes glittered at him even as he tried to catch his breath.

"You," she rocked her hips.

"Are," grind and slide.

"My," she lifted up.

"Pussy!" and she slammed back down.

"Fuck me," he grunted.

"I am, *pussycat,* and I will. Always. Mine."

Me-ow.

EPILOGUE

"Whoa, wait a second," Lucy said and looked from Leo to Sheila and back again. "So, you're a Prince and you mated Sheila?"

"Yes," Leo nodded.

"Yes," Sheila echoed, and rolled her eyes.

Leo was a Prince. She explained it ten times already. So, what was the big deal, anyway? He was also a detective, a Lion Shifter, and wonder of wonders, he was her one true and fated mate.

Phoenix scoffed.

Thor looked carefully blasé about the whole thing.

Brock was noticeably absent.

Cole pinned Leo with his silvery stare for all on two seconds before giving her the thumbs up.

"Oh my gods! You're a fucking Princess," Weylin snorted, and Phoenix grinned too.

"Idiots." Lucy rolled her eyes and popped another French fry into her mouth and chewed, then her pregnant cousin-in-law reached for her iced tea.

The rest of the guys just sat there quietly once they'd stopped making rude noises. Most of them with a beer in hand. Only her cousin was missing. Derrick had gone back to make sure the alarm had been activated at *Serious Moonlight* since everyone came running when she'd come to the Pack House to share her news.

"I just can't believe you mated, Sheila." Weylin faux gagged, and Sheila smacked him upside the head.

"That's my mate you're talking about," Leo growled.

"Shit on a shingle, can't you boys control yourselves? Sheila is a woman now and Leo is her mate," Lucy growled and closed her eyes. Then she yelled for her mate.

"Derrick!"

Her mate hauled ass not one second later through the back door, claws out he looked around and tried to control his breathing. Holy cow.

Remind Sheila to never scream for her mate like that unless she was in actual trouble.

"Dammit, woman, are you okay?" Derrick growled and walked to her side.

"Yes, I'm fine. Derrick, it's gotta happen," she said, and her purple eyes flashed at her mate. Everyone in the room felt the intense bond between the Alpha pair.

"Now?" he questioned, but he should have known better than that, in Sheila's opinion. Not that she had any idea what the fuck Lucy was on about.

"Yes," the feisty Bobcat insisted. "Right now."

"The cubs?"

"They're fine. Thor, get the box," she called out, and pushed herself up out of the chair.

"What's going on?" Leo asked.

"Uh, I think Lucy is going to get her tattoo," Sheila said with wonder in her tone.

"Tattoo?" Leo asked.

"Yes, it's a sacred Dire Wolf ritual," she whispered. For some reason, it felt disrespectful not to.

"Like a tradition?"

"Yes, but deeper, much deeper than that. Thor, our Enforcer, is more than just muscle. He's got *the touch*, the graybeards called him *favored by the gods*."

"Really?" Leo's eyebrows raised, but she could tell he was taking it all in stride.

Modern times or not, all Shifters believed in magic. How could they not when they shared their souls and switched bodies between human and other? Magic existed. They were living proof.

"When Thor channels the Fates, they answer. They work through his skilled fingers to depict a Shifter's true heart through ink and blood, until he connects with that person's *matebond* and shows them their path," Sheila explained.

She watched as Leo's eyes dilated, then flashed gold. It was clear his Lion was interested in her story. Then, without pause, he surprised her with his next request.

"I want one," he said.

"Are you sure?" she didn't dare give in to the hope that threatened to spill over in the form of tears yet. Not until he answered her.

"About you?" her Lion asked and grinned wickedly. "Sheila, you are about the only damned thing in this world I am sure of," he said and claimed her mouth with his even as he stood and led her into the living room.

"It hurts, you know, getting ink," she said and laughed when Leo looked affronted.

"Little Wolf, I'd crawl through glass, walk through fire, go to Hell and back for you, a little ink is nothing, my love. It means a lot, but the pain is worth it. As are you."

He touched her face and kissed her quickly.

"You sure?" she asked one more time.

"*Absofuckinglutely,*" Mr. Law and Order answered, and Sheila laughed aloud, wondering what horrified expressions the guys would make if they heard him talk like that.

He stood up and turned around, leaving her to follow him into the huge living room of the Pack house. It was no Palace, but it was the first home she'd ever known.

As of about an hour ago, however, Sheila and her mate were the proud owners of a three story colonial just down the road. Leo agreed that they couldn't live in the Pack house, or in the rented place he occupied in town. They needed privacy. Of course, proximity to Serious Moonlight and his Pride had been a priority.

The recently abandoned house fit all their needs. Yes, it needed a shit ton of work, but surprisingly, she looked forward to building a home for the two of them. Leo seemed keen, too. Sheila inhaled slowly as she took in the scene and her Pack surrounding her. The Dire Wolf MC was a group of rare Shifters who understood what it meant to be part of something. She was so proud of them all, and she was proud to be among them with her mate.

Lucy was sitting on a chair with Thor kneeling by her leg. He'd taken ink and bamboo needles from the metal box with the original Dire Wolf Pack glyphs etched on the outside. It was a sacred relic of theirs, as was the magicked ink he used to complete the mating ritual according to Pack law.

The large bald Wolf had dozens of tattoos across his enormous body. The most prominent being the wrath of flames circling his neck. His eyes were glazed over as he continued to repeat the same phrase in an ancient language that few knew or recognized as a special dialect of the Dire Wolves of old.

In his trance-like state, Thor etched a scene onto the pregnant Bobcat Shifter's calf. It showed her, her mate, and their cubs all in their animal forms. It was a tinier version of Derrick's tattoo, although in hers she was feeding their cubs, and he was watching over them tenderly.

Everyone was silent in the circle they'd formed around the pregnant Alpha fem, only Derrick approached, cradling her in his arms and claiming her lips with a soul-searing kiss that had even the men teary-eyed.

Normally, Thor was wiped out after one tattoo, but he held out one muscled arm and pointed a finger in Sheila's and Leo's direction. She looked at her mate and saw he was already removing his shirt, revealing his tanned, muscled perfection.

Dear gods, she loved his body. He was so handsome, big, strong, and powerfully built. Perfect for her in every way. Sheila wasn't exactly all sunshine and roses to deal with, but he managed her just fine. The past month had proved that.

He looked at her with his large golden eyes sparkling, and he winked before he made his way to the center of the circle. Thor turned him around so that his back was facing the big man and Sheila sucked in a breath.

Nerves made her tremble as the sheer overwhelming thought that this was actually happening occurred to her. This was more than just a big deal. It was bigger than kissing, biting, and even fucking. This was the real claiming as far as Dire Wolf tradition went.

This was their true mating night. She bit her lip as Thor lifted the ink and poured some into a clean bowl. He took a new bamboo needle and dipped it into the magickal substance before he began carving the path of Leo's destiny across his broad back. Her Lion didn't make one single move.

His face remained still and impassive as the huge Dire Wolf behind him cut through his skin and marked him permanently. Unprecedented in her time and never in her memory, Thor raised his left arm, and he pointed a finger at Sheila. She looked at Derrick, who nodded at her to step forward.

The Enforcer tugged her arm and tore the sleeve, causing a slight rumble from Leo, who quickly ceased the sound when she touched his hand. As Thor continued to draw with ink across Leo's shoulders, he began marking her using the same long arches with the sharpened bamboo. Prick after prick with the wooden blade, Thor worked. His pace was furious and sweat soaked through his shirt before he was finished. The Pack remained present, witnesses to the ritual, until finally the big man laid down his tool.

He breathed heavily, collapsing onto the floor as sweat dripped from his brow. Leo and Sheila looked at each other, awestruck and completely in sync. She felt their *matebond* pulsing around them, a living thing it warmed and protected, sheltering her in his love as she sheltered him in turn.

He was her clarity, her focus, her one true and fated mate, and she would do her best to make him happy. It was all she could promise, and it was enough. It was everything.

"I love you," she whispered as he reached for her.

"Love you, mate." He cleared his throat, and she gasped.

"Sorry, I didn't mean to touch it," she said and turned him around to look at the scene Thor had created with guidance from the Fates themselves.

A mighty Lion stood in a mossy field with a Dire Wolf at his side. They were standing together, equals in all and everything. The Wolf's head was turned towards him, her gaze looking at her future, and the Lion was focused solely on her as well. Sheila's heart pounded as she turned her right arm to see what it was she'd been tattooed with, to her consternation the scene went up her shoulder.

"What is it?" she asked, and she almost howled when no one answered.

Leo pressed a kiss to her skin before he spoke. She heard the awe in his tone, and it filled her with love and joy.

"Oh, baby, it's a Wolf's paw, a Dire Wolf's paw, and it's right over a heart that's surrounded in a mane of flames. I've seen that before, it's a depiction of a Lion's heart. My heart. Your claw isn't a threat, it's not piercing the heart, it's uh, it's carrying me. You're lifting me up, little Wolf. Just like you do, every single minute you're with me," his voice tightened, and she trembled, near to bursting with emotion, but he wasn't done.

"Sheila, baby, there are glyphs too. A circle with two wavy lines intertwined—"

"That's the symbol for fated mates," she said with a ridiculously happy bark of laughter.

"And another one, this one I recognize. It's the ring of circles, like on my bedroom door at the palace. The symbol for greatness," he whispered, and she felt the grin in his voice as he kissed her shoulder.

"Well, I am pretty great," she said, and he turned her around and claimed her lips. Breaking her sass with three little words she hadn't heard him say since the night they'd mated under the full moon.

"I love you, little Wolf."

"I love you too," she returned. And she did. With all her heart.

The end.

Liked this story? Want more Dire Wolf Mates?

Grab the next book, Pinch of Sass, at https://www. cdgorri.com/books/pinch-of-sass.

Or

Follow the whole series at https://www.cdgorri.com/seres/ dire-wolf-mates.

Thank you and happy reading!

BEWARE... HERE BE EVEN MORE DRAGONS!

The Falk Clan Tales began as my stories surrounding four dragon Brothers and how they find their one true mates, but when a long lost brother arrives on the scene, followed by a few more Shifters…what can I say? The more the merrier!

Each Dragon's chest is marked with his rose, the magical link to his heart and his magic. They each have a matching gemstone to go with it.

She's given up on love. But he's just begun.

In *The Dragon's Valentine* we meet the eldest Falk brother, Callius. He is on a mission to find a Castle and his one true mate, one he can trust with his diamond rose....

His heart is frozen. Can she change his mind about love?

In *The Dragon's Christmas Gift* our attention shifts to Alexsander, the youngest brother of the four. He has resigned himself to a life alone, until he meets *her*.

Some wounds run deep. Can a Dragon's heart be unbroken?

The Dragon's Heart is the story of Edric Falk who has vowed never to love again, but that changes when he meets his feisty mate, Joselyn Curacao.

She just wants a little fun. He's looking for a lifetime.

We finally meet Nikolai Falk and his sexy Shifter mate in *The Dragon's Secret*.

**Now available in a boxed set.*

Guess what…. I've got more Dragons on the way!

Look for The Dragon's Treasure. Now available.

Coming in 2022 The Dragon's Dream and The Dragon's Surprise.

HAVE YOU MET MY BEARS?

Looking for a Paranormal Romance series that is loads of growly fun?

Meet the Barvale Clan first in the Bear Claw Tales! A complete shifter romance series about 4 brothers who discover and need to win their fated mates!

Followed by two more spin off series, the Barvale Clan Tales and the Barvale Holiday Tales!

No cliffhangers. Steamy PNR fun.
Go and read your next happily ever after today!

OTHER TITLES BY C.D. GORRI

Other Titles by C.D. Gorri

Paranormal Romance Books:

Macconwood Pack Novel Series:

Charley's Christmas Wolf: A Macconwood Pack Novel 1

Cat's Howl: A Macconwood Pack Novel 2

Code Wolf: A Macconwood Pack Novel 3

The Witch and The Werewolf: A Macconwood Pack
Novel 4

To Claim a Wolf: A Macconwood Pack Novel 5

Conall's Mate: A Macconwood Pack Novel 6

Her Solstice Wolf: A Macconwood Pack Novel 7

Werewolf Fever: A Macconwood Pack Novel 8

Also available in 2 boxed sets:

The Macconwood Pack Volume 1

The Macconwood Pack Volume 2

Macconwood Pack Tales Series:

Wolf Bride: The Story of Ailis and Eoghan A

Macconwood Pack Tale 1

Summer Bite: A Macconwood Pack Tale 2

His Winter Mate: A Macconwood Pack Tale 3

Snow Angel: A Macconwood Pack Tale 4

Charley's Baby Surprise: A Macconwood Pack Tale 5

Home for the Howlidays: A Macconwood Pack Tale 6

A Silver Wedding: A Macconwood Pack Tale 7

Mine Furever: A Macconwood Pack Tale 8

A Furry Little Christmas: A Macconwood Pack Tale 9

Also available in two boxed sets:

The Macconwood Pack Tales Volume 1

Shifters Furever: The Macconwood Pack Tales Volume 2

The Falk Clan Tales:

The Dragon's Valentine: A Falk Clan Novel 1

The Dragon's Christmas Gift: A Falk Clan Novel 2

The Dragon's Heart: A Falk Clan Novel 3

The Dragon's Secret: A Falk Clan Novel 4

The Dragon's Treasure: A Falk Clan Novel 5

The Dragon's Surprise: A Falk Clan Novel 6

The Dragon's Dream: A Falk Clan Novel 7

Dragon Mates: The Falk Clan Series Boxed Set Books 1-4

The Bear Claw Tales:

Bearly Breathing: A Bear Claw Tale 1

Bearly There: A Bear Claw Tale 2

Bearly Tamed: A Bear Claw Tale 3

Bearly Mated: A Bear Claw Tale 4

Also available in a boxed set:

The Complete Bear Claw Tales (Books 1-4)

<u>The Barvale Clan Tales:</u>

Polar Opposites: The Barvale Clan Tales 1

Polar Outbreak: The Barvale Clan Tales 2

Polar Compound: A Barvale Clan Tale 3

Polar Curve: A Barvale Clan Tale 4

Also available in a boxed set:

The Barvale Clan Tales (Books 1-4)

<u>Barvale Holiday Tales:</u>

A Bear For Christmas

Hers To Bear

Thank You Beary Much

Bearing Gifts

Also available in a boxed set:

The Barvale Holiday Tales (Books 1-3)

<u>Purely Paranormal Romance Books:</u>

Marked by the Devil: Purely Paranormal Romance Books

Mated to the Dragon King: Purely Paranormal Romance Books

Claimed by the Demon: Purely Paranormal Romance Books

Christmas with a Devil, a Dragon King, & a Demon: Purely Paranormal Romance Books

Vampire Lover: Purely Paranormal Romance Books

Grizzly Lover: Purely Paranormal Romance Books

Christmas With Her Chupacabra: Purely Paranormal Romance Books

Purely Paranormal Romance Books Anthology

<u>The Wardens of Terra:</u>

Bound by Air: The Wardens of Terra Book 1

Star Kissed: A Wardens of Terra Short

Waterlocked: The Wardens of Terra Book 2

Moon Kissed: A Wardens of Terra Short

*Now in a boxed set and in audio!

<u>The Maverick Pride Tales:</u>

Purrfectly Mated

Purrfectly Kissed

Purrfectly Trapped

Purrfectly Caught

Purrfectly Naughty

Purrfectly Bound

Dire Wolf Mates:

Shake That Sass

Breaking Sass

Pinch of Sass

Kickin' Sass

Wyvern Protection Unit:

Gift Wrapped Protector: WPU 1

Standalones:

The Enforcer

Blood Song: A Sanguinem Council Book

Spring Fling (co-written with P. Mattern)

EveL Worlds:

Chinchilla and the Devil: A FUCN'A Book

Sammi and the Jersey Bull: A FUCN'A Book

Mouse and the Ball: A FUCN'A Book

The Guardians of Chaos:

Wolf Shield: Guardians of Chaos Book1

Dragon Shield: Guardians of Chaos Book 2

Stallion Shield: Guardians of Chaos Book 3

Panther Shield: Guardians of Chaos 4

Witch Shield: Guardians of Chaos 5

Vampire Shield: Guardians of Chaos 6

Howl's Romance

Mated to the Werewolf Next Door: A Howl's Romance

The Tiger King's Christmas Bride

Claiming His Virgin Mate: Howls Romance

<u>Twice Mated Tales</u>

Doubly Claimed

Doubly Bound

Doubly Tied

<u>Hearts of Stone Series</u>

Shifter Mountain: Hearts of Stone 1

Shifter City: Hearts of Stone 2

Shifter Village: Hearts of Stone 3

<u>Accidentally Undead Series</u>

Fangs For Nothin'

<u>Moongate Island Tales</u>

Moongate Island Mate

Moongate Island Christmas Claim

<u>Mated in Hope Falls</u>

Mated by Moonlight

<u>Speed Dating with the Denizens of the Underworld</u>

Ash: Speed Dating with the Denizens of Underworld

Arachne: Speed Dating with the Denizens of Underworld

Asterion: Speed Dating with the Denizens of Underworld

Hungry_Fur_Love

Hungry Like Her Wolf: Magic and Mayhem Universe

Hungry For Her Bear: Magic and Mayhem Universe

<u>Shifters Unleashed Boxed Sets</u>

Check out these amazing anthologies where you can find some of my books and the works of other awesome authors!

Midnight Magic Anthology (Water Witch)

Rituals & Runes Anthology (Air Witch)

<u>Island Stripe Pride</u>

Tiger Claimed

Tiger Denied

Tiger Rejected

<u>NYC Shifter Tales</u>

Cuff Linked

Sealed Fate

<u>A Howlin' Good Fairytale Retelling</u>

Sweet As Candy (single edition coming soon)

<u>Coming Soon:</u>

Hungry As Her Python: Magic and Mayhem Universe

If The Shoe Fits: A Howlin' Good Fairytale Retelling

Chickee and the Paparazzi: FUCN'A

The Wolf's Winter Wish: A Macconwood Pack Tale

The Hybrid Assassin

For Fangs Sake

Tempted By Her Protector: WPU 2

Alien Protector: WPU 3

Elvish Protector: WPU 4

Thrilled By Her Protector: WPU 5

<u>Young Adult Urban Fantasy Books:</u>

Wolf Moon: A Grazi Kelly Novel Book 1

Hunter Moon: A Grazi Kelly Novel Book 2

Rebel Moon: A Grazi Kelly Novel Book 3

Winter Moon: A Grazi Kelly Novel Book 4

Chasing The Moon: A Grazi Kelly Short 5

Blood Moon: A Grazi Kelly Novel 6

*Get all 6 books NOW AVAILABLE IN A BOXED SET:

The Complete Grazi Kelly Novel Series

Casting Magic: The Angela Tanner Files 1

Keeping Magic: The Angela Tanner Files 2

<u>G'Witches Magical Mysteries Series</u>

Co-written with P. Mattern

G'Witches

G'Witches 2: The Harpy Harbinger

G'Witches 3: Summoning Secrets

EXCERPT FROM WOLF SHIELD: GUARDIANS OF CHAOS

What a day! Fergie McAndrews headed towards the pick-up truck she'd borrowed from her roommate for work that morning.

Of course, the thirty-thousand dollar certified used luxury car she'd splurged on earlier in the year was in the shop. Again.

Just another in a long line of bad decisions. After leaving a perfectly good job for a startup company, she was laid off three weeks ago and had to borrow money from her parents to pay rent. Wasn't that humiliating?

"This is the last time, Ferg," her step-monster had said after she'd Venmo'd the money to her.

God forbid the mechanic call and tell her the car

was ready. She wouldn't be able to pick it up for another week. That was when she got her first paycheck from her newest gig at L-Corp. Not a startup, but an older company with new offices in Bayonne, which was only a half-hour commute.

But to commute, you needed a car. Fergie had no choice but to borrow the old pick-up from her best friend and roommate, Jessenia Banks. It wasn't like she needed the truck. She worked from home these days. Besides, Fergie promised to fill it up and have it washed.

She huffed out a breath. It'd been a really long day. A crappy one too. Fergie wanted to love her new job. Really, she did. But so far, it was the pits. If Fergie wanted to be a librarian, she would've been one.

Research was her jam. Well, when it was interesting. She had a knack for sniffing out information and compiling easy-to-read spreadsheets and timelines. It wasn't the hard work that annoyed her. Her complaint was the content. The actual stuff her new boss had her looking up. It was beyond boring.

Why an enormous conglomerate like L-Corp needed old land surveys, cross-referenced with newspaper reports on accidents, crimes, etcetera.

She had no idea. She'd been at it for weeks now. So far, she'd researched six locations given via GPS coordinates across Hudson County. Her new boss wanted everything, every little insignificant piece of information she could dig up.

That was the easy part. It was the hassle of the actual job that really made her want to give up. Every day she had to drive to Bayonne to pick up her work laptop she'd dropped off the night before with all of that day's findings. Every single night they wiped her computer clean.

Like she was going to run away with the secrets of what happened on 2nd and Washington sixty-years ago. Can you say paranoid? Ugh.

Fergie had always looked forward to working for a huge global company. It was supposed to be her ticket out of the Garden State. Traveling the globe, seeing new things, visiting far-off places was always a secret dream of hers. Well, that, and having her own walk-in closet full of gorgeous designer shoes.

Best secret dream evah! In her opinion, anyway. What woman didn't love shoes? Fergie hummed as she daydreamed about rows and rows of Blahnik's, Jimmy Choo's, Garavani's, Ferragamo's, and her personal favorites, Louboutin's on every shelf!

Don't judge. Fergie wasn't shallow, she just liked pretty things. Haters gonna hate. But every time she ran across a thrift or second-chance store, she'd search high and low to see what they had. That was how she'd scored the pumps on her feet.

They made her feel good about herself. Being five-foot two-inches short with more curves than a racetrack, Fergie had had more than her fair share of self-esteem issues growing up. Alright, so she was chubby. She could admit that proudly now.

If everyone looked the same, the world would be one boring as hell place. Fergie liked herself perfectly fine these days, in spite of all the times her step-monster tried to make her diet growing up. So she liked food and shoes. Big deal.

She worked hard to feed and clothe herself, so as far as she was concerned, no one had a right to comment. So what if she wanted some excitement in her life? Fergie was aware she was better off than most, but what was wrong with having goals?

She'd spent a lot of time thinking about how a woman like her could have an adventure. Travelling was the only thing she could think of. Of course, she'd been hoping this job would be the answer to that. Even travelling for work was better than being stuck.

Sigh.

So far, her plans had fallen flat, but hey, at least she was earning a paycheck. Her new boss, Mr. Offner, might be a strange man, but he signed her checks, and that was enough for now. Fergie had never seen more than a glimpse of him. All of her instructions usually came via email.

Most of the time she was able to compile her research quickly, then she'd head back to the office to organize it into neat little spreadsheets, and finally, she'd hand it all in with her laptop. But not today.

Mr. Offner sent her an email detailing everything she could dig up on one of the oldest places on record in the county. Of course, land surveys that old, along with police reports, newspaper articles, deeds, and sales records were nowhere she could easily access them.

After wasting hours at both the court house and municipal building, Fergie had been directed to the *second* public library. Apparently anything over a hundred years old was filed away in the godforsaken place. She'd been shocked to find an entire room filled with musty old archives. And wouldn't you know it, there was no cell service and no internet access. Plus, their phone lines were down. She'd had to photograph each page using her cell. When she got home later, she would send those photos like a fax to her boss along with her spreadsheet. If she could manage that before collapsing into bed.

Grab your copy at https://www.cdgorri.com/books/wolf-shield

EXCERPT FROM PURRFECTLY MATED

How the fuck did I wind up here?

It was all Elissa could do not to slam her face down on the table as she pondered that question for the umpteenth time since leaving her cozy Hoboken apartment to go on this so called date.

"So, babe," the over-stuffed, heavily-cologned, and downright fugly man said.

Her date of the evening looked like something out of a bad sitcom as he tried to lean over the stained tablecloth of the rundown hotel buffet room, he'd driven two hours to get to. Waggling his cater-pillar-like eyebrows, he gave her the once over and Elissa's skin crawled.

Oh, hell no.

"I got a room upstairs, you know, for *after*," he told her, nodding his head, and biting his lower lip in a manner she assumed he thought was provocative.

At best, it was nauseating.

FML.

How was this guy Elissa's date for the evening? What had she done to deserve this?

Little Gianni. Yup, that was how he'd introduced himself. And here she was. On a blind date with a guy who had the word 'little' in front of his name.

Well, what did she expect? Roses and champagne? In this economy? She didn't know where Cinder-fucking-ella got her prince, but it sure as fuck wasn't in Jersey.

Elissa could only blame herself for agreeing to go on this blind date. Initially, the whole Little Gianni fiasco had been intended for her roommate.

Wait a second. Scratch that thought.

It *was* all Gretchen's fault. That ungrateful cow!

She tried to play it off like she was some sweet little homegrown maiden. Oh, just wait till Elissa got home. Gretchen was never going to hear the end of it.

She owed Elissa. Big time. Like a whole month of

washing the dishes big time. The rat trap they shared in her hometown of Hoboken was all the two women could afford, and for the most part, they got along just fine.

In fact, they'd grown to be close friends over the three years they'd lived together. It was the only reason she'd ever agreed to this date from Hell.

Elissa sighed and looked over at Little Gianni. Maybe he wasn't all that bad?

"*BEEEELLLLLLLLCHHH!* 'Scuse me, doll. Better out, am I right?"

Gianni winked and Elissa wished for a black hole to open up and swallow her up right through the floor.

OMFG.

The man just burped out loud like he was in a frat boy belting contest, only those days passed him up about thirty years ago.

For fuck's sake. Gretchen, you so owe me.

Elissa cursed her roommate and tried not to groan. But Little Gianni wasn't quite done. The grown ass man lifted his leg and let one rip.

Right. Fucking. There.

Elissa was going to die before the end of the night.

Literally.

This is what you get when you do a friend a favor without asking for details! Idiota!

The voice of her Italian grandmother sounded in her brain. She tried to ignore it, willing herself not to wince at the man while he sucked air, and who knows what else, noisily through his coffee-stained teeth.

Ew. So gross.

That was the perfect word to describe it. The only word, in fact. The entire date was just so fucking gross. She still couldn't believe her sweet little roommate from Iowa, *Gretchen Kaepernick,* she of the wispy hair and baby blues, had set her up with this guy!

What the actual fuck was up with that?

Little Gianni was a slob. Actually, he looked just like her Uncle Nico, and that was not a good thing. Seriously, not good at all.

He wore his hair slicked back in a too tight ponytail that emphasized his rapidly receding hairline. As if that wasn't enough to put her off, he was sporting an enormous paunch. Now, being a curvy girl, Elissa appreciated food and was in no way against men showing the same appreciation.

She liked bigger men. Always had. But bigger did not mean you had to be sloppy. Little Gianni's stomach was literally hanging out from under a tight tan golf shirt that had definitely seen better days.

The man didn't even look like he had ever played a sport of any kind. With it, he wore brown polyester pants that were three inches above his ankles and unbuttoned at the waist.

He didn't look like he tried at all for this date. What kind of guy did that? His shirt collar was bent and wrinkled, and all three buttons were open to his chest, revealing a mat of oily, dark hair and pimples.

Somehow, he'd managed to tuck the back of the shirt in, but the front simply would not hold in that stomach. What worried her more were the tight brown pants.

As he sat back and stretched, she wondered if she should take cover. They looked like they were one bite from exploding off his body. Elissa shuddered at the image.

Please God, if You have an ounce of mercy, don't let that happen, she prayed.

"Hang on, doll, I gotta take this," he said, and turned to answer his cell phone.

It was ringing to the tune of '70s disco music she

hadn't heard since the last family reunion. Her eyes kept going to the huge stain on the front of his shirt. It was a little game she liked to call *what the hell is that.*

Coffee, she guessed.

"Up your ass, Bruno. I gotta have it by Monday," he cursed into the receiver.

Elissa winced at the spectacle he was making of them both. There were only a handful of people there, but still.

Deep breaths.

Ew. Maybe not.

She coughed as the strong body spray, that he'd obviously used a ton of in lieu of a shower, bad move in her opinion, invaded her lungs.

Oh, this was so bad.

Elissa was, by no means, a snob. But this guy looked like he'd stepped out of a bad 1980s mafia spoof film. What's worse, he kept smacking his lips together as he hung up the phone and looked her over from head to chest.

Thank fuck for the table, she thought, wishing she could hide her bosoms from his view.

"Sssss," he hissed, like it was sexy or something.

She just grimaced. Elissa might be able to forgive a lot of quirks, but she hated mouth noises. Really hated them. It was a super pet peeve of hers. Never mind his totally inappropriate and unwelcomed leer.

She started counting the minutes, willing the date to be over already. Plenty of people would tell her she shouldn't be so choosy, but really? She was not this desperate.

Not yet anyway.

So, she was curvy and a little mouthy too. But was it wrong to want a man with good table manners? Even if men were thin on the ground for someone like her.

As a chef, she'd worked in a lot of restaurants and even as a personal cook for professional couples. She'd seen her fair share of unhappy couples and downright uncomfortable marriages. But as far as she was concerned, all relationships went downhill when good table manners were dismissed.

Good manners were merely a sign that a person was thoughtful and respectful. At least, that was what Nonna had told her. Gianni here had clearly missed that lesson as a child. Elissa had to work not to groan in disgust as he slurped a raw clam down his gullet.

Shudder.

Was there no end to his feeding? That's what it reminded her of. Feeding time at the zoo.

OMG. That was rude, she scolded herself. But it wasn't like she said it out loud.

All she wanted to do was go home. At least she was comfortable. *She'd* worn her softest pair of black leggings for this disaster date, paired with one of her favorite tunics on top.

It was dark green with tiny black buttons down the front and showed just the right amount of cleavage. She'd gone for neat and tidy as opposed to downright sexy.

Good call, in her opinion. Elissa looked perfectly fine for a nice *getting to know you* dinner, which is what she thought she was getting when her roommate asked her to step in for her on a blind date that one of her best client's had set up for her.

Elissa shuddered now, thinking how good old Gianni here would've reacted to the red dress and heels she'd contemplated before checking the weather report.

Gulp.

The lewd man was already salivating, and she was so not having it. Fending off his unwanted advances was not how she wanted to finish the night.

Ew again.

Elissa shivered, slightly chilled despite the fact

they were indoors. It was a cold, gloomy evening, and the forecast called for even more rain later that night. Not at all unusual for this time of year in the Garden State.

November was always chilly in the evenings, rainy too. Elissa tended to run warm, but she was glad she'd brought a jacket with her. Especially since her date refused to turn the heat on in the car.

When she'd asked, he'd looked offended and told her it wasted gas.

Um. Okay.

She checked her phone. It was only seven o'clock, but the two hour drive was still ahead of them. Maybe they could make it home before ten if they left soon.

Ugh. Did he just blow his nose?

"Allergies, doll. Say, you gonna eat that?" he asked before scooping a fry from her dish and swallowing it down.

Elissa was gonna kill her roomie. Gretchen was a hair and nail stylist. A lot of her clients were elderly, and they just loved her. They were always offering to set her up on blind dates with their nephews and grandsons.

Mostly, the sweet old ladies were kind. They swore they could find her curvy roommate the right man, assuming she was single because she was new to town. Well, when Elissa got home tonight, she was going to tell Gretchen she needed to fire the old lady who set this date up from being her client.

Like *ASAP*.

No one who liked Gretchen would've sent her out with this guy. Gianni reached over and touched her hand and Elissa pulled back, reaching for the napkin.

Gross.

"I sure hope you ain't a cold one, doll," he said, shaking his head.

"What?"

"Ain't gonna matter. I know just what you need, doll."

She was still wiping the greasy residue he'd transferred to her skin from the food he ate sans utensils. This was too much. Elissa was beyond uncomfortable with all the leering and bad attempts at innuendo.

Plus, she was starving. One look at the dump he'd taken her to, and she knew she could never eat there. The chef in her wouldn't allow it.

To think they drove two hours for this! She'd practically frozen to death in his maroon Cadillac, listening to a CD of the Rat Pack, while Gianni crooned loudly, and off key, to the music.

Normally, she was a fan of the famous group of legendary singers. Having grown up in Hoboken, she couldn't not be a Sinatra fan. Though, to be honest, Dean Martin had always been her favorite.

Still, Elissa was a firm believer that there were just some people you did not try to imitate. Especially not if you were Little Gianni. While he was belting his heart out, he'd been trying to get his right hand on her thigh. She'd asked him politely to stop.

Twice.

Then she'd been forced to try something a little more drastic. Like spilling her hot tea on the offending hand the third time he'd tried it. Finally, he'd removed his hand from her leg. Not making a fourth attempt, which she was grateful for.

Elissa should've taken that behavior as a sign and gotten out of the car. But no. She'd wanted to do Gretchen a solid. So, against her better judgement, she gave the creep another chance.

Idiota, her grandmother's voice echoed in her brain again.

The old woman had loved her. Elissa knew that without a doubt. She'd raised her after her own parents had passed on in a tragic automobile accident when Elissa was just twelve.

Her grandmother was a no-nonsense kind of lady who dished out priceless wisdom with brutally honest insights. It was the same way she dished out huge bowls of pasta with her amazing meatballs and homemade sauce. Not to mention a side order of back-breaking hugs that Elissa still missed.

Nonna cooked like that all the time. She made a huge pot of sauce every weekend, and she was happy to serve it to Elissa and her teammates and friends, especially after games and tournaments.

Soccer had been her sport of choice, and cooking had soon become her favorite hobby. Her grandmother had encouraged her in both pursuits. Guiding her in one and cheering her on in the other. Elissa still missed her terribly.

"Hey babe, ain't you gonna eat nothin'? You know they charge twenty dollars just to sit down," Little Gianni interrupted her train of thought.

Elissa was forced to turn her mind back to the present, which unfortunately included watching, *and hearing*, him as he sucked on his teeth and stuffed another breaded shrimp down his throat.

"I'm fine," she answered with a polite smile plastered on her face.

Just get home, Lissa. Just get him to take you home.

Elissa closed her eyes when he looked back down at his dish. Thank God for small favors, she mused. At least he was more interested in eating at the moment.

He'd taken her to the rattiest looking hotel and casino she'd ever seen in her life. And the buffet room?

Ew.

Seriously, the place had to be violating at least a dozen health codes. When Gianni had said Atlantic City, she'd thought at least the atmosphere would be exciting. But they were so far from the real glitz and entertainment, they might as well be anywhere else.

She sighed, looking at the plate she'd made for herself. Elissa couldn't even fake an interest in the food. As a chef, it was hard enough to dine out.

She was always judging the food, the service, the ingredients. How could she not? It was her business. And that was when the food was good!

This was not good. Not at all.

She'd been to hospitals that served better food. Old yellow lights buzzed and blinked around the buffet, giving it an abandoned kind of feel. The menu was made up of mostly frozen then fried or baked cuisine.

Reheated actually. It was like a giant TV dinner buffet where every item was previously frozen when already cooked and warmed up in an oven.

It was the kind of food sold cheap at restaurant supply stores in bulk. Yeah, this was much worse than hospital food, in her opinion.

There was a worn carpet on the floor, a handful of scattered tables in the dining room, elevator music on in the background, and the entire place smelled like canned soup.

Not to mention not one of the five people there besides them was under sixty years old.

"Gianni," she said, leaning forward so as not to hurt his feelings.

"I thought you mentioned something about seeing a show tonight. Is it here?"

Please don't be here.

If he was taking her somewhere else, she could beg off and hire a cab to take her home. There was no way she was sitting through anything else with this man. Not now. Not ever.

"Ah, I see, babe, you want some entertainment first, I get it," he snickered loudly, and she blanched.

Whatever he thought was going to happen wasn't. She needed to disabuse him of the notion, and fast.

"Alright, alright. Lemme finish this, babe. Then we'll go up to the room I got for us," he said.

Before she could make sense of the ludicrous statement, he slurped another fried shrimp, don't ask how. Then he grabbed her arm and yanked her from the seat before she could even react.

Elissa tugged on his hold, but the man was immovable. Tossing a five-dollar bill on the table, Little Gianni snatched a toothpick from the hostess stand before dragging her outside.

Great, he was a cheap tipper, too.

All she wanted was to go home. Figuring the best way to do that would probably be to get him to the car, she let him lead the way.

Once inside, she would ask him to drive back to Hoboken so she could wring Gretchen's neck. Fuming, she pulled her arm out of his hand and walked behind him.

The rain was really pouring, and the cheap bastard had refused valet. Elissa ducked her head so she wouldn't get so wet. Of course, the jacket she'd brought was light and had no hood.

Gianni had an umbrella, but he didn't offer to hold it for her, and honestly, she did not relish the idea of getting any closer to him than necessary.

Seriously, not happening.

Now all she had to do was break the news. She had no intention of watching a show or returning to the hotel with him.

What could go wrong?

Grab your copy at https://www.cdgorri.com/books/purrfectly-mated!

EXCERPT FROM BOUND BY AIR

Troy Waman looked down at his smartphone to the little red arrow blinking on his map app, indicating he had reached his destination. He frowned pensively before shaking his head.

"What a fucking shithole," he murmured to himself as he exited the nondescript black SUV his Station Master, Rex, had given him for the job.

"Try not to scratch it," the tough Bear shifter had said with a barely contained growl after their meeting the day before last. After a thousand years of waiting, The *Wardens of Terra* were being called to duty and this was Troy's first assignment.

It took him a day and a half to make his way to Shadowland, New York from the little suburb in Virginia Beach where his Station was located. There were dozens of them across the continental United States and even more overseas, though he'd rarely been out of the county himself.

Troy rolled his shoulders and exhaled. He was the first from his Station to be called to duty. A fact that left him both proud and humbled at the same time. He'd trained damn hard since he was a child waiting for such an opportunity. Now he had it, and it was almost too much to bear.

Fuck and damn. It's time Troy, get your ass in gear. That was all the sympathy he had for himself. Why the hell should he have any at all? Troy Waman was no tenderfoot normal. He was a Warden of Terra. He didn't need to remind himself of the honor and duty that went along with his position.

The *Wardens of Terra* were an ancient group of elite warriors. All of them Shifters. Identified in their youth and trained throughout their preternaturally long lives, they were guardians as well as fighters. *Station Masters* led teams of Wardens across the planet.

Though they'd been deactivated sometime in the last millennium, Wardens were born, chosen, and trained every day with the distinct knowledge that someday, they'd be called upon to defend the earth. That day was here.

Troy Waman had been trained as a Warden since before he learned how to spell the word. His heritage was a mix of Anglo and Native American. His father's blood was a mix of tribes including Algonquin, Lenape, Cherokee, and a few others. He hadn't stuck around long enough for anyone to learn the rest.

He supposed he could get a DNA test, but that might raise too many questions with the normals. Especially in this day of advanced technology in biogenetics.

Besides, it was quite common in today's world to find Native American peoples descended from multiple tribes. Troy Waman was uncommon for an entirely different reason. He was a Shifter, a special race of dual natured beings with one foot in the supernatural world and one in the human. Troy was a *Thunderbird Shifter* to be exact. Something unique even amongst Shifters.

He stretched his long, lithe body as he stepped away from the vehicle. It was already dark out despite it being fairly early in the evening. *Daylight savings my ass.* He sniffed the frigid air. The unusually high winds made the cold seem even more bitter. The street lamp stuttered on the corner, a rusty fence squeaked, and a black cat crossed the street, ducking under some parked cars. Troy's frown deepened.

It looked like the setting of a B-horror flick. All it needed was some half naked co-ed to run down the street with a masked bogeyman stalking behind her, traditional blood-coated knife in hand. *Oh yeah.* They might call it *Shadowland Nightmare* or something equally cheesy.

He stopped his musings and used his heightened senses to take in the downtrodden area around him. It would seem upstate New York wasn't all orchards and sprawling suburbs. He smirked as the "I love New York" song ran through his head. *Yeah, right.*

Apparently, parts of the Empire State were as fucked up as the street where he was born in Newark, New Jersey. He'd visited that shithole back when he was in his teens just out of curiosity. What a mistake that had been! He'd left almost as soon as he'd arrived. His extended family had been, shall we say, less than welcoming.

His gray-haired grandmother had screamed and crossed herself when he stepped over her threshold. He was what they called a *skin walker*. They feared and loathed him as something evil. Him evil? Like he was the motherfucker who knocked-up some unsuspecting normal and left her ass with a Shifter baby.

He was not evil, but he was something they did not understand. He'd been angry and ashamed that day. He'd crashed through his grandmother's kitchen to hitch a ride back down to his Station in Virginia Beach.

In his youth it was more like a military training camp, but it was all he knew of home. After all, it was where he'd lived his entire life. He'd made his peace and settled fully into his life there.

The incident with his grandmother had happened over a decade ago, when Troy had stolen his records out of Rex's office. Still, the memory remained fresh in his mind as if it were only yester-day. The fucked-up street where he was standing only brought back the painful reminder that he'd come from the same kind of squalor. *Fuck this*, he thought.

The pungent scent of despair washed over him. *Reminding him.* A young man with a hood pulled up over his head, eyed him from the street corner. *Drug dealer. Shadowland* indeed. It was an apt name for this shamble of a neigh-borhood.

The young man continued to stare until Troy allowed his beast to shine through. His golden eyes pinned the errant youth through the inky darkness of the night. Startled, the kid dropped the bag he was holding and ran down the alley.

Punk. Troy walked over and picked up what he had so hastily left behind. A couple of grams of crack cocaine and heroin, *probably cut with Fentanyl.* There were also various sized baggies full of what smelled like some below average marijuana and half-rotted psychedelic mushrooms.

Just your garden variety of illegal substances to be found on most street corners in neighborhoods like this one. *Fucking normals.* He frowned and dumped the still sealed contents down the closest storm drain. He sent a quick text to Rex earmarking the location.

Rex would make sure the local police department got an anonymous tip to retrieve the narcotics before someone got hurt. Recreational drug use, mainly the opioid epidemic, was wreaking havoc amongst the humans with more and more of them succumbing to their addictions.

It was troubling, but not Troy's problem. Shifters were extraordinarily hard to kill. Most human drugs had little to no effect on supernatural beings. *Normals,* he growled the thought, *such weak creatures.*

To be fair, Shifters had vices too. He just had little

experience with it. Cecil, a Station-mate of his, had an adrenaline addiction. He was always putting himself in dangerous situations, even during simple training exercises. Fernandez, a Jaguar Shifter, was always trying to get into some chick's pants. *Sex addict.* And he knew of others who channeled their energies into ways he considered to be mostly unproductive.

His opinion, for sure. He'd always been something of a loner by nature. There weren't many Thunderbird Shifters around. Hell, he was the only fucking one he knew of in this part of the world.

He didn't blame or judge his Station-mates for their proclivities. Most of the Shifters he knew had large appetites which included food, exercise, and sex.

Troy had certainly explored that part of him. He wasn't a man-whore or anything, but he'd had his share of women. None of them mattered to him. Just a means to satisfy the occasional itch.

Troy was determined to live his life as a Warden of Terra alone. He never expected to find anyone willing to share what was a potentially deadly existence.

Those who followed the Darkness and evil were always looking for ways to gain the upper hand and it was his job to stop them. The way he saw it, it was an honor and a duty to serve.

He shared this great responsibility with the entire organization. The core belief of the Wardens was based on one indisputable fact Shifters had walked the earth since the dawn of time, even before humankind; therefore, they were responsible for the well-being of the entire planet and all its inhabitants. Especially those who were inherently weaker. Mainly females and *normals*.

There were other supernaturals who believed humans, or normals as they referred to them, were a blight on the planet. Those creatures wished to destroy them and take over.

Demons, Dark Witches, and a whole plethora of evil beings sought the destruction of the normals and the world they lived in. *Idiots! Did they even realize if they destroyed the world, there would be nothing left? Where the fuck would they live?*

Of course, the supernatural world had many agencies that worked towards the common goal of saving the planet. The *Order of the Guardians,* for example, were responsible for policing the various factions of supernaturals.

Shifters generally tended to ally themselves with the Guardians. Sure, there were *bad* Shifters, but he'd never come across any willing to follow the Dark. Simply because most agreed the destruction of the world could not be allowed to happen.

Different Packs and Clans, etcetera, of course, had different ideas. Some wanted to remain secret, others wished to come out, and other still wanted to rule the weaker humans. It was a whole fucking thing, and they argued about regularly.

Troy didn't know from any of that. He spent little time in the human world. His efforts better spent making himself worthy of being a Warden. Training, exercise, and following orders. That's what Troy lived for, it was why he was chosen.

Thunderbird Shifters were very rare. *Special*. He scoffed at the stray thought. But no matter what way he looked at it, Troy was indeed unique. In more ways than one. He was born *marked* by the stars. A *Shifter of Terra*.

From infancy, he was told he carried the power of his sign within him. *Aquarius* ruled his destiny and it would aid him in the never-ending battle against the forces of darkness.

Every single Warden he knew was a Shifter like him. They were the fiercest warriors on the planet. Like many others throughout the last thousand years, Troy, *a Shifter child who was marked*, was taken from his parents and trained by his Station Master until the time when he would be called into use.

All that time, he thought, *and here I am.* He tried to ignore the pressure building inside of him. He felt anxious. His animal pressed against his psyche, comforting him with his presence.

The significance of the moment was not lost on him. The Wardens had waited a millennium to be called to act. *He* had been waiting his entire life.

"Do not fear the future, Troy," the Herald who had visited his Station said to him when he'd brought word that they had been activated, *"Your destiny awaits."*

Troy wondered if the old man referred to the Wardens finally being called to act, or if the elder spoke of yet another legend. Troy had been shocked to say the least when the Herald had entered their tidy little Station in Virginia Beach with his flowing white hair. After he told them the news, he turned to Troy and recited another old tale.

"Young Thunderbird, you are the first to return us to Terra. Do not doubt your worth. Your destiny has been written in the stars since before you were born, Troy Waman. Remember, a Warden discovers his true measure when his fated mate is thrust upon him."

Whatever the fuck that meant. Troy looked down at

his phone, then to the street sign on the corner, and finally, to the faded numbers painted on the mailbox in front of the ramble of a house his map app had brought him to.

Fuck, am I thinking? Fated mates are myths. Stories made up so orphaned Shifters would sleep through the night. He scoffed at the thought. Memories of tales the head nurse, Sr. Maria, had told him at the training camp he'd called home for years invaded his brain.

Memories were pesky things. Sometimes eternal, and always fucking portable. But he was no longer a child. *No more stories, Sister. Now, I act.*

"A thousand years we've waited, and I'm walking into a fucking scene from a bad episode of *Hoarders*," Troy shook his head and frowned at the decrepit house that sat a few hundred feet away from him.

It was cold as fuck outside and his leather jacket did little to warm him. Avian Shifters did not carry around the same bulk as other types of Shifters. He ran hotter than normals, but the single digit temperature froze him to the bone.

True, he wasn't beefy like some of his fellow Shifters, but he was just as incredibly strong, and he was wicked fast. Much stronger than any average male. He paused briefly gauging the atmosphere.

There was something off about the place. He scented *Magic* and something else. His Bird bristled beneath his skin. *Easy now.*

Lightning flashed in the darkened skies, allowing him to see the worn shingles, and cracked siding of the beaten-up colonial in greater detail. More than one window had been smashed and boarded up with cheap plywood.

If anything, it enhanced the creepy haunted house feel of the place. The porch sagged danger-ously. He wondered how the place had managed to not be condemned by the town. One thing was certain, it was an ugly little turd of a house.

Who the hell put gray siding on their house anyway? Maybe it wasn't always that color. Maybe the owner liked gray. *Whatever.* He couldn't give two shits about the siding.

His only concern was the increased supernatural activity in the area over the past two weeks. Ever since the owner, a *Mrs. Renalda Curosi,* passed away. *A haunting?*

A creaking sound floated up to his ears and he stilled his movements. The sound developed into more of a *moaning* noise. An unearthly wail. It grew louder as the lightning continued to flash in the sky.

Troy had never seen a ghost. True, there were a

lot of things in the universe he had never seen nor heard of, but that didn't make them any less real.

If ghosts were real, and they made noises, he imagined that pitiful wail was damn close to what it would sound like.

No such thing as ghosts. Yeah, well, most people had never heard of Shifters either. And yet, there he stood.

His Thunderbird shifted once more beneath his skin, the beast flexing his senses as the lightning in the air drew him to the surface. *No.* He told his other half. His human needed to be in control now. He walked across the street, keeping to the shadows.

Something was indeed off about the creepy old house. He inched further to the black door. The knocker was in the shape of a face or mask. No discernible features, just a vague impression of eyes, nose, and mouth. *Shadowland indeed.*

He listened with his enhanced hearing and frowned. There was a distinct voice somewhere beneath the moaning and creaking. A *female* voice. His curiosity was piqued.

From what he'd seen in her file, Mrs. Curosi was ninety-seven when she passed. Her closest living relative was a half-sister, a *Magdelena Kristos,* and she lived over three hours away in New Jersey. The half-sister was cut from Mrs. Curosi's will recently. She'd bequeathed her entire estate, house, bank account, and all her earthly belongings, to someone named *A. Kristos. Another sister? Maybe.*

Troy hadn't given it much thought until now. A crash sounded from inside the house. He perked up as the feminine voice he'd thought he'd heard earlier screamed in pain. *Time to act.*

Grab your copy at https://www.cdgorri.com/books/bound-by-airbooks/bound-by-air!

ABOUT THE AUTHOR

C.D. Gorri is a USA Today Bestselling author of steamy paranormal romance and urban fantasy. She is the creator of the Grazi Kelly Universe.

Join her mailing list here: https://www.cdgorri.com/newsletter

An avid reader with a profound love for books and literature, when she is not writing or taking care of her family, she can usually be found with a book or tablet in hand. C.D. lives in her home state of New Jersey where many of her characters or stories are based. Her tales are fast paced yet detailed with satisfying conclusions.

If you enjoy powerful heroines and loyal heroes who face relatable problems in supernatural settings, journey into the Grazi Kelly Universe today. You will find sassy, curvy heroines and sexy, love-driven heroes who find their HEAs between the pages. Werewolves, Bears, Dragons, Tigers, Witches, Romani, Lynxes, Foxes, Thunderbirds, Vampires, and many more Shifters and supernatural creatures dwell within her worlds. The most important thing is every mate in this universe is fated, loyal, and true lovers always get their happily ever afters.

Want to know how it all began? Enter the Grazi Kelly Universe with Wolf Moon: A Grazi Kelly Novel or pick up Charley's Christmas Wolf and dive into the Macconwood Pack Novel Series today.

For a complete list of C.D. Gorri's books visit her website here:

https://www.cdgorri.com/complete-book-list/

Thank you and happy reading!

del mare alla stella,
    C.D. Gorri

Follow C.D. Gorri here:
    http://www.cdgorri.com
    https://www.facebook.com/Cdgorribooks

https://www.bookbub.com/authors/c-d-gorri
https://twitter.com/cgor22
https://instagram.com/cdgorri/
https://www.goodreads.com/cdgorri
https://www.tiktok.com/@cdgorriauthor